A FELLHOUNDS OF THESK STORY

MOON CROSSING

by

Cathy Farr

This book is published by
Grosvenor House Publishing Ltd
28-30 High Street, Guildford, Surrey, GU1 3EL.
www.grosvenorhousepublishing.co.uk

A CIP record for this book
is available from the British Library

ISBN 978-1-78148-515-6

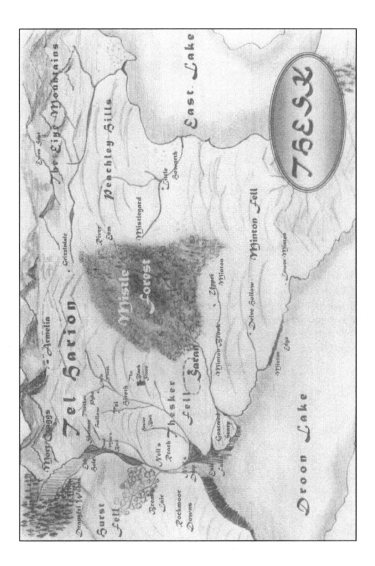

About Cathy Farr

Cathy Farr has always loved stories; listening to them, reading them and writing them. She lives in South Wales with her husband and her Irish Wolfhound, Finn, who has provided much of the inspiration for the magnificent Fellhounds that play such a big part in her books. Finn is 9ft long nose to tail and weighs almost fifteen stone; Cathy is almost 5ft 7inches but her weight remains a closely guarded secret.

Moon Crossing is Cathy's second book and also the second of the *Fellhounds of Thesk* stories.

For Ali

CHAPTER ONE

The One Left Behind

Godwyn Savidge was standing with his back to the fireplace in Lovage Hall, under the portrait of the Hall's owners Lady Élanor, her younger sister, Tally, and their father, the late Lord Lakeston. Sweat glistened on his bright red forehead. He was livid.

'I just can't believe you've brought him back – *after what he did to my son!*' Godwyn continued to rant.

Despite the early spring sunshine, Lady Élanor's housekeeper Martha had insisted on lighting a fire the minute she had heard that the Order of the Magewizen of Saran were on their way. Martha bustled across the room and tossed another log on the already blazing inferno. Then she bustled back again to retrieve a plate stacked with slabs of dark cake from the dresser and, mouthing words of encouragement, offered it around the rest of the stony-faced gathering.

'He was going to be married. Poor Olivia,' said Godwyn to no-one in particular. Morten Mortens, the Grand Wizen of the Order, perked up at the sight of Martha's famous honey cake and unashamedly selected the largest piece on the plate – his third. Martha beamed and waved the plate under the noses of the other members of the Order, all of who were pink from the heat of the fire. Godwyn found his voice again.

'If that boy had done his job… Too busy trying to be a hero! I knew it was a mistake.' Oswald Beck dismissed Martha's offer with a wave of his hand. She dodged right to avoid Godwyn's pointing finger. 'We should have hung him when we had the chance…' Agatha Peasgood politely took a very thin slice and put it on her plate where it remained untouched.

To one side of the fireplace sat Lady Élanor. Her pale blue eyes were fixed on Godwyn who had been on his feet now for some time. 'We were too soft, Mortens,' he growled. 'I warned you, but would you listen?'

He paused for breath and Lady Élanor seized the opportunity to cut in, her soft voice a stark contrast to Godwyn Savidge's snarling rage.

'I can only guess at what it must be like to lose a child, Godwyn.'

Godwyn stared into the fire, gasping laboured breaths. Oswald, Agatha and Morten Mortens nodded. Lady Élanor's voice hardened.

'But your son was an experienced Fellman. And I can assure you all that Wil Calloway was not to blame.' She gestured across the room to where a teenage boy was concentrating very hard on his piece of honey cake. 'He is here at *my* invitation – to help rescue my sister!'

She paused. In her hand, she clutched a ragged scrap of parchment. Godwyn took advantage of the brief silence.

'Well, I don't see how–,' Godwyn hissed, stabbing his finger towards Wil. But Lady Élanor cut across him.

'We all know how keen Giles was to prove himself, Godwyn,' she said even more firmly. '*That* was what sealed his fate!' Her expression softened again. 'We have had this conversation many times these past winter months, Godwyn. *It really wasn't Wil's fault* – Giles made a huge mistake and unfortunately paid a heavy price.'

The room fell silent. Wil, with his back against a vast dresser crammed with books, coloured jars and bunches of dried herbs and flowers, shifted uncomfortably. Godwyn wiped his soggy forehead with the back of his hand and glared at the fire. For all the man's blustering and his sweating red face, Godwyn's eyes were lifeless; his only son had been attacked during a Moon Chase and no-one really knew what had become of him. Wil's own father had been taken by Lord Rexmoore, the grasping ruler of Thesk, six years earlier because Wil's parents couldn't pay their taxes. To this day Wil didn't know what had really happened to him. For a brief moment Wil felt very sorry for Godwyn Savidge.

An abrupt knock on the Hall's heavy oak door broke the sad silence. Martha shot a questioning glance at Lady Élanor who nodded. Leaving the plate of cake precariously balanced on the cluttered dresser, the housekeeper went to investigate. With a suspicious peek out into the dark evening Martha's face expanded into a broad smile and she threw the door wide open. The hinges objected with a loud creak.

'Master Merridown!' Martha beamed. 'Well, I'll be… it's a while since we've seen you up here! How did you get on with those pink mustard seeds – did you do them with the salmon, like I suggested? And what about that tarragon butter…'

Martha's culinary inquisition continued as a tall, athletic young man strode confidently into the room.

'Yes, Martha, and it was delicious, thank you,' he grinned, searching the faces around the room until he seemed to find who he was looking for.

'Wil, I *knew* we'd see you again!'

Mortimer charged forward, arms wide. Wil got to his feet just in time to be gathered up into a huge bear hug.

3

'It's good to see you too, Mortimer!' wheezed Wil.

Mortimer released his grip and Wil stepped back gasping but smiling. It really was good to see his friend again.

'Bryn told me that Lady Élanor had gone to fetch you. Sooner than I thought, but I knew we'd see you again, Wil Calloway,' said Mortimer.

The last time Mortimer and Wil had spoken was before the winter, on the day Wil had left Saran to return to his own village, Mistlegard. It was also the day he had last seen Gisella Fairfax. Wil was hoping that she might have come with Mortimer but Martha had shut the door and it was obvious Mortimer had come alone. With a familiar twinge of regret – the parting with Gisella had not been one of Wil's finest moments – he decided not to make enquiries in their present company.

'And how's that Fellhound of yours – Apophinis? I hope you haven't let him get into any bad habits!'

'Phinn's fine – my mother *might* forgive him one day for chewing her favourite bedspread – well actually, her only bedspread!' Wil answered with a sheepish grin. 'My fault. I left him in the yard when the washing was on the line. Won't do that again – he can reach the sheets *even* when the line is on the tallest pole!'

Mortimer laughed.

'Well, where is he then? I didn't see him in the garden. I bet he's grown! Mia – Phinn's sister – remember? She's brilliant – big, too, like her Dad – Tarek would have been so proud!'

A shadow flickered across Mortimer's face at the mention of his old Fellhound. Wil carried on.

'Well, Phinn's easily as big as Seth's hound, Farrow! He's up in the stables with Pickles and Alana – Alana's pups are *massive*, Mort!' He held his arms at waist height to demonstrate. 'I can't believe they've grown so much. The last time I saw them they were sat on Tally and me – they're far too big for that now!'

But before they could go on Lady Élanor cut in with the same acid tone she had used on Godwyn Savidge a little earlier. 'Gentlemen, I'm sorry to interrupt this hound-filled reunion but we *are* here to discuss how we can make sure my sister gets the *option* of whether or not Alana's pups can sit on her lap in the future!'

'Sorry, yes, Lady Élanor – that's why I'm here,' said Mortimer, suddenly serious. 'If I can be of service, please, count me.' He bowed solemnly.

'Thank you Mortimer,' said Lady Élanor returning the bow. 'I just hope we can find her before Lord Rexmoore's wife gets near her!'

She looked down at an old map laid out over the floor in front of the fire. Her back stiff and her fingers in an almost permanent knot, Lady Élanor's anxiety was obvious to everyone in the room. She had already told Wil a little about Lord Rexmoore's domineering wife – her aunt, Imelda – earlier that day when she had arrived in Mistlegard to ask Wil for help. She had shown him the note she now clutched in her fist: '*Give up the legacy or I will make your precious sister tell me where it is!*'

But Wil also knew that only three people knew the whereabouts of Saran's legacy – and Tally was not one of them. From what he had heard so far Wil couldn't help thinking that Lady Élanor was right to worry.

He watched her draw her mane of silver hair back over her shoulders in order to study the worn parchment. During one of his rants earlier Godwyn had carelessly stepped on one corner. The large muddy print of his boot was plain for everyone to see – although nobody mentioned it.

5

The map showed the entire kingdom of Thesk. Wil could see Mistlegard tucked away on the far side of Mistle Forest, beyond the River Eem. Earlier, before Godwyn had disrupted the meeting with his *very* vocal objections about Wil, the Order had been discussing possible routes to Armelia with Lady Élanor – the most obvious being north along the edge of the forest and then north-west over Tel Harion.

Oswald Beck certainly favoured this route, as did Lady Élanor – although Godwyn Savidge and Agatha Peasgood were in firm agreement that this was by far the most dangerous option.

Wil shivered. The putrid stench of the Wraithe Wolves that inhabit the stark hills of Tel Harion still lingered in his nostrils, serving as an almost constant reminder of the Moon Chase he had been forced to join the previous autumn. In these past cold winter nights Wil would lie alone in the dark trying to silence the terrifying howls that still rang loud among his memories.

'… so how far is that, Wil?'

Mortimer's question jolted Wil from his nightmare thoughts. Everyone was still studying the map.

'Sorry, how far is where… from, eh, where… sorry?' asked Wil, trying to look as though he had been listening.

Mortimer repeated his question while he traced his finger across the top of the map: 'How far is Armelia from Mistlegard if you go via Grizzledale?'

Wil thought for a moment.

'Er, I'm not sure – I've never been to Armelia. I know it takes a day to get to Grizzledale because the river's too fast through the forest so you have to go all the way up. There's a bridge there somewhere,' he said, waving one hand vaguely over the middle of Mistle Forest while taking a piece of cake with the other as Martha swept past again. Then he added,

'Well, there was – it got swept away in all that rain last month. I think it would probably take a couple of days now to go round.' He took a bite of cake but then remembered. 'Oh, they had heavy snow in Grizzledale last week. Garth Fengal, one of our Elders, got stuck there for four days!'

'Hmm, well we can rule that one out then!' said Mortimer squinting down at the grubby map. 'If we do go straight over Tel Harion as Lady Élanor suggests, well, it's no more than a good two-day ride from here – and I know those hills.'

'Two days!' said Lady Élanor. 'They took them yesterday morning! Lord Rexmoore's going to have a very long time to discover that Tally *really* doesn't know where the legacy is! Oh, why did I say she could go out on her own with Tanith?'

Wil remembered Lady Élanor's beautiful, golden horse that he'd met up in the stables above Lovage Hall. Wil frowned.

'Well, if it was Rexmoore… well, they won't be in Armelia yet then – will they?' he said, wondering if he'd missed something. 'I mean, you can still see a lot of snow up on the Fells… if Tanith's anything like the horses in our village, he'll really struggle. They're ter–'

Wil's voice tailed off – Mortimer was glaring at him and a glance in Lady Élanor's direction told Wil that he had probably said a little too much. Morten Mortens leant forward, still clutching his crumb-dotted plate.

'Well, they do have the advantage of a head start, I agree. But the fact they have Tanith will work in Tally's favour, my Lady. Believe me,' he said glancing at Wil, 'Tally will be over Tel Harion and away from the dangers of the weather *and* the Wraithe Wolves in no time.'

Agatha Peasgood brightened, 'And we don't *know* if it was Rexmoore's men who took her.' Although she seemed to realise almost immediately that this suggestion wasn't helpful and took a long sip of her tea.

'And if it *was*,' said Mortens pointedly, 'Rexmoore still may not have Tally yet. After all, he's about as likely to leave Imelda's side as I am of jumping over the twin moons!' He paused to hand Martha his empty plate as she tiptoed past and then continued while brushing crumbs from his magenta robes. 'I am more concerned that once his Lordship – or rather *his wife* – realises that Tally is ignorant of the whereabouts of the legacy, she will try to use Tally in some way in an attempt to make *you* give it up, Eli.'

'But why?... How…?' said Lady Élanor, looking utterly forlorn.

Morten Mortens looked suddenly sad.

'When your mother passed away, Imelda was convinced that somewhere in Armelia was a vast hoard of gold that your father had hidden from her – in fact she became quite obsessed.' Wil got the impression the Grand Wizen's words were for the benefit of the whole room. 'Nonsense of course, but it didn't take much for her to convince Rexmoore to help her look; after all he had been in love with her for years. But she only took an interest in him when he suddenly became useful. So, you see, Eli, now that Rexmoore thinks he is getting close to helping his wife satisfy that obsession, he will not give up easily.'

Lady Élanor sat forward and opened her mouth as though she was going to say something but then seemed to change her mind. Instead she pressed her lips together and stared at her hands.

It was Mortimer who broke the silence, taking the opportunity to move on to more positive talk.

'So, if that is the case, my Lady, I am assuming that you will be staying here in the safety of Lovage Hall – unless you want to risk walking straight into Rexmoore's dungeons – which, by the sound of it, might be what he's hoping for.'

Lady Élanor kept her eyes fixed on the parchment in her tightly clenched fist and said nothing.

Agatha Peasgood nodded.

'Mortimer is right, Lady Élanor. If this is a trap we could lose you, Tally *and* Tanith in one misadventure!' She attempted a thin smile. The paleness of her face seemed to exaggerate the worried look in her shining eyes that darted between Mortimer and the Grand Wizen. After a moment's hesitation, she added gently, 'I really do think it would be best for you to stay here in the safety of Saran, my Lady.'

The Grand Wizen took a deep inward breath before he voiced his agreement.

'Agatha is right, Élanor. I made a promise to your father that I would watch over you and your sister. You are much safer here. Lord Rexmoore may have Tally for the moment but we will get her back.'

Lady Élanor raised her eyes to the ceiling and then bowed her head. Wil watched as a single tear trickled down her ivory cheek and dripped onto her pale fingers. The ink on the parchment blurred. Turning a silver ring around her finger, she made no move to wipe the tear away. 'But staying here makes me feel so helpless!' she whispered.

Then, with a sharp breath she fixed Wil with her blue eyes, her voice still barely a whisper. 'Bring her back, Wil. Bring Tally and Tanith back for me.'

Wil met her unblinking stare. He nodded.

Mortimer looked relieved.

'Right, well if that's settled,' he said, and without waiting for confirmation, set about planning. 'We'll go tomorrow at first light – sorry my Lady, but it's far too late to even think about leaving now *and* it's pouring with rain! Wil, we'll take four Fellmen and their hounds, plus you and Phinn. We'll cross over to Mistle Forest and head up to the Black Stone using the cover of the trees for as long as we can. Then we'll make for Mort Craggs, keeping Tel Harion on our east side,' he said pointing out the route on the map as he talked. 'Wraithe Wolves *hate* water, so if we hit a problem we'll cross Dead Man's Beck and keep going north from the other side!'

Oswald Beck shook his head.

'But that would take us into Drangfel Woods,' he said. 'I'm really not sure if I'm happy about that.'

'Does that mean that you'll be joining us, Mister Beck?' asked Mortimer without taking his eyes off the map.

'If one of the four Fellmen is Leon then yes, I don't want *my* boy going the same way as Giles!'

Godwyn Savidge, who had been smouldering quietly for quite some time, was once more on his feet. Agatha Peasgood dropped her cup.

'And just what do you mean by that, Beck? That *I* should have been on that Moon Chase? That *I* should have been there – for *my boy*?' said Godwyn in a dangerous voice. His bloodshot eyes blazed red in the light of the fire. Oswald met his glare but Morten Mortens got in first.

'Oh, I'm sure Oswald didn't mean anything of the sort, Godwyn,' said the Grand Wizen pleasantly. But his normally pink and jovial face had gone the colour of the white china plate he held in his hand. 'Why don't you take a seat and have a glass of elder wine. I'm sure Martha has a bottle ready to open somewhere?'

He raised his eyebrows hopefully at Martha. She took his cue and scuttled out to the kitchen. But Godwyn was not going to be placated that easily.

'What I don't understand is why *this boy* is so important?' Godwyn hissed through gritted teeth, jabbing his finger towards Wil. '*Or* for that matter why, Morten, you are prepared to risk the safety of Saran for a fourteen-year old girl – who is not even Saran-born – and an old horse! And as for this legacy of yours, *your Worship* – even as a member of the same Order, I am obviously not worthy enough to share the secret of its whereabouts or, in fact, *what it is!*'

For the first time that evening Morten Mortens' face coloured with anger.

'Now, really, Godwyn, that's–'

But Godwyn Savidge was not to be stopped.

'No, Mortens! I've only ever done my best for Saran – with my own gold, too! And how do you repay me? You keep secrets. You have my son destroyed. And now it seems you are suggesting that somehow *I* might be to blame! Well, *this* member of the Order will *NOT* support this fool's errand – and if I were you,' he snarled, turning to Mortimer, 'I wouldn't worry about how to get to Armelia, son, Rexmoore's men will destroy you before you reach the slopes of Tel Harion!'

Then without another word he marched to the front door, grabbed his cloak off its hook and swept out into the fading light of the late afternoon – leaving the door wide open behind him.

A loud *POP!* came from the kitchen – followed by the clinking of glasses.

With Godwyn gone and a glass of ruby red elderberry wine in front of everyone, the mood in the Hall lifted considerably. Lady Élanor and Oswald Beck eventually got their way – largely thanks to Mortimer who seemed very keen for an excuse to get back out onto the Fells. Wil guessed that the Fellman must have had something of a quiet winter.

With the route finally agreed, the decision that Mortimer would head the rescue was largely academic. They were to leave at first light. Wil and Phinn were to join him, together with Fellmen Leon Beck, Curtis Waller and Becky Lum; and although Mortimer made absolutely no effort to hide his objection, Oswald remained adamant that he was to join the party.

As he listened, Wil desperately wanted to ask why Gisella wasn't going but shied away from mentioning her name in case he looked stupid; Wil wasn't sure how people would react if he appeared to be too keen to see her. He was surprised that the disappearance of Gisella's mother, Fermina Fairfax, had not been discussed. It was one of the other pieces of dramatic news that Lady Élanor had shared on her arrival in Mistlegard that morning. But as the subject had not come up at all at the meeting Wil guessed that Gisella's mother must have turned up and had not come to the meeting for some other reason. Instead, Wil asked why Seth Tanner hadn't been included, but it was everyone's view that Seth's mother wouldn't let him go – particularly after the last Moon Chase! Wil couldn't disagree.

The formulation of a firm plan seemed to calm Lady Élanor but Wil got the distinct feeling that something was still troubling her. Time and time again during the evening she had asked how long the rescue mission would take. But each time no one was able to give an answer.

As everyone finally got ready to leave, Lady Élanor touched Morten Mortens on the elbow, 'Morten, before you go, could you just spare me a minute – I would like to discuss the linen stocks for the infirmary.'

'Er – right now, my Lady?' said the Grand Wizen, throwing his cloak over his shoulders. 'It's just that Millicent is cooking the first of the spring lambs – it's always a bit of a celebration in our house, you know – new season's lamb, new potatoes and spring greens – one of my favourite meals as it happens.' He smiled wistfully and fastened his cloak under his chin. 'We've kept a bottle of mead from last year, too – should be quite a treat!'

A shadow passed over Lady Élanor's face. She turned; her voice fading as she walked into the kitchen.

'Well, if your meal is more important than the cleanliness of the town's only hospital, *particularly* during this latest outbreak of chicken fever, then of course you must go, your Worship.'

With a sigh, the Grand Wizen undid the clasp of his cloak and plodded after her.

Agatha and Oswald followed Mortimer down the garden path and Martha shut the front door. She stood with her hand still on the latch, looking puzzled.

'Funny, there's a mountain of clean linen in the laundry – did it myself yesterday,' she frowned. But then a thought struck her. 'Oh my, I hope those blessed swallows haven't been nesting in there again – it's the same every year – droppings everywhere! Better go and check – I'll be so cross if I have to wash all those sheets again! It's not as if her Ladyship hasn't got enough to worry about as it is…' And, completely ignoring Wil, she too headed for the kitchen – the quickest route to the infirmary – leaving the door slightly ajar in her haste. Unsure quite what to do, Wil sat in one of the huge wooden armchairs and gazed into the glowing remnants of Martha's blazing inferno.

Lady Élanor's worried voice drifted out from the kitchen.

'I know that, Morten, and her disappearance troubles me, too. But with the Alcama only a few nights away – we *must* get them back. Goodness knows what will happen to Saran without–'

The door was closed quietly and, try as he might, all Wil could hear was the crackle of the glowing embers of the fire.

CHAPTER TWO

Dawn Flight

A rush of freezing air smacked into Wil's face like a wave of icy water. Robbed momentarily of breath, he opened his eyes but the darkness smothered everything in a blanket of black. He was sure he was in the air – how high, he didn't know – and certainly didn't want to know! He was also sure he was travelling *very* fast – *downwards* – and braced himself ready to hit the ground. But then, almost leaving his stomach behind, he was suddenly hauled upwards into a long climb. The wind roared in his ears; his eyes streamed in the freezing blast and his nose was so cold it burned. Wil screwed his eyes tight shut in case he got a glimpse of just how high – *or low* – he was to the ground as he soared and swooped. But then he felt himself tumble into another dive and instantly regretted that last piece of honey cake. He retched, lurched sideways and landed with a thud on the floorboards of the bedroom in Lovage Hall.

Utterly bewildered, he squinted into the more comfortable darkness of the bedroom. He could hear rain hammering against the window. From down the hall light footsteps raced towards his room and Lady Élanor's voice called out.

'Wil, are you alright? Can I come in?'

Dazed and shaking, Wil clambered back into bed, 'Er...hang on...yer...er …'

The door flew open and Lady Élanor stood in the light of the lamp she was clutching in her raised hand.

'What was that noise? Wil – are you alright? You haven't seen any more prowlers in the garden, have you?'

'No – a dream… I think… I fell out of bed,' Wil admitted. Lady Élanor's words made him feel even more foolish – the last time he had spotted someone trying to break into Lovage Hall he had raised the alarm by banging Martha's precious copper pots together and had scared everyone witless in the process!

'I… I thought I was flying,' he said. His cheeks blazed red.

Lady Élanor opened her mouth to speak but a sudden, sharp tap on the window made them both jump. Waves of rain hurled against the leaded glass. The tapping got louder and slightly more irritable. In the darkness on the other side of the tiny glass panes Wil could just about make out the shape of a very wet raven.

'Pricilla!'

With a wide grin, Wil scrambled to the end of the bed and opened the window.

'Crronk! Crronk! Prruk!'

The soggy raven hopped, dripping, onto the bed, spread her wings and flapped – for several seconds. Wil grabbed the covers to fend off the spray of icy water and waited until she had made her point. The images from his dream fell into place.

'Well, if that was your idea of a welcome, Pricilla, I'm glad it was dark! You know how much I hate heights!'

The huge bird shook herself again and gave Wil's big toe a light peck. Then she flapped over to the washstand and took a long drink from the water pitcher.

'Heights – what do you mean, Wil?' asked Lady Élanor with a frown. But she wasn't listening for an answer. She stood, gripping the window latch and stared out of the open window into the drenched black night. Rain trickled over her small white hand but she didn't seem to notice. Wil answered anyway.

'I was dreaming that I was in the air – flying – I must have been reading Pricilla's mind – you know, while she was flying here.' He watched Pricilla sploosh water over the bedroom floor. 'I never realised how cold it is up there!'

Lady Élanor didn't speak. Her pale eyes searched the night sky and rain splashed off the window sill onto the brightly coloured quilt at the end of Wil's bed.

'Don't worry about Tally, my Lady,' said Wil, guessing her thoughts – he could read the minds of animals in a somewhat haphazard and barely controlled way, but reading the minds of humans was definitely Lady Élanor and Tally's area of expertise.

'I'm sure she's OK,' he added.

But even to Wil, his words sounded lame. The lamp flickered, caught by a sudden gust and Lady Élanor pulled the dripping window closed.

'I hope so, Wil,' she whispered and walked to the door. Without a backward glance she said softly, 'Pricilla, I have a dead mouse downstairs. Would you like it?'

Pricilla cocked her head to one side, gave Wil a disdainful look and fluttered off the washstand. Wil heard her noisy landing on the bare boards out in the hall and then Lady Élanor's voice as the bedroom door closed with a soft click.

'Good night, Wil.'

'Night,' replied Wil and kicked the soaked quilt off the end of his bed. But as he listened to the rat-tat of Pricilla's claws across the floorboards a thought struck him, '*Funny, it wasn't raining up there.*'

Puzzled, he sank back onto the soft pillow and breathed in a vaguely familiar flowery scent. But before he could place the smell, Wil was fast asleep.

The next time Wil was woken up, the day was only just breaking. A heavy pounding on the front door downstairs jolted him out of a very nice dream in which he and Gisella were floating on a boat on East Lake. They were laughing and she was about to give him a piece of the apple she had just cut up when Wil heard a man's gruff voice interspersed with the indignant voice of Lady Élanor's housekeeper. Shaking himself awake, Wil got out of bed as quietly as he could and dressed quickly in the thin dawn light. Then he retrieved his hunting knife from under the pillow, grabbed his cloak and hurried out of the bedroom – boots in hand.

At the bottom of the stairs he barged into Mortimer who was standing just inside the doorway that led into the living room. Wil opened his mouth to speak but Mortimer pushed him flat against the wall, pressed his finger to his own lips and crooked his ear with his other hand. Wil got the message and nodded.

This time it was Lady Élanor's steady voice, crystal clear through the walls.

'Sorry, who? Wil Calloway? There is no one here by that name, I can assure you, Sire.'

A man's voice replied.

'We know he's staying in this house, my Lady. There is no point lying to us. The boy must be taken to Armelia immediately. Lord Rexmoore is waiting.'

'Well, I can only repeat that he is not here! What does his Lordship want with this boy anyway?'

Wil wondered the same thing – he had never even been to Armelia, and had certainly never met Lord Rexmoore. How did Rexmoore even know Wil's name – let alone that he might be in Saran? Wil lived in Mistlegard!

Then a second man spoke.

'Look, you can make this easy and give him up, woman, or we'll come in and search for 'im!'

A chill crept down Wil's spine – that voice – he was sure he'd heard it before. He held his breath and strained to listen in case the man spoke again. But instead Wil heard the familiar creak of a hinge and knew that Lady Élanor had opened the front door wide.

'You are welcome to search, gentlemen! Where would you like to start?' Lady Élanor's voice could not have been more welcoming.

'Right, where's the stairs? I heard something up there just now – someone moving about. I'll bet he's under the bed – they're always under the bed – unless you've got an attic!'

Wil and Mortimer exchanged the same horrified look – they both knew that the only way to the bedrooms of Lovage Hall was right where they were standing – it was also the only way out!

Then Wil heard Lady Élanor's voice again. This time there was something very odd in her tone.

'But wait, Sires. Before you start I am sure you would welcome a cup of mint tea… and some breakfast, perhaps? It is only just dawn. You must be *starving.*'

The words rushed into Wil's ears. Images of warm bread heaped with freshly churned butter and sweet raspberry jam floated in front of his eyes. Memories of all sorts of delicious tastes wound around his tongue as hunger engulfed him. Unable to resist Lady Élanor's invitation, he moved forward. But as Wil took his first step, a chubby hand grabbed his arm. Salivating, he looked round. It was Martha. Her other hand was wrapped around Mortimer's elbow – he, too, seemed to be heading in the same direction as Wil. Without a word Martha pulled them away towards the library.

Lady Élanor's hypnotic voice drifted from the living room as she continued to tempt Rexmoore's men with talk of hot buttered toast, home-made marmalade, scones, scrambled eggs... but as Martha dragged Wil and Mortimer away the voice, and the gnawing starvation, dwindled to nothing. By the time they reached the balcony at the far end of the library, Wil felt as though he had already eaten a perfectly satisfying breakfast.

'What on earth was going on back there?' whispered Mortimer with a bewildered look back towards the stairs.

'Yer! That breakfast sounded fantastic, but now *I don't feel hungry at all*!' whispered Wil, utterly confused. Martha chuckled.

'Oh, that's one of Lady Élanor's little tricks,' she answered loudly.

Wil and Mortimer exchanged another horrified look and Mortimer tried to clamp his hand over the housekeeper's mouth, hissing 'By the moons, Martha. Do you *want* to give us away?'

Quite unperturbed, she brushed him aside and continued, her voice as loud as before.

'Oh, don't worry about that – they can't hear us.' She gave a wicked chuckle and her eyes were suddenly filled with mischief. 'They'll be tucking in to scrambled eggs and bacon in no time – won't even remember why they've come here! I've seen her do that with naughty children before now... although it doesn't seem to work quite so well on Tally nowadays for some reason!' She frowned. 'Not sure how the chap with only one hand'll cut his bacon though? *Or* butter his toast, for that matter?'

Her face was filled with genuine concern but her words gave Wil the clue he needed. He knew that voice was familiar – it belonged to the man who had grabbed hiss ankle when he and Gisella were trying to escape from the deer rustlers on the Thesker Fell, after the Moon Chase.

And, thought Wil, *that* must be how Lord Rexmoore knew about him! That man must have told Rexmoore that ridiculous theory dreamt up by Sir Jerad Tinniswood, about Wil being a seer. Of course! That was why Rexmoore was looking for him now – to help him find the legacy if Tally wouldn't. Maybe Rexmoore thought Wil would be able to read her mind? But Wil knew that he couldn't – whenever he and Tally linked minds the effect was so bad that Wil seriously thought he was going to die!

The ancient ladder that led up to the library balcony had been something of a problem for Wil in the past. Even this time, despite the threat that Rexmoore's men may find them at any moment, Mortimer had to go up and down three times before Wil could be persuaded that the rickety rungs wouldn't collapse under him! And once at the top, Wil felt anything but safe.

The tiny space was absolutely jam-packed with books and papers and Wil was in no doubt that with the three of them adding even more weight, they would go crashing back down into the library below at any minute.

Despite his aversion to heights, Wil stood right on the edge and clung to the rail. Martha, however, seemed determined to go even higher. Ignoring his protests, she hopped up onto a precarious stack of books, reached for a dusty volume entitled, '*A Hundred and One Ways with Carrots*' and tipped the book towards her. To Wil's horror the bookcase started to creak.

'Get down! The balcony's collapsing!' he yelled – any memory of Rexmoore's men wiped from his mind.

But Mortimer stayed where he was. Instead Wil heard him mutter, 'Well, I'll be…'

The creaking had stopped only to be replaced by the most terrible grinding and scraping and Wil turned just in time to see the bookcase shoot up into the attic leaving a huge plume of dust in the space it had just filled.

As the dust settled, Wil could see the entrance to a dark tunnel. There was also a sudden and very strong smell of damp. Martha wrinkled her nose and peered towards the murky blackness.

'Thought we'd better take the back route out of the Hall – I put extra cream *and* a good glug of gooseberry gin in that porridge to keep those two quiet for a while, but it never harms to be too careful!'

Then she clambered back down the little book staircase and clicked her fingers. Immediately little orange lights burst into life all along the passage walls on both sides.

'Glow worms,' she said with a satisfied smile and hitched her skirt up to reveal a pair of ancient boots and thick grey stockings. 'Follow me – and don't worry about the cobwebs – I keep meaning to pop in and give it a dust over but there's never enough hours in the day for some jobs, don't you find?'

Mortimer glanced at the cloak and boots Wil was still clutching – in the rush he hadn't thought to put them on.

'I hope you don't need to go back for anything!' said Mortimer and ducked through the low doorway after Martha without waiting for an answer. Wil hauled his boots on. His bag was back in his room, but deciding that it may not be a good idea to go back, he too ducked into the tunnel and ran after Mortimer and Martha.

As he caught up, Wil glanced back over his shoulder – the narrow tunnel was once more in silent darkness.

It had quickly become obvious that being taller than the dumpy little housekeeper (by quite a lot) was a distinct disadvantage. Wil heard a dull bump up ahead. Mortimer cursed; then Wil banged his head – probably on the same low beam. Thankfully, after only a few more minutes Wil could see daylight, but by then his mouth was full of gritty cobwebs.

Dusty and not a little bad tempered, Wil and Mortimer stepped out into the lobby of Lovage Hall's infirmary – right opposite the door into the ward.

Untangling a particularly thick cobweb from his eyebrows, Wil heard Lady Élanor's voice. It had the same tone his mother always used if she was talking to someone either very ill or very old.

'There – you have a rest now. Perhaps that third bowl of porridge wasn't such a good idea after all.'

Wil peered through the barely open door into the ward. A chain-mail clad man clutching his stomach was staggering towards an empty bed – his face had a decidedly green hue. Opposite, another man was lying on his side sucking his thumb. Already sleeping peacefully, his other arm was tucked under his chin. Wil jerked away from the door, he had been right – there was no hand at the end of the man's arm. Mortimer gave Wil a questioning glance but Wil shook his head and said nothing.

Martha hauled open the heavy oak doors that led out into the beech wood and chuckled.

'Sounds like the gin worked! Come on, Bryn's waiting for us.'

Bryn was indeed waiting – together with Seth and Gisella.

'Where are the others?' demanded Mortimer, his expression suddenly thunderous. To Wil's surprise Mortimer completely ignored Gisella.

Gisella threw Wil a fleeting glance that gave absolutely nothing away and turned her attention to a pure white Fellhound standing at her side. Around the hound's neck was a broad iron collar which Gisella seemed to find terribly interesting.

Completely thrown, Wil felt suddenly awkward.

Seth, however, didn't seem to notice the frosty atmosphere and launched into an excited gabble.

"Rexmoore's men took them – they're all over the village, Mort! They're arresting anyone who even looks like a Fellman! I heard one of them asking about you, Wil. Martha woke me up and told me to come and meet you here – she told me we're going to rescue Tally. D'you think Farrow looks good? Her ear's miles better now.' Seth patted the flank of another Fellhound, grey and bigger than the first, that sat head-height next to him. 'I've just seen Phinn – he's massive! What've you been feeding him?'

While Seth continued to chat away, seemingly oblivious of any danger they might be facing, Farrow got to her feet and wagged her long tail lazily. She had a neat split almost down the length of her right ear – a scar from the fight that nearly cost Wil his own life. She was wearing a collar much like the white hound – a collar Wil knew that had once saved her life.

Despite a growing feeling of anxiety at Mortimer's sudden change of mood, a strong sense of joy swept over Wil as the huge hound ambled towards him – at least *she* was pleased to see him.

'Is Phinn alright, Bryn?' said Wil, at the same time trying to catch Gisella's eye. But Gisella kept her attention stubbornly fixed on the white Fellhound.

'Ey, e's bin chasin' Alana's pups roun' the paddock! I were tellin' Martha ony lars nigh',' replied Bryn with a nod towards his wife. 'Gorra good instinct for the chase, thar un! Bur e's a bi' keen wir 'is teeth – given a couple o' the pups a nasty nip – playin' I know, bur e din alf make em yelp!' Bryn chuckled as he spoke in his strange accent. 'Ir'll do im good to be wi Mia an' Farrow 'ere fer a while – teach 'im some manners 'ey will!'

Gisella was still preoccupied so Wil decided to go for a more direct approach.

'So is this Mia, then?' he asked, in what he hoped was a friendly and relaxed tone.

But Mortimer stepped in before Gisella could open her mouth.

'Yer, this is Mia. How come you've got her, Gisella?'

Wil was stunned. Gisella didn't look up. She ran her pale fingers over Mia's velvety ear.

'Seth was trying to bring her up here in case you needed her. But she wouldn't come for him so he came to get me. Rexmoore's men were arresting everyone – I thought you'd need me. Seth's brought Rhoani, too, but I couldn't find Shadow. I guessed he was up here – didn't the blacksmith call yesterday?'

Mortimer barely even acknowledged that Gisella had spoken.

'Did Kenton shoe my horse, Bryn?'

Bryn's dark eyes flicked between Mortimer and Gisella.

'Ey! Four new shoes, too – luck'ly. You'll be needin' 'em where yer goin'! e's in Tanith's stable. Martha, come an' gi me an 'and! Pickles is still nor eatin' – missin' his mistress too much!' And with a sad shake of his head, Bryn turned away and headed off towards the stable block. Martha scuttled after him and Mortimer's thunderous expression made Wil sorely temped to follow – this certainly *wasn't* the reunion he'd been imagining during the long winter nights!

'And do your parents know where you are *this* time, Seth?' snapped Mortimer.

'Er, well, yer… sort of. Martha said she'd tell them. Anyway, they'll see that I didn't have a choice. Everyone except Olivia and Gisella were being carted off – I saw them all tied up!'

'So why didn't you bring Olivia?'

'Well, I don't think Olivia's really up to anything, Mort – she's still missing Giles and anyway Gisella was closer and, well, I er… didn't think you'd mind – after all, you and her *have* been training Mia for most of the winter. I thought you were… um, well… I thought you two were, well… going out?'

'What!' chorused Wil and Gisella.

Mortimer rounded on Seth.

'Well, we're not! And *you* should have just come alone, Seth!'

And with that Mortimer stomped away towards the stables. Mia padded over to Gisella and leant against her.

'Mia, come!' barked Mortimer without turning round.

Seth looked utterly crestfallen.

'Oh dear, I'm so sorry Gisella. I didn't realise. It's just with your mother gone… well…you and Mortimer have spent so much time together over the last few months that everyone just assumed…'

'Well, they were wrong,' snapped Gisella. 'You were *all* wrong! And it looks like *my* assumption that we were all friends was wrong, too!'

CHAPTER THREE

A Bitter Reunion

Anxiety and disappointment consumed Wil as the gloomy group rode out of the yard. He had imagined his next meeting with Gisella many, many times through the winter and had rehearsed his speech so often that even Phinn knew it backwards – but now that had all melted away. Depressed and distracted, Wil had climbed up onto Shadow behind Mortimer without a second thought for either his dislike of riding *or* his fear of heights.

Even the arrival earlier of four saddle-packs – one for each of them – stuffed with blankets, food and flasks filled with water and elder wine, did nothing to lighten the mood at the stables as they had made ready to leave.

'Lady Élanor made me pack these last night. I think she was expecting something like this to happen,' Martha had muttered as she jammed another plump pasty into Wil's bag. 'I've put your first aid kit in, Wil…Mortimer – I packed some extra herbs and spices in yours.'

Mortimer had made no comment, but Wil nodded a thank-you. He had first discovered the very special first aid kit when Pricilla had helpfully presented Wil with one just after the Moon Chase – and it had proved vital on more than one occasion.

As the housekeeper made sure they were not going to starve on the journey, Bryn had handed out four new crossbows together with as many bolts as they could all carry. Wil had stuffed most of his into his jacket and the rest down into his boot where he could grab them easily if he needed one in a hurry – either to load into his crossbow or to throw.

'You still go' thar 'unting knife Tally gi' you fur the Moon Chase?'

Wil patted a leather sheath on his belt.

'Don't worry, Bryn – I wouldn't be without it!'

'I pur a collar on Phinn too, 'ope you don' mind bur i' could come in 'andy.'

On a patch of grass at the end of the stable block Wil had spotted Phinn rubbing his neck along the ground and shaking his head. Then, wearing a distinctly unimpressed expression, the hound had flopped down, flat to the ground – his face and the collar thick with fresh mud.

'Don' think e likes i' much though,' Bryn had added unnecessarily.

And yet despite the bustle and all the help from Bryn and Martha, when Mortimer had finally spoken, it was clear that he hadn't cheered up at all.

'Right, come on. Wil, you ride with me. We need to get going before Rexmoore's men find their way up here. We won't get to Mort Craggs before nightfall, the rate we're going!'

Wil had watched his angry friend checking Shadow's feet – for the fourth time – then the sharpness of every bolt head and the tightness of the cords of his own and Wil's crossbows.

'*Anything but look at Gisella,*' thought Wil. But then, as now, Wil decided he might be better off keeping thoughts like that to himself until he could get to the bottom of his friend's dramatic mood change.

The unhappy group were picking their way out of the beech wood and into Mistle Forest just as it started to rain; the drenching drizzle only adding to the bleak atmosphere. By the time the first oaks of the forest came into view the rain was pounding down like stair rods and branches all around them bowed under the weight of their soaking leaves. Mistle Forest looked even darker than usual.

As soon as they had said goodbye to Bryn and a very tearful Martha in the stable yard, Mortimer had made it quite clear that he didn't want to talk so Wil brooded in silence. After all they had been through, he thought – the Moon Chase, Wraithe Wolves, deer rustlers… *What could possibly have happened between Mortimer and Gisella that could have wiped all that away?*

With no conversation to lighten the mood, the rain sounded like it would never stop. Shadow and Rhoani splashed over the waterlogged ground. Mia and Phinn padded behind them utterly bedraggled, while Farrow did her best to stay under the cover of the trees – no matter how low the branches got.

Wil pulled his cloak over his head and hunched behind Mortimer. In a way, he was grateful for the noise of the rain – at least the air was filled with the sound of something, even if it wasn't the happy chatter of four friends who hadn't seen each other all winter!

Suddenly Farrow, Mia and Phinn stopped dead, their amber eyes fixed on the same patch of the gloomy forest. Mortimer pulled Shadow to a halt and held up his hand for Seth to do the same. Shadow snorted and stamped his foot.

'Steady boy,' said Mortimer quietly.

A second later a springing branch shot a cascade of water right across the path. Rhoani spooked. He leapt sideways, catching Seth and Gisella completely off balance. They both landed with a soggy splat on the mud.

'Who's there?' demanded Mortimer.

On one knee in a flash, Gisella already had her bow raked back ready to shoot. Seth tripped but managed to grab at the reins of his frightened horse. Farrow gave a warning bark.

'Do not be alarmed,' said a familiar voice. A slender figure emerged from the trees in front of them and pushed her hood back off her long silver hair.

'Lady Élanor!' exclaimed Seth. Gisella lowered her bow and got to her feet. Farrow gave a sweeping wag of her tail and, as if reassured, Mai and Phinn wandered off to shelter under a leafy branch. Lady Élanor opened her mouth but Mortimer spoke first.

'Are you alright, my lady? Rexmoore's men – Seth said they've arrested the Fellmen – what about Leon? What happened to those two at the Hall? How–'

But Lady Élanor held up her hand for quiet.

'I am fine, thank you. And Seth is correct. The Fellmen are in Saran jail – but Leon and Olivia are not among them. Morten is trying to find out why the others have been arrested – it seems Rexmoore's men are really only interested in you, Wil.' She nodded towards Wil but changed the subject by answering Mortimer's final question with a wry smile. 'And as for my visitors... they enjoyed rather too much of Martha's gooseberry gin porridge and took my invitation to enjoy a restful nap. They will not bother anyone for a while yet.'

'Won't they guess you tricked them?' asked Gisella, wiping her muddy hands down her cloak.

'Probably. And I am sure they will soon realise that Wil really is *not* in Saran. But by that time you will be well on your way to Armelia and...,' she paused and tapped her finger on her lip, 'Well, it seems that Rexmoore's men really aren't having a good morning. Can you believe that every one of their horses has lost a shoe? And as bad luck would have it, the blacksmith was called to Upper Minton long before dawn this morning. They will not be going anywhere for a while yet.'

'So what happened to Leon and Olivia?' asked Wil.

'Apparently Olivia has gone to stay with an aunt in Lower Minton – she left yesterday afternoon. Fortunately, Leon and Oswald managed to get away before Rexmoore's men got to their house. They will meet you at the Black Stone before nightfall.'

Then with a wary glance over her shoulder Lady Élanor took another two steps forward. She rested her hand on Rhoani's muzzle.

'There is something else I must tell you... I assume that you have all heard of the Alcama?'

Mortimer, Gisella and Wil nodded. Seth looked as if he was trying to recall a distant memory.

'Isn't that when the twin moons become one?' he said searching the sky as if expecting Thesk's two moons to be hanging there at that moment. 'My mother told me about it. She said it doesn't happen very often – I missed the last one 'cos I was in bed with mumps – I can't really remember what happened.'

'Yes, Seth – once every seven years the two moons cross and for a brief moment they become one. Long ago the people of Thesk believed the Alcama to be a time of evil. They would sacrifice animals and lock their doors on the night of the moon crossing.' Her face became sad. 'Children born on the Alcama were cast out as witches.'

Seth looked slightly unnerved.

'I don't remember my mother saying anything about witches!'

Lady Élanor brightened.

'No, I am not surprised. Thankfully, although the Alcama is still treated with suspicion, in the main, fears of witchcraft and sorcery have long since faded.'

'So if it's not like that now, what's the Alcama got to do with us rescuing Tally?' asked Mortimer.

'That is a reasonable question, Mortimer,' said Lady Élanor. 'No doubt you will see evidence of what I am telling you when you get to Armelia; however, there are some who wish to keep the fear alive – my aunt is one of these. People can be controlled when they are fearful.' She paused, stroking Rhoani's nose in long sweeps. Then she added, 'She knows this… she also knows that my sister was born on the night of the Alcama.'

'Oh,' said Mortimer. Realization crept over Wil, too.

'But we don't even know if Tally is in Armelia?'

'Wil, the Alcama is in three nights' time. If Tally *and* Tanith are not there by now, they soon will be,' she said patiently. 'I have no doubt that Imelda will use Tally any way she can to establish the substance and whereabouts of Saran's legacy and I live in dread of what will happen if she is successful.'

Seth looked confused.

'Legacy? I didn't know Saran had a legacy. Does that mean there's loads of gold hidden away somewhere?' he asked. But Wil knew not to expect a direct answer. Tally had told him once that only three people knew what and where the legacy was and that she was not one of them. Wil wondered how much Mortimer and Gisella knew. After all, Gisella's mother was a member of Saran's Order – or at least she had been before she disappeared – and, like Godwyn Savidge, Wil had heard Fermina voice her displeasure at being kept in the dark on the subject of the legacy.

Lady Élanor answered Seth's question just as vaguely as Wil had anticipated.

'The legacy ensures that the people of Saran are kept safe and well, Seth. *What* and *where* it is are nothing to be concerned about. Tally is as ignorant about this as you, and I intend to ensure she stays that way.' She turned back to Wil. 'My concern is Imelda's knowledge of Tally's birth date. She will use it, Wil. I do not want either my sister *or* Tanith to be in any position where danger has been created by superstition. I can only be sure that they are safe if they are home – at Lovage Hall – with me.'

There was real fear in her pale blue eyes. Wil nodded.

'We'll bring them back, don't worry, my Lady.'

Her gaze flitted from Gisella to Mortimer, and Wil was sure he heard the words, 'Not if you are not acting as one.' But at the same moment an angry shout echoed through the trees. With both hands Lady Élanor shooed them away.

'Stay inside the forest for as long as you can,' she said quietly and melted back into the dense woodland of Lovage Hall.

It was only then Wil noticed that it had stopped raining.

CHAPTER FOUR

Friends No More

The ride through Mistle Forest was lightened considerably by Phinn and Mia. Son and daughter of Tarek – the Fellhound that Mortimer had tragically lost on that fateful Moon Chase – they tirelessly charged through the trees and bounded into the long grass at the edge of the forest, returning on command when they looked to be straying too close to open country.

'Well, they certainly seem to like each other!' said Wil in an attempt to get Mortimer talking.

'Yep!' was Mortimer's curt reply.

A yelp came from somewhere behind them. Wil turned. Mia had Phinn pinned to the ground, her huge jaws around her brother's throat.

'Mia, gentle!' roared Mortimer. Mia immediately let go and with a single booming bark jumped backwards, lazily wagging her huge tail. Free of his sister, Phinn lunged, ducked behind her and nipped her on the rump. It was Mia's turn to object with a loud yelp. Then both hounds raced at full pelt in a huge circle, darting between the trees, their massive strides covering the ground at breakneck speed.

Taking advantage of the antics of the young hounds, Wil made yet another attempt to get Mortimer to talk.

'It's great to see Phinn playing with something his own size. At home he's got the choice between the Peachley herding dogs or the tiny Grizzledale Terriers – or the sheep, of course… well, he *thinks* the sheep are one of the choices anyway!'

Mortimer said nothing.

Inwardly cringing, Wil recalled a particularly embarrassing afternoon back in Mistlegard when Phinn tried to *play* with the sheep – thank goodness they weren't lambing at the time! Fortunately, Phinn had grasped Wil's instruction that he wasn't allowed to hurt the sheep – unfortunately, not chasing them or pinning them down by the throat were instructions Phinn chose to completely ignore! After that, Wil kept Phinn in the confines of an unused sheep fold. But he wasn't on his own for long – the smaller village dogs soon overcame their fear of his huge size and their daily visits meant he was never short of company for a game of chase. But the only time Wil could let Phinn really run free was out on Peachley Hills or in the forest. There Phinn could run for miles without doing any harm.

Now, riding through the damp trees, Wil gave up trying to get Mortimer to talk. Instead he watched Phinn and Mia in their own frantic game. Stretching every sinew to gain ground, Phinn tucked his nose under Mia's ribcage and lifted her clean off her feet. Once brought down, his massive jaws closed around her throat; then, almost as if he were counting to three, he would jump away to let her take up the chase. The game went on for quite some time and Wil was delighted to hear Gisella's laughter behind him. Every now and then she shouted encouragement to Mia. But each time her voice rang out Mortimer stiffened. Confused, Shadow danced sideways thinking that Mortimer was urging him into a canter and on more than one occasion Wil nearly toppled off.

As dawn matured into morning the young hounds finally started to flag. Only then did Farrow join them and for a long while all three ambled along behind the horses, sniffing every tree stump and grassy mound that flanked the path.

Suddenly Farrow took off into the dark forest at full pelt.

'Oh, I think she's seen lunch!' said Seth beaming proudly. Almost immediately Farrow reappeared. Something dead was swinging limp from her jaws.

'There we are Mortimer, a marbussal!' shouted Seth as Farrow delivered her prize – a plump, deer-like creature covered in red feathers. He turned to Gisella, 'My aunt cooked one for us last yulefest. I was really surprised – it was really nice!' His eyes shone at the memory but Mortimer's terse response wiped the smile straight off Seth's face.

'We won't have time for cooking, let alone plucking. Martha gave us food – eat that. The hounds can share *that* later!'

Seth slowed his horse, took the marbussal from Farrow's mouth and then fell-in a little way behind. They rode on in silence.

Mortimer's bad mood continued to cast a shadow over the morning and Wil knew he was going to have to say something. At last he thought he'd found the right words.

'Look, Mortimer, I don't know what Gisella's done but I'm not sure it's fair to take it out on Seth like that!'

Mortimer's jaw twitched but he didn't say a word.

Although it had stopped raining, the going was frustratingly slow through the forest. All around them, the trees released heavy drops of freezing water like tiny ice bombs – every one precisely aimed to chill the neck of an unsuspecting rider as they passed under the green canopy. For a very short time it was quite amusing. Wil listened jealously to Seth and Gisella's squeals and giggles the first few times icy water trickled down their necks; but it wasn't long before the novelty wore off and their mirth turned to peevish complaints about the cold.

A lifetime later Wil noticed that the trees were not as densely packed and brighter light indicated that they were right at the edge of the forest. His thighs ached and his bottom was completely numb. All he wanted to do was get his feet back onto solid ground so that he could stretch his legs.

'I really think we need to stop for a break, Mortimer,' he said hopefully.

Mortimer's reply was reasonable, Wil noted, but still stubbornly sullen.

'No. We have to get to the Black Stone before dark. You heard Lady Élanor, Wil. Leon and Oswald'll be waiting for us – it's too dangerous to be that close to Tel Harion without any hounds! And it's not as if our own back-up is that great!' he said throwing a malevolent glance over his shoulder.

As straws went, that was the last for Wil. Without another word, he let go of Mortimer's waist and slid backwards right over Shadow's rump. Landing hard, he hobbled around while the feeling returned to his legs and feet – *never* in the whole of his lifetime would he *ever* understand why people rode horses for pleasure!

Mortimer looked down at Wil in complete astonishment.

'What the…! *What* are you doing, Wil?'

But before Wil could state his case, Seth reined-in Rhoani.

'Well, I agree with Wil!'

Almost before Rhoani came to a halt, Seth swung his leg over the horse's neck. He jumped to the ground and darted behind a bush. Farrow followed.

'Go on girl! Can't a boy have a little privacy?' said Seth from the thick greenery.

Wil saw the smallest smile flash across Mortimer's face but it evaporated in a heartbeat.

Defeated for now, Mortimer dismounted and hurriedly untied the saddle-packs. Wil looked around. Rhoani was standing alone.

'Shall I make up a fire then, Mort?' he asked, putting as much cheer in his voice as he could muster in an effort to distract Mortimer – Gisella and Mia had also disappeared.

'No, we'll have a quick break and then head out over the Fell. We'll take it at a gallop to make up the lost time.'

Starving, Wil was already munching on a soft bread roll from his pack. He choked at Mortimer's words. The thought of giving his already aching muscles a rest had cheered him immensely; the thought of a bone-jangling gallop across Thesker Fell did not!

He had also been looking for an opportunity to have a quiet word with Gisella – to try to find out what was going on between her and Mortimer. Despite the prospect of discovering that they really were going out together – or at least, *had been* – Wil had already decided that the prospect of going over Tel Harion and meeting a Wraithe Wolf with two people who apparently hated each other was far more terrifying. Lady Élanor was right; if they weren't working together any attempt to rescue Tally would end in failure – if not disaster. Wil had to try to find out what was going on – *and* do something to try to put it right, and fast.

'Oh, no!'

The abject horror in Seth's thick voice dragged Wil from his own worries. The sandwich in Seth's hand was missing a large bite-sized chunk.

'Martha's put tomato chutney on my ham – *I hate tomato chutney* – yech!'

Seth spat the contents of his mouth into the grass and threw the rest of the sandwich into the trees with a look of disgust. Mia immediately padded off and sniffed at the discarded sandwich. Gisella jumped to her feet.

'Seth, you really should know better than to give them food just after exercise! No Mia!'

She grabbed at the hound's collar and bent to retrieve the bread. A bolt thunked into the ground inches away from her outstretched fingers.

'What the…!'

Mortimer was on his feet, bow in hand – his face was sheet white.

'If I want you to interfere with the training, or welfare, of *my* Fellhound, Gisella Fairfax – I'll ask you! OK?'

Wil and Seth watched, unable to speak – Wil was barely able to breath.

Gisella unwound her fingers from Mia's collar, picked up the bread and walked towards Mortimer. She stopped only a few feet from him and held out the half-chewed sandwich. When she spoke, her voice was dangerously calm.

'Oh, I'm sorry, Mortimer. Did *you* want to eat it?'

And in a blur of movement she hurled the food into Mortimer's face.

'Whoa!' breathed Seth. Wil stood statue-still. One of the bread slices stuck briefly and then slid to the ground leaving a trail of tomato relish down Mortimer's nose.

'*That* wasn't funny!' said Mortimer in a choked voice and, in a flash, he raised his hand.

'*NO!*' shouted Wil. He lunged forward. At the same moment Mia leapt between Mortimer and Gisella and let out a low warning growl. Wil took one step back; he could feel the hound's confusion – the two people she loved most in the world were fighting and she didn't know which one to protect.

Mortimer looked as if *he'd* been slapped. He dropped his hand to his side.

'It's alright Mia. Down,' he said with a softness that surprised Wil.

The hound hesitated, flicking her eyes briefly towards Gisella then back to her master. Gisella kept her own defiant glare fixed firmly on Mortimer. He repeated his order as softly as before.

'*Down*, Mia.'

As if it was in his own body, Wil felt the hound's heart rate ease. She lowered her body to the ground and lay, sphinx-like – but Wil could still sense her confusion.

Farrow and Phinn stood a little way off, their eyes fixed on their own masters.

Without a word, Mortimer wiped the tomato relish off his cheek with the back of his shaking hand and turned away. Mia sprang up and trotted after him. Wil followed too leaving Gisella with silent tears streaming down her cheeks. As he headed after Mortimer, Wil heard Seth's frightened voice behind him.

'Gosh, Gisella, what was *that* all about?'

Anger bounced around Wil's brain. Battling against the almost overwhelming desire to charge over and punch Mortimer, he watched him roughly strapping his pack back onto Shadow's saddle. For a fleeting moment the surly Fellman reminded Wil of Giles Savidge – the urge to march over and belt him got significantly stronger!

Wil couldn't understand what had gone wrong in only a few months. Why were two of the people he considered to be among his best friends at each other's throats when only a few months before they had been fighting to save each other's lives?

Despite the very strong sense of satisfaction he knew he'd feel if he *did* hit Mortimer, Wil managed to calm his boiling rage. Instead he took a very deep breath and made another attempt to get his friend to talk.

'Is Mia OK there, Mort? She didn't eat any of the bread, did she?'

'Er… no, she's fine.'

Wil could see Mortimer's hands were still shaking.

'Good job Gisella got to it in time then, wasn't it? We don't want a hound with bloat just at the moment, do we?'

Mortimer stopped yanking on the buckle that he'd been struggling with, but didn't turn round.

'Yer. It's a good job she's so quick – she's always looked after Mia like that. Though… I know why, now!'

He said those last words so quietly that Wil thought he'd misheard. Mortimer resumed his struggle with the buckle.

'What do you mean, Mortimer? You know why – *why, what?*'

'Look Wil, it's got nothing to do with you! We need to get a move on or we're not going to be there for Leon and Oswald – *they need us!*'

'Yes, and so does Tally! But if you and Gisella don't sort this out, *no-one*'s gonna to get rescued!'

Mortimer finally turned. He looked past Wil to where Seth was comforting Gisella and his face filled with loathing.

'She's trouble, Wil. She's trying to make Mia obey her instead of me so that she can get me killed on the next Moon Chase!'

Wil felt as if someone had just clutched hold of his heart and squeezed it with both hands. He could not believe what Mortimer had just said.

'Mortimer, I'm not sure who you've been talking to, but they're messing with your head!' Wil was whispering now –

desperately hoping that neither Gisella, nor Seth would overhear this ridiculous conversation. He could hardly believe he was hearing it himself! '*You don't honestly believe that Gisella is planning to get you killed?*'

Mortimer's jaw twitched.

'Olivia told me that–'

'Olivia! Olivia Drews? *Giles Savidge's girlfriend? Ha!*'

Gisella and Seth looked over. Wil kept his voice low.

'You remember what she said up on the Fell, Mortimer? For goodness sake – *she blamed Gisella for what happened to Giles!* Don't you think it might be sensible to be just a *little* bit sceptical about anything she says against Gisella?'

It was so obvious that Wil laughed again. He really was struggling to believe he was actually having this conversation – let alone that there was the remotest chance that Mortimer might be taken in by the heartbroken Chaser over one of his best friends!

'It makes sense Wil! You haven't been here. She's hardly left my side when ever I've been with Mia – some days it's all I can do to get Mia to listen to me. I tell you – if I'd let it go on any longer… I'd definitely have lost control of that Fellhound and goodness knows what might have happened on the next Moon Chase!'

With that Mortimer sprang back up into Shadow's saddle – Wil got the distinct impression that the conversation was over.

'Come on,' said Mortimer, his voice loud enough for the others to hear. 'We've got to get going. They'll be waiting by now!'

Astounded and frustrated, Wil walked away rubbing his hand down his face. '*This cannot be happening!*' he thought. '*I bet there's nothing in any of our bags to deal with this one!*'

Gisella's gentle voice came from a little way behind him. 'Come on, Wil. We've got to go.'

Once again sitting astride Rhoani, behind Seth, Gisella's tear-stained face was pale. She mustered a weak smile.

'Come on, Tally needs us,' she said quietly.

Mortimer rode up and held out a stiff hand. At that moment Wil would have preferred to do absolutely anything else but he had no choice.

Wil was barely back in the saddle when Shadow, followed closely by Rhoani, exploded into the bright sunshine – out onto the wide open expanse of Thesker Fell.

CHAPTER FIVE

The Black Rock

The ride across the Fell was one Wil hoped never to repeat. Every time there seemed the remotest sign that they might slow down, Mortimer kicked Shadow on harder and faster. The freezing wind bit into Wil's cheeks and his eyes streamed as he clung on for dear life.

The hounds flanked them, easily matching the horses' pace as they raced over the open ground, scattering rabbits and wild deer as they bounded over fallen trees and swerved around boulders and bushes. In any other circumstance Wil would have been impressed by Phinn's speed and agility, but right now he just wanted it all to end so that he could get off Shadow.

Even Seth managed to stay in the saddle – although it was touch and go when Rhoani unexpectedly jumped an exposed tree root to get out of a stream!

Then, just as Wil was seriously contemplating falling off and walking the rest of the way – no matter how far it was – Mortimer finally slowed Shadow to a walk. The sun hadn't quite managed to break through during the afternoon, but as it drifted into the horizon somewhere in the west it cast a pink blush across the clouds.

'The Black Rock,' said Mortimer. Up ahead a dark, towering rock stood in perfect silhouette on the hilltop. Just to the left and dwarfed by the huge monolith stood the dark shape of a figure also silhouetted against the evening sky.

'That must be one of them, up there – look!' said Gisella pointing. As if in answer, the figure waved and then disappeared into the shadows.

'They'll be holed-up on the other side out of this wind,' said Mortimer. Wil's eyes had started to clear now that they had slowed down. All around them the ground was peppered with frost and snow snuggled against the rocks out of reach of whatever sun did manage to shine on the barren Fell. Seth drew Rhoani alongside Shadow.

'Well I hope they've got a big fire going,' he panted. His cheeks were a startling shade of red. 'I swear to you, Mortimer, once we get to that rock, I am not moving another step until I've had something decent to eat!'

The daylight was almost spent by the time they climbed the gentle slope that swept up to the base of the huge rock.

'You're late!' growled a voice and a dark figure with a loaded crossbow stepped out of the gloom. Phinn stopped in his tracks and sniffed the air suspiciously; the other two hounds padded towards the voice, their huge tails sweeping from side to side.

Wil recognised the stocky shape of the speaker – it was the Bearer from the Moon Chase, Leon Beck. He recalled how Leon, together with Gisella and Giles Savidge had stayed back as Bearers armed with crossbows. Mortimer's plan had been for Wil to accompany them while they waited for Mortimer, Becky, Emmet and Curtis to ride out onto Tel Harion to draw down a Wraithe Wolf. Unfortunately Giles had decided to change the plan without telling anyone and it had all gone horribly wrong. And then Seth had turned up and things had got a whole lot worse. But, even though everyone knew the truth, Wil knew that Leon had always blamed him and Gisella for what had happened to Giles that night.

Leon acknowledged Mortimer with an abrupt nod.

'What took you so long?'

Then he noticed Seth and Gisella. Giles's expression showed that they were not who he had expected.

'*What the hell have you brought these two for?* It's bad enough that Calloway had to come!'

'Rexmoore's men – Emmet and Curtis didn't get away in time so it seems Lady Élanor made a few *changes*,' said Mortimer. He spat on the ground near Shadow's feet and dismounted. Wil gingerly hauled his aching leg over Shadow's rump, gripped the saddle with both hands and very slowly lowered himself to the ground. Leon addressed Mortimer, obviously enjoying Wil's painful descent.

'Yeah, we saw them take Emmet. Becky, too. They must have taken the others after we'd gone. I'm betting *someone* tipped them off after yesterday's meeting – *can't think who!*'

'Well, no prizes for guessing who Leon thinks *that* might be!' said Gisella icily. 'Well, for your information, Beck, I didn't even *know* about the rescue until dawn this morning when Seth woke me up!'

'Sadly, we only have your word on that, Fairfax! And I'll bet your mother had something to do with it, too!'

'Leave my mother out of this!' said Gisella in a high voice, her eyes glistening again.

'Well, if she's so innocent, where is she? My father said she's been missing for days – and *before* … well, missing a few buns from a baker's dozen, I heard!' Leon laughed at his joke but Gisella didn't see the funny side *at all*.

'Well, at least she hasn't been having cosy meetings with Godwyn Savidge!'

'What–'

'Oh, come on, Leon – they were down by the courtroom two days ago. I heard Savidge say that Morten Mortens is too old for the Order. Savidge is desperate to be the Grand Wizen – I heard him talking about *special privileges* if your father helps him?'

Wil thought about Oswald and Godwyn's row at Lovage Hall the night before and closed his eyes – things were rapidly going from very bad to even worse!

'And what special privileges might those be, *Miss Fairfax?*'

Wil opened his eyes. Oswald Beck – a crocodile smile on his face – was standing behind Gisella. She went to say something but closed her mouth quickly. To Wil's great relief it was Mortimer who spoke next. He was looking into the blackening sky. The sun had set leaving behind a star-lit horizon that threatened a very cold night.

'Look, I'm sorry Mr Beck, but we really don't have time for this. We're going to have to make a move again in a couple of hours.'

Wil could see that Oswald was about to take up the argument but before anyone could say anything else a relieved voice from somewhere below them piped up, 'Thank goodness for that, I'm starving!'

While they had all been arguing, Seth had found a sheltered ledge and was busily building a fire.

'I would have thought you'd have done this by now!' he was saying as Wil and Mortimer dropped down onto the ledge carrying their saddle-packs over their arms. Leon followed, empty-handed.

'What do you mean '*by now*'?' said Leon.

Gisella dropped her bag close to the fire and stomped off in the direction of a stream that Wil could hear babbling at the base of a nearby gully.

'We saw you waving from way off,' said Mortimer pointing back across the Fell in the direction they had come. For a split second Leon looked utterly confused but rallied almost instantly.

'Oh, *then!*' he said quickly. 'Oh yer, I saw you *then*. But, well, you know… we had to unload our things and I needed to get water for the horses. We just hadn't had a chance to make up the fire. Anyway – Seth's doing a great job without my help!'

Red-faced, Oswald tottered into the makeshift camp carrying both saddle packs.

'Hard ride, Mister Beck?' Wil asked pleasantly while they all watched Seth trying desperately hard not to burn himself.

'Yes, boy – beat you to it, though!' he said triumphantly and lifted his flask to his lips. Wil watched a small trickle of dark liquid dribble down the man's chin as he took a deep draught.

'You certainly did!' said Wil and headed off towards the sound of the brook.

From the edge of the gully Wil could see Gisella's slender frame below. She was barefoot and up to her knees in the stream, splashing water over her face and arms. The shallow brook tumbled noisily over the rocks, drowning any surrounding sounds – if Wil was going to speak to Gisella, now looked like the time.

There was no real path down the bank and, with darkness closing, in the going wasn't easy. Even Phinn picked his way cautiously, with his body so low that his deep ribcage brushed the ground.

Wil reached the water's edge at the same moment that Gisella looked up – just in time to see the large flat boulder to which Wil had just committed all of his weight, rock sideways. There were two spectacular splashes – one was Wil; the other was Phinn whose enthusiastic leap to follow Wil strongly suggested that he thought this was some great new game.

'Well, that's one way to get my attention!' said Gisella.

Wil spat out a mouthful of the river.

'It wasn't quite what I had in mind.'

The stream was deeper than Wil had expected and within a second his boots were brimful of icy water. Wading happily beside him, Phinn ducked his nose and blew out a lungful of bubbles until, with a drenching jerk, he raised his head and coughed loudly. Then he did it again.

Wil, meanwhile, was trying in vain to get to his feet but he hadn't noticed that his waterlogged cloak had wrapped around a tree root. He fell for the second time. This time Gisella laughed out loud.

She waded over to him and untangled the cloak.

'You should be able to get up now. Here!' she said.

Wil took her outstretched hand – cold and slender, it felt weird in his rough palm – nice, but weird.

Back on his very soggy feet, Wil waded to the bank. He plonked down on a twisted tree root, leant back and lifted both legs into the air. Water cascaded out of his boots and over his trousers – together with the half a dozen bolts that he had jammed into his boot earlier. Gisella laughed again.

'Well, as long as someone thinks it was funny,' said Wil, with a good-natured grin.

Gisella's voice lost its mirth and her smile vanished. She waded back to the bank and picked up her boots.

'Well, it's certainly the funniest thing I've seen all day!'

Wil folded the edge of his cloak over two of the bolts to make a tight twist and squeezed about a bucket of water out of the cloth.

'Just what *is* going on with you and Mortimer?' he said.

'I would have thought that *you* knew the answer to that, Wil!' snapped Gisella.

Wil continued to squeeze his dripping cloak.

'Well... if I did, I wouldn't... be asking... would I?'

Gisella gave a derisory snort.

'You don't honestly expect me to believe that, do you, Wil? You and Mortimer have been thick as thieves all day!'

She was still standing in the stream waving her boots over her head – Wil could see that there was a distinct possibility he wasn't going to be the only one to end up soaking wet!

'Maybe *you'd* like to tell *me* what's going on because I *really* haven't got a clue!'

'Look Gisella, I'm asking you because Mortimer just won't talk about it. Seth's as confused as me and to be honest, unless it gets sorted out, I really don't hold out much hope of us rescuing Tally. In fact, at this rate, *she's going to be in more danger if we go than if we don't!*'

Gisella stopped flinging her boots around for a moment and stared into the busy stream.

'Do you think I hadn't thought of that, Wil? Look – all I know is that Bryn asked me to help Mortimer with Mia – after he, you know – lost Tarek so suddenly – then next minute he's best friends with Leon and I'm left out in the cold!'

'So, you and Mortimer... you aren't... I mean... you weren't... well, of course – you were just helping him with Mia, weren't you?' Wil's words tumbled out in a rush. Gisella frowned.

'That's what I just said, Wil?'

'Yes, but Seth... eh... Seth said that he thought that everyone else assumed–'

'Wil, for goodness sake, I am not *now* – and *never was* – going out with Mortimer Merridown – if that's what you are so ineptly trying to ask!'

Gisella was wielding her boots again so dangerously that Wil felt compelled to duck in case she let go – accidentally, or otherwise!

'No… of course not… I didn't think that you were, of course – I just thought, you know… I'd better check, er, to make sure there was no… er… misunderstanding.'

'The only misunderstanding around here is that I *thought* I was coming to help my friends rescue Tally – but apparently no-one wants me here!'

With that Gisella hurled one of her battered boots into the water right in front of her.

'*I want you here!*' thought Wil. He watched the boot bob a short distance down stream before it snagged on a fallen branch, filled with water and sank.

'Do you want me to go and get that?' he asked after a moment's silence.

'No, I'll get it!' she answered, her face sullen. Still clutching the other boot, she took a precarious step and gingerly placed one bare foot on a rock in the middle of the stream. 'Honestly Wil, you've got to believe me. I went to see Bryn because I want to train as a Chaser. He was already worried about Mortimer taking Mia on so soon after Tarek so he suggested that I could help Mortimer to train Mia – that way I could keep an eye on him and learn about Fellhounds at the same time. And my mother was…' she frowned and took a deep breath, 'wasn't well… so it was perfect to get me out of the house.' She sploshed her foot back into the water. 'For a while Mortimer seemed fine but then one day I went to join him out on Nell's Reach and he completely ignored me. It was awful, Wil. I don't know what I've done and now he won't even look at me ...' She broke off. With another deep, this time, shaky breath she retrieved her boot and swooshed a handful of water over her face.

Wil sat on the bank contemplating what she'd just told him. Mortimer had said that she wants to become a Chaser!

'*But that didn't mean that she wanted to take Mortimer's place,*' he reasoned. '*...and it certainly didn't mean that she wanted him dead... Did it?*'

'Did you tell anyone else about this, Gizzy?' he asked out loud.

'Only Olivia – I went to see her. I know she said some horrid things about me on the Moon Chase after Giles... you know... but I'm sure she didn't mean them – we were always okay before.'

Still barefoot, Gisella tottered back along the rocks, clambering over the tree roots that cluttered the riverbank. 'She doesn't want to be a Fellman any more, Wil. Now Giles is gone she wants to leaving Saran for good when she gets to her eighteenth summer. She told me and then made me promise not to tell anyone, so I haven't... until now. That's next summer, Wil. I thought it would be a great chance to take her place without upsetting anyone – and we already know that Seth wants to be a Bearer rather than a Chaser, so he could take *my* place – as long as we could convince his father, of course!'

The root – Wil's makeshift seat – bounced as Gisella plonked down heavily and emptied her boot into the swirling pool below her feet.

'Well, it certainly sounds like you've got it all worked out, Giz – but why didn't you tell Mortimer?'

'I promised Olivia and, anyway, I wanted to make sure I could handle a Fellhound first. If I was hopeless I wouldn't stand a chance – and I'd look stupid. So I asked Olivia not to tell anyone until I was ready and she said that she wouldn't.'

Wil stared down into the dark water below him as her words flowed over him. He knew that she was telling the truth.

'*She has no idea that Olivia broke her promise; Olivia must have told Leon who twisted the truth to suit himself,*' he thought. All he needed to do was to go to Mortimer and explain what had happened. But if Mortimer's mind had already been swayed by Olivia's broken promise, it might be difficult to convince him – *especially* when the deliverer – Leon – was about to accompany them up onto Tel Harion!

As Wil deliberated on what to do, a handful of earth and stones rolled past into the stream. Farrow was first to appear, but almost immediately Seth's familiar voice drifted out of the darkness.

'Wil… Gisella… are you down there? Come and eat something – we'll be off again soon! Farrow, come here now!'

Wil didn't think it would be a good idea to antagonise Mortimer any further by making it obvious that he and Gisella had been talking. He lowered his voice to a whisper.

'You go up – I'll have a quick wash and be up in a minute.'

'But aren't you clean enough from your dunking?' said Gisella with a mischievous giggle. But without waiting for an answer she pulled on her boots and left him where he sat. He listened to her scrambling up the bank and wondered again what had happened to Gisella's mother, Fermina. He heard Gisella swear in the darkness and another flurry of rubble cascaded past him.

Phinn, bored of rooting about in the river bank, splashed over and nudged Wil's knee with his very wet nose.

'*It would be much easier if Leon wasn't with us,*' he thought stroking Phinn's damp ear. Without Leon, Wil knew he would be able to explain the misunderstanding to

Mortimer this minute and everything would be okay; but just what story *had* Olivia and Leon cooked up for Mortimer? And the fact that Gisella really did want to become a Chaser was going to make it harder to convince Mortimer that Leon's version was a lie – *and* what on earth were Godwyn Savidge and Oswald Beck planning for the Order? With both Leon *and* Leon's father around, Wil thought, finding out was going to be even more difficult.

CHAPTER SIX

A Gift from Above

'… far too dangerous, Leon! If we go that way we might as well paint ourselves in deer's blood, too, because the Wraithe Wolves will have us for supper!'

Mortimer stopped talking and looked up as Wil walked into the little camp.

'Where've you been?' he asked suspiciously, glancing over at Gisella who had suddenly found something very interesting in her bag.

'Went for a wash but I slipped and fell in the stream – I've been *ages* wringing out my clothes.'

Wil draped his wet cloak over a bush for extra effect before delving into his own bag.

Leon nodded towards Gisella. 'But *she* went down there, too?' he hissed, his voice loaded with accusation.

'Oh!' said Wil in feigned surprise. He took a bite out of the pork and apple pasty that Martha had packed for him – he was cold and suddenly ravenously hungry. The huge pasty was absolutely delicious! He spoke again with his mouth full. 'I didn't see you, Giz – but come to think of it,' he swallowed, 'I did hear someone splashing about further upstream. But it was too dark to see who it was.'

Taking care not to catch anyone's eye, Wil munched hungrily. Even though the pasty was stone cold, he could feel the food warming him through.

'Did anyone else have one of these, they're really good!' he asked, taking another huge mouthful.

'What was in yours, Wil? I had corned beef – *my favourite!*' chirped Seth. He was looking a lot happier now he had a full stomach.

'Pork and apple – I think?'

'Ew! That sounds yech!' exclaimed Seth, sticking his tongue out in disgust.

'I thought you might say that!' Wil grinned and popped the last scrumptious morsel into his mouth.

With supper finished, Mortimer suggested that they get some rest before heading on. The fire was still glowing but Wil wasn't convinced that he would get any sleep at all on the frozen ground. He hauled his still damp cloak around him and glanced over at Seth. The sleeping boy's hair was coated with a light dusting of frost that glistened in the moonlight; however, despite the ice Wil could feel knitting into his own eyebrows, within less than a minute he too was fast asleep.

But Wil's dreams were far from restful. Stomach-churning flying scenes made way for rows of teeth; then a putrid smell filled his nose and he was being chased by at least a hundred Wraithe Wolves. Next Phinn was locked in a vicious fight with an Eagard that picked him up and carried him up over Mort Craggs; Phinn was yelping helplessly and just as the giant bird flew over what looked like the ruins of a castle, it let go–

Wil woke with a jolt. In that split second between being asleep and being wide awake, Wil had the feeling he was being watched. He shook his head and blinked into the dark. The only sound around him was the regular breathing of sleeping people. Farrow and Mia were sprawled out a little way off, seemingly oblivious to the ice beneath them.

Then, in the light of the dying fire, Wil spotted Phinn's shining eyes fixed on him – the hound's long eyebrows sparkling with frost. Wil grinned to himself; he should have known it would be Phinn. The young hound stayed with his chin flat on the floor between his huge, outstretched paws. Reassured, Wil closed his eyes but the cold crept into his bones and his mind just wouldn't shut up. It kept asking him questions about Gisella and Mortimer, the journey they were about to make, and Tally – *how would they know where she was? Or even if she was still alive? What was Armelia really like?*

Wrapped tight in his cloak, Wil tucked his arm under his head and did his best to focus on nothing but the darkness around him. Suddenly something hit his cheek. He brushed his face in case it was a midge – although he knew that it was too cold and too early in the year for midges – by about two full seasons!

He tried to settle again but something else stung his temple.

'What the…?' he whispered crossly and sat up. Phinn raised his head as well. A third stinging tap right on the crown of Wil's head made both he and Phinn look up.

'Crronk!'

The familiar noise came from the top of the Black Rock high above them somewhere in the starless night sky. Phinn sat bolt upright on his haunches.

'*No, DROP!*" Wil thought.

To his absolute amazement Phinn immediately lay down and dropped his chin back on the ground. He watched Wil intently.

'Well I'll be… that's a first!" muttered Wil, casting his mind back to those frustrating hours in the sheepfold at Mistlegard when training sessions with Phinn had not gone to plan – well, not *Wil's* plan anyway!

From above them, another impatient *Crronk!* echoed out of the dark and something dropped out of the sky, clipped the face of Black Rock loudly and landed right on top of him. Startled, he lunged to grab the missile before it rolled off his cloak and scrambled to his feet. At the same moment, Wil caught sight of Oswald. Lying nearest to him, the man was on his side staring directly at Wil.

Not knowing what else to do, Wil gave a weak smile and offered up what appeared to be a long, straight stick by way of an explanation as to why he was dancing about in the freezing moonlight. But Oswald just held his wide-eyed stare; then, after a few seconds he turned over and snored loudly.

Wil held his breath but no-one else stirred. He looked at Oswald again – the man's deep, regular breathing suggested that he was fast asleep. Slightly spooked, Wil decided not to check if Oswald's eyes were still open.

In the clear sky the twin moons shed a pale light across the sheer granite. In a few nights time they would be full – and, for a brief spell, would cross and shine as one huge silver orb. Wil wondered what the Alcama would be like in Saran. He remembered the last one in Mistlegard. It was his ninth or tenth spring and his parents had taken him to Garth Fengal's home where the village had gathered for the event. Round and built of stone like all of the houses in the village, it was a good deal bigger than most. The central house was surrounded by a cluster of little extensions – almost like a troop of mushrooms. Set in its walls were tiny, recessed windows – into each of which had been placed a sheep's skull illuminated by a candle. Wil's mother had explained that if the candles burned all night they would all have good luck for the next seven years. Later that evening when Wil opened the door to get some more pear juice from the larder one of the candles had blown out – just over a year later Rexmoore's men had come and taken Wil's father away and Wil never saw him again.

A flutter of wings above his head jolted Wil out of his sad memory. He had the strongest feeling he was being watched and scoured the night in search of Pricilla. But in the darkness he had little hope of seeing the jet black raven, even if she was making her presence obvious. Wil's curiosity was also now getting the better of him – he wanted to take a closer look at that stick. So, worried he might wake the others, Wil tiptoed around to the other side of the Black Rock. Phinn hauled himself to his feet and padded after his master.

'So, what do you think we've got here, Phinn?' whispered Wil. It was difficult to get a good look in the thin light, but the stick – or staff, if that's what it was – felt surprisingly light. Phinn sniffed the curious object with interest. Wil closed his fingers around the smooth wood at the head – it was worn… and warm, as if the hand that had carried it for many years had only just given it up. The hairs on the back of Wil's neck prickled. He folded his fingers around the wood and ran his free hand down its length. It narrowed almost to a point. In stark contrast, the tip was ice-cold – some sort of metal, Wil assumed; square with knife-sharp corners and a flat base. With the tip on the ground the head came up to Wil's elbow.

Quickly deciding that the staff must have come from Lady Élanor via Pricilla, Wil immediately dismissed any suspicious thoughts – after all, she did have a habit of delivering things to him when he was out on the Fells, although what the purpose of this latest gift might be – he had no idea. Knowing Pricilla – *that* would become evident in time!

CHAPTER SEVEN

Eagards!

Voices drifting through the darkness told Wil that everyone was awake and getting ready to leave. So, carrying the staff as nonchalantly as he could, he rejoined the others. Leon eyed him with suspicion.

'Where've you been?'

'Oh, you know... just needed a private moment.'

'Oh, yer, er… right. Well, you'd better get packed up – we're not waiting!'

Wil swept his cloak over his shoulders and pushed his flask down into his pack. Right at the bottom of the deep bag his fingers brushed against something soft. It felt like fine rope. Unfortunately with so much food crammed in on top of it, try as he might Wil was unable to get a closer look just at that moment. So, silently resolving to eat more, he pulled the drawstring tight.

Strapping the bag back onto Shadow's saddle, it dawned on Wil that he wasn't going to be able to carry both his crossbow *and* the newly-acquired staff without the risk of blinding Mortimer – and neither would fit into his bag.

'What've you got there?' Mortimer asked. His mood had greatly improved since they had met up with Leon and Oswald.

'I'm not sure yet,' answered Wil. He was failing to tie the staff to his bow.

'I'm pretty sure it's from Lady Élanor,' he added in a low voice, not wanting Leon or Oswald to hear.

'Oh! Well, if it's *half* as useful as that first aid pack she gave you on the Moon Chase, it'll be worth struggling to hang on to it!' said Mortimer while Wil wound the strap of his bow around the staff. But when he tried to hang them both over his shoulder the staff just twirled to the ground. Wil tried again – the same thing happened. Irritation rising, he hooked the strap over his shoulder and rammed the staff through the fastenings – the cord snapped and bow and staff clattered to the ground. Leon and Oswald looked over. Wil gave them a casual wave.

'Just dropped my bow!'

They nodded and resumed their own conversation.

'Oh, well done, Wil! Look! You've broken it already!'

Mortimer was pointing down at the staff. It was lying on the ground, snapped in two places and bent almost into a triangle.

'Oh, great!' sighed Wil. Angry, he snatched up the broken staff. It snapped back into a perfectly straight, rigid rod.

'Whoa!' said Mortimer, stepping back. 'How did you do *that*?'

'I don't know,' answered Wil. Very gently, he flexed the staff again – it bowed but did not break. With a frown he let it go. It hit the stone and flicked back into its triangular shape. Wil picked it up and squeezed the corners gently – the triangle folded into a neat bundle, about a third the length of the original staff.

'Well, that should do it!' He slid the staff neatly into his bag.

Mortimer raised his eyebrow, 'Hmm, I have to admit, Wil, I'm struggling to find uses for a collapsible stick just at the moment!'

To Wil's relief the journey through the reminder of the night, while swift and extremely uncomfortable, was at least uneventful. They even managed to cross the river on Tel Hireth without Seth falling in!

By dawn Mortimer seemed satisfied with progress and it didn't take much for Oswald to persuade him that they should stop for a rest. It was obvious that everyone was flagging.

With sweat running down his face, Oswald was the first to dismount. He stood for quite some time with his hands on his knees, breathing very heavily, before he carefully lowered himself to the ground and leant back against a rock. He flexed his knees and winced.

Leon bent to speak to his father and while Wil wasn't near enough to hear, Oswald's bad-tempered answer gave Wil a clue as to what Leon might have said.

'For the last time, boy – I'm absolutely fine!'

Oswald splashed water from his flask onto a rag which he dabbed over his face and neck.

Looking slightly hurt, Leon turned away. He dragged a cloth bundle from his saddle pack and stomped off towards Mortimer, who was stationed under a tree. Mortimer was devouring one of Martha's pasties; his broadsword and bow abandoned for the moment, leaning against the trunk behind him.

Grateful to feel solid ground under his feet, Wil idly wondered what filling Martha had put into Mortimer's pasty as it was Wil's guess that she had cooked to everyone's individual tastes. With high expectations, he delved into his own pack and was not disappointed. His hand immediately found a slab of honey cake – one of his particular favourites – and, nestling against a boulder, he began his breakfast. Phinn flopped down beside him and immediately fell asleep.

'The hounds'll need a couple of hours to rest and eat,' said Mortimer, sprinkling crumbs down his chest, 'So once we've had some food we might as well all try to get some sleep.'

'Good plan, Mort!' said Leon and waved a stripped chicken leg in mock salute.

To Wil's increasing frustration, Leon and Mortimer had become inseparable since Leon and his father had joined them. It was proving impossible for Wil to talk to Mortimer about Gisella – although he was forced to admit to himself that he had no idea how to broach the subject, or what to say once he had.

Wil's failure to help Mortimer and Gisella reconcile their differences was doing nothing to quell his worries about how they were going to rescue Tally. Lady Élanor's words kept coming back to him – '*Not if you are not acting as one,*' she had warned. But with Leon and Oswald starting to bicker and no sign of Mortimer even breathing near Gisella, Wil felt that the prospect of them all working together was, at that moment, remote to say the least.

'When do you think we'll get to Armelia?' Leon asked Mortimer through a mouthful of bread.

'Well, we're right above Skelmer Hollow now,' said Mortimer. Wil felt his stomach drop into his boots – Skelmer Hollow was where Wil had fought for his life in the Moon Chase. Suddenly he didn't want the rest of his breakfast.

Mortimer continued, oblivious of Wil's alarm. 'Once we get to the tip of Thesker Pyke we should be able to see Mort Craggs.' He scoured the distant hills as if expecting to see the

Craggs at any moment. 'That'll give us a better idea of when we're likely to get to the city.'

'So where's the castle? Is it actually *in* Armelia?' asked Seth. He and Gisella were sitting on a rocky ledge a little way off. Gisella had fixed her gaze out over the frost-coated grassland. Mortimer raised his pasty in Oswald's direction.

'Well, I don't really know, but I'm hoping that Mr Beck here will be able to show us the way once we get to the Craggs!'

But Oswald's surprised expression suggested that this was news to him.

'What gave you that idea, boy?'

'Well, I thought... well, you've been to Armelia before, haven't you – as a member of the Majewizen?'

'Gracious, no! There's never been any need – I think Mortens went once or twice, but Rexmoore always sends his men out if he wants anything – I thought you knew that?'

'Er, no, but ... well... I thought you knew the city – that's the only reason I agreed that you could come with us!'

Mortimer took another huge bite out of his pasty.

Without saying a word Oswald got to his feet and walked right up to Mortimer – the older man's face had been red before, but now even his eyebrows were beetroot.

'I was not aware that I needed *your* agreement!' he said and turned away. Then he turned back and pointed directly at Mortimer.

'Make no mistake, boy, the errors you made on that last Moon Chase will *not* be repeated while I am here!'

Mortimer swallowed hard. His eyes flicked to Leon who stared at the ground; then to Wil, who held his friend's gaze but didn't dare say anything. Then Mortimer opened his mouth to speak – the remains of his breakfast forgotten in his up-turned hand. But whatever he was about to say went unsaid.

A shrieking cry shattered the awkward silence.

'No! Mortimer, *LOOK OUT!*"

The shout came from Gisella. But before Mortimer had time to raise his head a huge grey and black shape swooped down.

'*Eagards!*' yelled Seth.

But it was too late. One eagard grabbed at Mortimer's wrist. He cried out. Blood gushed down his hand. The great bird wrapped its talons around Mortimer's arm. Wil could see it was trying to get airborne again. Leon must have seen it too. He was on his feet in a flash. But, as if something had lifted and discarded him, Leon suddenly flipped backwards and lay flat on the ground with his arms over his head.

'*NO!*' Oswald yelled and ran to his son, oblivious of the eagard's massive wings – each one easily the length of a full-grown man.

In the chaos of barking hounds and Mortimer's agonized cries, Wil grabbed his bow and cursed – the bolts were no longer in his boot. He must have left them on the river bank after his chat with Gisella. All his others were packed away in his bag – but Rhoani and Shadow had bolted out onto the Fell as soon as the eagards had attacked. In desperation, Wil yanked his knife from his belt but Mia was now frantically leaping and snapping at the bird, making a clean throw impossible.

Wil could see Mortimer was trying to get to his sword. His desperate fingers brushed the hilt as the monstrous bird hauled him off his feet. With a metallic clang, the sword slid away, out of reach.

Mia threw herself up at the eagard's neck but was knocked backwards by an easy beat of the bird's giant wing. Gisella was standing on the ledge above Wil jabbing her finger to his left.

'Wil – my bow – *use my bow!*'

Wil whirled around – Gisella's bow was only a few feet from him and there in the stock, ready to load, lay a silver-tipped bolt.

'You are truly wonderful, Gisella Fairfax,' he muttered and dived for the bow. At the same moment two more eagards came out of the sky – only to be met by Farrow and Phinn. One pulled up just in time to avoid Farrow's snapping jaws. But as it abruptly changed course and took off into the safety of the sky, it collided with Gisella and sent her tumbling out of sight.

The other eagard was less fortunate – Phinn snapped his jaws around its throat and dragged it efficiently to the ground where, with a gush of dark blood it slumped lifeless at the Fellhound's feet.

But there was no time for praise. Wil looked around frantically but couldn't see any sign of Gisella, and Mortimer was now being dragged away. Mia, back on her feet, was joined by Farrow. They charged after her master and with a lunge Mia grabbed a mouthful of tail feathers in her teeth and held fast.

Adrenalin seared through Wil's veins. He dragged the bow string back until it clicked. An ear piercing screech made him look around. Hurtling straight towards him on an absolute collision course was the third eagard. It streaked through the sky with its wings set in a dive position – the image of a helpless mouse sprang into Wil's mind. He took aim.

Then, just as he was about to shoot, with his bow ready Seth rose up between him and the stooping bird. Seth took aim. Wil yelled at the back of Seth's head.

'Seth, look out! Get out of the way! I can't get a shot!'

He wasn't sure if Seth had ignored him or just didn't hear him but in the next breath Seth released his bolt. The bird screamed and went into a spiral. Seth ducked – Wil, however, didn't.

Chapter Eight

A Stitch in Time

Though very blurred, the sight of Gisella's face and the feel of her cool hand on his arm eased the splitting headache that also greeted Wil when he woke up. He moved to sit up but felt Gisella's hand resist his efforts. He lay back down.

'I think it might be best if you stay there for a while, Wil. I'm still not sure you haven't got a few broken ribs – the way that eagard ploughed into you. It's a good job it was already dead!'

'What? Is there a difference in being hit by a dead Eagard to a live one then?' croaked Wil. His aching ribs certainly told him that he'd been hit by something very heavy. Gisella shrugged.

'I hope we don't find out! At least you're not going to have any scars.'

Ignoring Gisella's protestations, Wil made a second, more successful attempt to haul himself up onto his elbow. Under the tree that Mortimer had been using as a back rest, Wil could see fuzzy shapes moving. He could hear Seth and Mortimer's voices. To the left was a larger shape, sitting on its haunches – Mia or Farrow, Wil couldn't say.

Blinking to try to clear his vision, Wil spotted Rhoani and Shadow, once more tethered to a tree closer to him. Next to them were more shapes – one lying on the ground next to the horses. He could hear Oswald talking in a low voice. His heart sank.

'Oh no, Giz! They didn't get Leon, did they?'

'Yes, Wil. But it's OK, he's not dead – well, I think it's OK.' Gisella frowned. 'He hasn't come round yet and Oswald won't let me near him. Honestly, Wil, I can't imagine what he thinks I'm going to do!'

At the sound of Gisella's voice, Seth looked over his shoulder.

'Wil! Welcome back! I really thought you'd get out of the way. I couldn't believe it when you didn't duck!'

He nodded towards three black and white mounds.

As Wil's eyes drifted in and out of focus he realised that the lifeless mounds were eagards. One was streaked with mud; one was caked in what, even through his misty vision, looked like drying blood and he was pretty sure the other didn't have a head. Then he saw Phinn and Farrow – lying sphinx-like alongside their trophies. Wil beamed proudly.

'Gosh! Well that wasn't a bad morning's work!'

But then Mortimer let out a low moan.

'You OK?' Wil called over, blinking hard.

Mortimer waved his arm. Wil could see something glistening crimson.

'Is that blood?'

'Yer, but I'm planning on living – if we can stop this!' answered Mortimer. His voice sounded flat. Squinting hard, Wil could just make out a bandage at the top of Mortimer's arm. It was fastened with what looked like a stick that Seth kept turning. Each time Seth touched the stick Mortimer took a sharp intake of breath through what sounded distinctly to Wil like gritted teeth.

'It's a tourniquet,' Gisella whispered, in answer to Wil's unasked question. 'It's bad, Wil. We can't stop the bleeding.'

'Have you looked in my bag?' asked Wil, equally quietly.

'No. Why would I do that?'

'Because Martha packed another first aid kit – didn't you hear her at the stables?'

'Er, no, I must have missed that,' answered Gisella.

'Can't think why!' sighed Wil and silently resolved that this argument between Mortimer and Gisella really had to be sorted out.

Without waiting to be asked Gisella jumped up and ran to Wil's pack. Within a few moments she returned and handed Wil a small, pink, silk bag – Wil recognised it immediately.

'Right, let's see if Lady Élanor has done it again,' Wil thought to himself and rummaged in the little bag. Almost immediately he felt cool glass and pulled out a tiny clear phial; swinging from its even tinier glass stopper was a label that was almost as big as the phial itself. He made an attempt to read the label:

For Feather Blindness:
Apply once and keep eyes bound
For four full days.
Do not allow sun or moon light
to shine on eyes during treatment.
Best before: The next gibbous moon.

Wil was confused. He glanced over at Mortimer and then at Gisella.

'How're his eyes?'

Gisella pursed her lips in thought. 'I don't remember him saying anything about his eyes – he certainly looked horrified enough when I went over to help him! So I'd say his sight is pretty good. Why, what's that?'

Wil held out the tiny phial of clear liquid. Gisella read the label and peered into his eyes.

'Must be for you then.'

Wil shut his eyes and looked away.

'It can't be – my eyesight's still a bit blurry but it's getting better all the time!'

It was a lie – his sight wasn't a bit blurry, it was *very* blurry.

'Maybe that bump confused the messages I'm giving the bag? I'll give it another go.'

He delved into the bag again, this time keeping his eyes firmly fixed on the fuzzy image of Mortimer's blood-soaked bandage. A sharp pain shot through his finger and he dropped the bag.

'Ouch!'

A pack of needles and a twist of extremely fine golden thread lay on the ground next to the bag. But, to his surprise, there was no label.

Gisella looked at the pack, her eyes wide.

'Gosh – I think you're meant to sew him up, Wil.'

'I think you're right. The only problem is – I couldn't darn a pair of socks at the moment, let alone Mortimer.' He blinked up at her. 'You're going to have to do it, Gisella!'

'NO! Absolutely no way!'

Mortimer tucked his injured arm behind his back. Gisella retreated. Still at Leon's side, Oswald cast a brief, unseeing glance across to where Wil, Gisella and Seth were trying to persuade Mortimer to let Gisella sew up his arm. Leon was still unconscious. Oswald mopped Leon's brow and then held the rag he had been using to his own face – Wil got the distinct impression the man was crying.

Turning his attention back to the horror-struck Mortimer, Wil did his best to stay calm – blood was now dripping down off Mortimer's elbow onto the grass.

'It's the only way, Mort! You know how Lady Élanor's bag saved me before – and you remember Gisella's leg? So if it's given us this – well, it probably means that if we were back at Lovage Hall, Lady Élanor would be the one stitching you up!'

'I know that, Wil, but *you* can do it!'

'I've already told you – I can't see clearly enough! For all I know, I could be sewing your fingers together!' Wil's patience was ebbing rapidly.

'Well, it's you or no-one and that's the end of it!' said Mortimer, his jaw set. But he was now deathly pale and beads of perspiration soaked his temple. Wil sat back on his haunches and chucked the pink bag to one side. If only Mortimer hadn't believed Leon and Olivia's lie! It was a good job that Leon was already unconscious, he thought, smouldering with anger, because if he hadn't been–.

'Wil, can you come here a minute.'

Gisella was standing a little way off. In one hand she held the little silk bag; in the other she held out a small square of clean white cloth. Like the phial, it had a label dangling from it. Mortimer was now shakily making his way over to Leon and Oswald. Seth was following behind, poised ready to catch him, if – or rather, when – Mortimer passed out.

Wil lifted the label but the words swam in front of his eyes.

'Sorry Gisella, can you read it for me?'

Gisella read in a whisper, 'Chloroform – *emergencies only*. Ideal for minor operations, *stitches*, extracting teeth or foreign objects. Get patient to take one deep breath and work quickly! Best before: Eternity.'

Wil pursed his lips.

'OK, so all we have to do is get Mortimer to put this over his nose and breathe in and everything else will be plain sailing!'

'Look Wil, I know he doesn't trust me at the moment but to be honest, I'm not sure he trusts Oswald. Maybe if you show him this and tell him that *Seth* will do the stitches – well, he might just go for it – then I can do them and he'll never need to know!'

'*Seth! Do you honestly think Mortimer's going to let Seth loose on any bit of his body with a needle?*'

'Well, in that case we'd better just wait until he passes out from loss of blood – which I don't think is going to be that long!' hissed Gisella. Mortimer had slumped against a tree. His face was ghost-white. Wil knew they didn't have a choice. Somehow, Wil had to convince Mortimer that Seth could do the stitches.

'Needles! Oh, no. I faint at the sight of needles – always have! I'm really sorry!'

Seth did look genuinely sorry. He had perked up significantly at the prospect of helping Mortimer but as Wil and Gisella had hastily explained their plan, his expression had gone from eager enthusiasm to genuine horror.

'But Seth, you don't have to do the *actual* stitches – just let Mortimer *believe* you're going to do them. Once he's taken the chloroform Gisella can do them!' Wil begged – his sight was clearing, but not nearly quickly enough.

'I really don't think–' Seth began, but Gisella cut in.

'How about, if Wil holds the needles – as if he's helping you? You can give Mortimer the chloroform, Seth – after all, he trusts *you*!'

Seth brightened but then frowned again.

'But won't he suspect something if you're with us, Gisella? And what about Oswald? I can't see him standing back if he sees you bearing down on his son's new best friend with a needle in your hand!'

Gisella threw a guilty glance towards Wil.

'Gisella's already thought of that one, Seth,' said Wil, managing to sound a lot more confident than he felt.

'How is he, sir?' asked Wil quietly.

He knelt down opposite Oswald and stifled a gasp. Leon was as still as a stone. Across both of his closed eyes were three dark red wheals. He looked like he'd been branded.

Oswald mopped his son's face and then dabbed his own eyes as he had done before with the same grubby cloth. He blew his nose.

'I couldn't do anything,' he whispered. 'I'm so sorry, son. I just couldn't do anything.'

'Why don't you come and help us, sir? Seth is going to stitch Mortimer's arm,' said Wil gently, although he was pretty sure that Oswald wasn't listening. 'Come on, sir. We could do with some help over here.'

Wil waited, praying that Oswald would refuse. If Oswald did agree to join them Wil would have to resort to his back-up plan, which he hadn't quite formulated yet.

Oswald let a tear run down his cheek unchecked.

'Come on, Mr Beck. *Please*, we need your help.'

Wil tried his best to sound desperate, which wasn't hard under the circumstances.

Oswald suddenly fixed Wil with a bloodshot glare.

'Did you say that *Seth Tanner* – the clumsiest Chaser that ever rode in a Moon Chase – is going to stitch our best Fellman?'

Wil was taken aback.

'Yes, er, yes, sir – Lady Élanor, um… gave us some… er… stuff – over there, sir,' Wil stammered and waved his hand vaguely in Mortimer's direction; the powers that Lady Élanor and Tally held were a closely kept secret and it was only now dawning on Wil that Oswald may not know about Lady Élanor's first aid bags.

'*No!*' snapped Oswald, so abruptly that Wil jumped. 'If there's any stitching to be done, *I'll* do it!'

Oswald was on his feet in a second.

Wil scrambled to follow. He had banked on Oswald staying put. Wil's idea had been to offer him a clean cloth for Leon, hoping that Oswald would do what he had done just now and blow his nose in it – Wil had been hoping he would breathe in the chloroform and be out cold while Gisella did Mortimer's stitches. *Oswald* volunteering to do the stitches was not in Wil's plan at all – his mind raced.

'Just a minute, Mr Beck – you'll need to wipe your hands with one of these.' Wil held out the chloroform-soaked cloth. 'To clean your hands, I mean… to do Mortimer's stitches. Lady Élanor showed me, er, back at the Infirmary.'

He smiled politely and offered up the soft white cloth. Oswald eyed it suspiciously.

'She said it was *really* important with open wounds,' said Wil hastily, raising his hand a fraction more. 'After all, she did a pretty good job with Giles Savidge, didn't she, sir?'

Oswald hesitated. Then, to Wil's relief he took the cloth and gave his hands a cursory rub before dabbing it on his tear-stained face. Suddenly his eyes widened. He held the ball of cloth to his nose and took a deep sniff. Wil wasn't sure if Oswald had suspected anything but it didn't matter. Oswald's eyes rolled back and he collapsed forward into Wil's arms.

In a trice, Wil had gently laid Oswald next to Leon and was racing back to Gisella and Seth.

Mortimer was now slipping into delirium, which at least meant that he hadn't seen Oswald fall. Gisella turned the tourniquet tighter but it had no effect on the constant crimson drip from the bandage – but he barely noticed that either.

'I don't think we can leave it any longer, Wil,' said Gisella, trying not to kneel in the growing pool of blood.

'Right, here's the cloth, Seth. Where are the needles?' Wil asked.

Mortimer's eyes snapped open. Suddenly he was lucid. He pointed at the cloth in Wil's hand.

'What's that? I know what you're doing! You're all in this together, aren't you? Well, you won't kill me that easily, Gisella Fairfax!'

He smashed his good arm into Gisella's shoulder and sent her toppling backwards. Then he threw a punch at Seth. But before Mortimer could do any more harm, Wil dragged him backwards and pressed the chloroform cloth over his nose. The Fellman's taut frame went limp.

'Sorry, Mortimer,' panted Wil. Frantic now, he set about the bandage but the blood quickly made his fingers sticky and the tight knot was impossible to undo.

'Goodness, who tied this?'

He reached for his knife. In one slice the knot gave way and the bandage unravelled. Immediately blood started to pump from the open vein in Mortimer's arm.

'Quick, Seth, put some pressure on this. Gisella, are you ready with that needle?... Gisella?'

Wil glanced round expecting to see Seth and Gisella poised ready to help, but they were just sitting there. A huge bruise was already coming up on Seth's cheek and Gisella was nursing her shoulder.

'Hey, come on!'

Wil pressed down hard on Mortimer's wrist but warm blood oozed between his fingers.

'It's only a bit of blood – surely you've both seen plenty of that before?'

'What did he mean, Wil? He said I was trying to kill him!' Gisella said in a shocked whisper.

'He said we were *all* trying to kill him!' added Seth.

'I know. I think it's the fever kicking in,' answered Wil without looking at either of them. 'I'm sure he didn't mean it.'

But Gisella wasn't convinced.

'No, Wil! He meant it. You've seen how he's been with me since we set off. I know *why* now!'

She held the needles absently in her fingers. Mortimer moaned.

'Look, it's to do with what you told Olivia, Giz. But we really haven't got time to talk about this now. Can we just sort Mortimer out and then you two can have a good chat later, hey?' begged Wil. He waved the chloroform under Mortimer's nose again. If they didn't do something soon, either Mortimer would come round or Gisella was unlikely to get the chance to have that chat ever again.

'Yes, but this means that he doesn't trust us!' objected Seth with a hurt look.

A little flame of anger flared in Wil's gut.

'Well, none of you trusted me on the Moon Chase – but I still helped!' He snapped. 'And if it wasn't for me at least *one* of you wouldn't be here now!'

His breathing was quick now from anger and frustration and his vision was coming and going in waves – if Gisella and Seth weren't going to do anything he was going to have to do it himself.

'Give me the needles then, Gisella. I am *not* going to sit here and watch one of my best friends die in front of me – even if you are!'

He thrust out his hand for Gisella to pass him the pack and the thread. Gisella looked as though she'd been slapped. She sat unmoving for a second and then got to her feet.

'No, Wil. I'll do it,' she said quietly. Mia walked over to Gisella and licked her hand.

'It's OK, girl,' said Gisella softly. 'He'll be OK, I promise.'

True to his word, Seth had passed out as soon as Gisella threaded the long, silver needle. The golden thread was as fine as a cobweb and it had taken her several attempts to get it into the needle's tiny eye. Once Gisella started sewing, though, the pin-point accuracy of her needlework was amazing to watch.

'Have you done this before, Gisella?' asked Wil.

'No,' answered Gisella. She sounded as impressed as Wil. 'I'm just pointing the needle – it's as if it knows what to do!'

With each stitch Mortimer's shredded skin sealed as the needle made contact. Only a neat red mark traced the line of the wound as she sewed. She worked quickly and within minutes the flowing blood had finally stopped; when she finished only a thin scar gave any hint that Mortimer had been injured at all.

Seth began to stir.

'Is it over yet?'

He looked decidedly queasy. His cheek was dark purple now and very swollen. He flexed his jaw, gingerly pressing his teeth with his finger.

'I think he loosened two of my teeth, you know!'

Wil finally allowed himself to smile.

'I'm sure you'll live, Seth. And yes, it's over and I think Mortimer's going to be OK – thanks to Gisella!'

She was peering into the pink bag again.

'I think we're supposed to give him this,' she said, holding up a small bottle of dark green liquid. 'The label says it's for heavy blood loss.'

Wil surveyed the dark pool surrounding Mortimer, together with the pile of soggy crimson bandages.

'Well, I'd say he's the ideal patient then!'

CHAPTER NINE

Time for Truth

'Look, I really am very sorry, Mr Beck, but I must have given you the wrong cloth!' said Wil, apologising for the third time.

Oswald had woken up just after they had poured the thick, green liquid down Mortimer's throat. Mortimer was still unconscious and the exercise had taken all three of them to avoid drowning him in the process.

Luckily Oswald's only real concern was for his son. Leon had still not stirred and Oswald had made only a cursory inspection of Mortimer's arm before very begrudgingly congratulating Seth.

'Oh, it's quite alright, Mr Beck. It was really rather easy,' Seth began, ignoring Wil's warning glare. 'My mother always said I could turn my hand to anything if I–'

But before he could milk Oswald's undeserved praise any more Leon suddenly coughed and sat bolt upright. His face contorted in terror. He started screaming.

'My eyes – they're burning! I can't see, I can't see!'

Oswald, Wil and Seth were at his side in a second. Leon pushed his father away then clutched him back. Closing and opening his eyes, Leon clung to Oswald with one arm and waved the other wildly.

'Father, what's happening? I can't see. Why can't I see?'

Pale and scared, Oswald made a brave attempt to calm the panic-stricken boy.

'It's OK, son. You've had a bit of a knock. Just sit back, you'll be OK. You'll be OK.'

But Leon wasn't listening. He kept on blinking his unseeing eyes.

'I can't see. *Why can't I see?*' My eyes – they're burning, arggh! Help me!'

Wil's ears were filled with the sound of Leon's rising panic. He could see that the marks across Leon's eyelids had gone right into his eyes – they were blood red. Gisella's urgent whisper came from behind him and Wil felt the cool glass of a phial being pressed it into his hand.

'Wil, the phial! Give Oswald the phial!'

Wil knelt. He grabbed Leon by the shoulders and spoke directly into his face, trying to keep a calm in his voice that he certainly wasn't feeling.

'Leon, it's me, Wil. Listen to me. Calm down and listen!'

But Leon carried on shouting. Wil tried again.

'Leon, calm down, please! It's me, Wil. I think you've got feather blindness, Leon – we can help you!'

'No! It's a trick! You did this! Oh, the pain. I can't see, I can't see! Get off me! Arrgh!'

He shoved Wil backwards. The phial span out of Wil's hand and rolled across the dirt. Wil managed to regain his balance but Oswald ploughed into him and pinned him to the ground. With his face in Wil's he began yelling, 'What are you trying to do to my son? I know what you–'

'Oh, for goodness sake,' said a calm voice right over Wil's head.

A tanned, slender hand holding a small white square of cloth appeared from behind Oswald's head. Oswald went limp. A second later Leon stopped shouting.

'I'm sure that much chloroform can't be good for you?' groaned Wil as Seth and Gisella lifted poor Oswald off him.

'Well, I had to do *something!*" Gisella said waspishly. 'We are *supposed* to be on our way to rescue Tally – unless everyone has forgotten!'

After knocking out Oswald with another lungful of chloroform, Gisella had done the same to Leon. This made it far easier to drip the feather blindness ointment into Leon's eyes.

Despite Wil's misgivings about the chloroform, he had to admit that it had worked a treat. Gisella had then taken the opportunity to bind Leon's head and eyes. Her intention was to keep out the light but Wil couldn't help worrying about how Leon might react to this enforced blindness when he woke up – especially when he found out that the dressings would have to stay on for the next four days!

Mortimer was still lying with his back against the tree. The effects of the chloroform were obviously wearing off and his cheeks were now a far healthier colour. He turned his hand over and flexed his fingers.

'Who did this?'

Wil and Seth answered at the same time.

'Seth.'

'Me!'

'Don't you remember, Mort?' Wil cut in before Seth got the chance to get too carried away. He was struggling with Mortimer's constant lack of trust although he did his best not to let it show. 'It was from the first aid bag. We gave you something for the blood you lost, too.'

Mortimer inspected the thin scar. Eventually he seemed satisfied.

'Hmm, well it feels okay so far – I guess I owe you a thank-you, Seth.' And for the first time in what seemed like a very long time, Mortimer gave Seth a genuine smile. 'That's one heck of a bruise, by the way! Did one of those birds get you too?'

A look of surprised indignation flickered across Seth's battered face then he beamed.

'Yep, but I managed to get out of the way before it did any real damage!'

Surprised, though very grateful to Seth for being so gracious, Wil knew this was the moment to tell Mortimer about Leon. The morning was rapidly becoming afternoon and they really needed to decide how they were going to get on and rescue Tally – and *who* would be going.

'The thing is Mort, Leon didn't – er, get out of the way, I mean,' said Wil. He braced himself for Mortimer's reaction.

For a split-second Wil thought it wasn't going to be too bad. Mortimer's words were both predictable and understandable.

'What! He's not dead, is he? Where is he? Where's Oswald?'

But then Mortimer was on his feet. With a look of wild-eyed revulsion, he grabbed the front of Wil's shirt.

'Did *she* have anything to do with this?'

Something in Wil snapped. He swiped Mortimer's hands away and pushed him with all his might. Mortimer tumbled backwards into Seth.

'What the–' Mortimer protested. But Wil cut across him.

'This… stops… now!'

He stormed over to the rocky ledge where Gisella had stationed herself under the pretext of acting as lookout. His chest was tight, and with every step rising anger pulsed through his body.

'Gisella, come down here! You and Mortimer are going to have that chat!'

Without waiting, Wil turned. He bore down on Mortimer. Once the words started, they wouldn't stop.

'Right, to start with, Gisella is NOT trying to kill you – Olivia lied to Leon and Leon believed her. Second, Gisella wants to be a Chaser – it was Bryn who told her to help you with Mia! For some bizarre reason these people seem to care about you!' Wil was now well and truly in his stride. 'And thirdly, it wasn't Seth who stitched you up, it was Gisella. And before you say *anything* – she probably saved your life – so I suggest your next two words are – *Sorry* and *Thanks*!'

He stood panting and unclenched his fists. Mortimer opened his mouth and then closed it again. Seth stepped between them. Mortimer was clearly struggling with the torrent that Wil had just delivered.

'Is this true?'

Seth nodded.

'Well the bit about the stitches and saving your life is – I was there! But Gisela didn't tell me about the other stuff,' he said and then added quickly, 'But I believed her anyway! Mia trusts her and that's good enough for me… and it *should* be good enough for you too, Mort.'

As if she understood what was happening, Mia licked Mortimer's hand and then walked over to Gisella and sat down pressing her long back against Gisella's leg. Gisella scratched the hound's ear gratefully and took a deep, visible breath.

'It's true, Mort. Olivia wants to leave Saran, she told me. And I told her I wanted to be a Chaser. I spoke to Bryn about learning so that I could take Olivia's place when she leaves. *He* told me to help you with Mia – you know, because you might still be missing Tarek – and I was supposed to learn at the same time,' her voice quavered with the struggle to hold back tears. 'True, I love Mia, but she's *your* Fellhound, Mortimer. All I wanted to do was ride with you and the others on the Fells and one day have my *own* hound.'

By now her tears were flowing freely.

Mortimer suddenly looked lost.

'Why would Leon do this?'

They let Mortimer's words hang in the air while he tried to digest what was happening.

'Why didn't you tell me you wanted to be a Chaser?' he asked eventually, keeping his eyes fixed on Mia.

'Because I wanted to make sure I could do it first – I… I didn't want anyone to laugh,' Gisella answered, gulping back tears. Her lip was quivering uncontrollably now.

'And you did my stitches – even though I've been so horrible to you. Why?'

Gisella swallowed and tried to speak but tears were streaming down her face now and words failed her. Wil answered for her.

'Because, like the rest of us, she cares about you, you complete idiot! And, because she didn't *know* what she was supposed to have done. She believed it would be alright in the end!'

'You didn't tell her, Wil?'

'You must be joking! I knew it was all because of Olivia's lie – I just couldn't work out how to get you both talking to each other to sort it out!'

Mortimer looked skywards, 'Well, I never thought I'd hear myself saying this, but – thank the moons for those eagards!'

He threw a sheepish grin at Gisella.

'Sorry, Giz… and… thanks.'

Gisella uttered a gulping sob and smiled a watery smile – again, words failed her.

'Right,' said Wil with a sigh of relief, the sun was now high in the sky and the twin moons had long since disappeared over the bleak horizon. 'Now that we've finally sorted that out – can we *please* get on with rescuing Tally?'

CHAPTER TEN

Separate Ways

With Gisella and Mortimer back on speaking terms Wil's mood lifted considerably. He sat and listened while Mortimer quizzed Gisella, and was relieved that Mortimer accepted Gisella's reason for why they had knocked out Oswald and Leon in the first place. Mortimer was more concerned about what might happen once the chloroform wore off and Leon was awake.

'How long did you say those bandages had to stay over Leon's eyes, Gizzy?' Gisella retrieved the now rather grubby square of cloth from a pocket in her breeches.

'Well, the label says four *full* days.'

'Does it say anything about moving him?' asked Mortimer.

Gisella turned the label over and shook her head. Mortimer glanced towards the tethered horses.

'Well, in that case, the way I see it he's got two choices. Either someone – I suggest Oswald – takes him home or they stay here and wait for us.'

It was clear from Gisella's shocked expression that she hadn't considered this; although given the recent events, her suggestion took Wil by surprise.

'But they can come with us – surely that would be safer?' Mortimer flexed his fingers as if testing them out.

'You know what Wraithe Wolves are like, Gisella. If they get the slightest idea that one of us is weak they'll be down in their droves! And once we get to Tel Harion…' he paused, his dark eyes searching the horizon. Then he shook his head. 'No, it's better if they turn back now – once they get to the Black Rock they'll be fine.'

Wil studied Mortimer's face – his confidence didn't quite make it to his eyes.

'Anyway, I can't see Oswald wanting to press on. He only came to protect Leon after all. It's my guess that Oswald'll be delighted when I suggest he take his son home!'

As it happened, breaking the news to Leon and Oswald hadn't been that bad – largely because Wil had found a bottle of dark purple liquid in the first aid bag that was simply labelled '*FOR PANIC! TAKE THREE DROPS!*'

As a precaution, Gisella had insisted that Mortimer take one drop – because, as she reasoned, he had already had one bad experience that day and he might suddenly go into some sort of delayed shock. So, very begrudgingly, Mortimer had opened his mouth while she tipped the bottle and tapped it once – Mortimer's tongue went bright purple. Seth muttered something about checking on Farrow and rushed away, coughing loudly. Gisella said nothing and carefully dripped the full dose onto Oswald's and then Leon's lips. Moment's later they both stirred.

Oswald, while very confused, was completely calm. He accepted without question Mortimer's story that he must have passed out after being overcome with worry. And Mortimer's suggestion that Oswald take his son back to Saran was met with positive enthusiasm.

Contrary to everyone's fears, Leon's reaction to his blindness second time around was very different from the first. True, he was worried that he could not see, but made no complaint of the pain or burning that had caused him such discomfort previously. He had no memory of the eagard attack and listened intently while Mortimer and Oswald recounted as much of the tale as they could piece together. He also calmly accepted Mortimer's instruction that his bandages were to be left on for four days in order to allow Lady Élanor's medicine to work.

Meanwhile, Wil kept an eye out for Pricilla, his aim being to send word to Lady Élanor that Leon was injured and on his way home with his father. But the skies remained stubbornly clear.

Oswald took up the reins of his own horse in one hand and gripped the reins of Leon's horse in the other while Mortimer helped Leon into the saddle.

'So, due south, you said, boy?' said Oswald gruffly.

Mortimer patted the neck of Leon's horse and nodded.

'Just take it steady, sir,' said Mortimer. 'Once you get to the Black Rock you should be able to see Mistle Forest. Keep it on the skyline and head south – you'll be back in Saran tomorrow.'

Despite being back on a horse, Wil was relieved that they were finally on the move again.

'Well you were right about Oswald,' he said to the back of Mortimer's head. 'Did you see the relief on his face when you suggested taking Leon back to Saran?'

'Yes,' said Mortimer without looking round. 'Although I'm sure Leon didn't really understand what was going on. I think Gisella might have been a bit heavy-handed when she gave him that calming liquor!'

'OK, I might have given him an extra drop or two, but after the way he was before… well, I just didn't want to take any chances!' admitted Gisella, with a guilty grin.

'Yer. What a performance!' said Seth.

'Well, he did wake up blind, Seth. Be fair!' said Mortimer.

'I know, but it couldn't have been that bad – I mean, he insisted on riding his own horse just now, didn't he? Let's hope Oswald doesn't let go of those reins!'

'Well, I thought that taking both horses was a bit selfish of them, actually,' said Gisella. 'I mean, I'm not sure if anyone else has thought about this, but if anything has happened to Tanith we're going to have a heck of a job getting five of us home on only two horses!'

CHAPTER ELEVEN

Another Attack

The problem of how to find Lord Rexmoore's castle was resolved far easier than any of them had anticipated. As they reached the snowy peak of Craggston Tor, Mort Craggs darkened the horizon. Below, the walls of Armelia spread like a shroud and there at the base of the Craggs, among the jagged rocks, lurked a sprawling castle shining golden in the late afternoon sunlight. Wil's heart sank.

'Oh, great,' he muttered. 'More climbing!'

But as they got nearer Wil could see that the castle tower appeared to be incomplete. To confirm his own thoughts, Mortimer spoke only a short time later.

'I think Rexmoore's doing some home improvements!'

He reined Shadow to a halt. Seth and Gisella pulled up alongside.

'Well I don't know how we're going to get the hounds in there, Mortimer,' said Seth.

'From here, I don't see how *we're* going to get in there either!' said Gisella. Wil silently agreed – from where he was sitting, there was certainly no obvious sign of a gap in the wall – or a gate. 'Please tell me *someone* mentioned that wall? Didn't Lady Élanor give you any clues as to how we're going to get in?'

But Gisella's question went unanswered.

'Ouch! What was *that*?' said Seth, slapping his hand onto his neck.

'What was *what*?' asked Mortimer.

A second later he, too, was nursing his cheek.

'What is wrong with you two?' asked Gisella.

'I'm not sure,' Mortimer answered waving his hands around his head, 'I think I've just been stung by something.'

'Well, I think we can safely say it wasn't a midge!' said Gisella, admiring the walnut-sized welt blooming on Mortimer's cheek when–

'Ow!'

Mortimer grabbed at the missile that ricocheted off Gisella's thigh. It really was a walnut!

With that, Wil felt a sharp sting on his own neck. Another nut – this time a hazelnut – rolled across the ground. At the same moment what sounded distinctly like a chuckle came from a thick copse of battered, snow-dusted trees – the only obstacle that stood between the riders and the wind-raked Fells of Tel Harion.

'What the–' growled Mortimer. He pointed towards the copse, 'Mia, Go!'

Mia didn't need to be told twice. She took off towards the trees. Without waiting for an order Phinn darted after her.

'Got your knife handy, Wil?' Mortimer said in a voice low enough not be heard from any distance.

Wil patted his boot, 'Yep, safe and ready for action.'

'Good, hang on!'

Wil hardly felt Mortimer move but Shadow went from a stand to a gallop in a heartbeat; in three more they were in the middle of the thick copse under a huge Thesk pine. Mia was on her hind legs, towering above Mortimer as she stretched up the trunk, keeping a keen grip on its orange-brown bark with her finger-long claws. Craning her neck, she sniffed along one of the lower branches and sneezed violently when the needles tickled her nose. Phinn sat on his haunches and offered up a deep bark that echoed out over the barren hills.

'Call them off! Call them off!' wailed a boy's voice from high above them.

Mortimer dismounted. Slowly, he strode around the ancient trunk, searching the cloud of needle-fine leaves, yellow-green from at least two centuries of Tel Harion winters.

'Who's there? Come on – show yourself!'

'Not until you call off those dogs!'

'How do I know that you won't shoot us?'

The voice didn't reply. Mortimer's eyes flicked down to Wil's boot. Wil took the hint and silently drew out the hunting knife.

After a few minutes one of the upper branches bounced as if something – or someone – was jumping up and down on it. Tiny crystals of old snow sprinkled through the ancient branches. Wil closed his eyes. Then he heard something else clattering down through of the tree and opened them again to see Mortimer jump backwards with his arms over his head. A small tin whistle, several different nuts and a sling-shot landed at his feet. Mortimer bent to pick up the whistle but Mia got there first.

'Leave, Mia!'

Mortimer's sharp command made Wil start. Mia immediately backed away and lay down, chin flat to the floor; her bushy eyebrows twitching as she watched her master retrieve the dropped items one by one. With a frown, he blew into the whistle. Brief but ear piercing, the blast was surprisingly loud. Mia and Phinn sat up immediately. Mortimer raised an eyebrow and tapped the whistle on the back of his hand.

'If you are unarmed you can come down. But I warn you, my friend here is a dead shot with a knife.'

'But how do I know those hounds won't eat me?' returned a nervous voice.

'You don't!' Mortimer answered. He winked at Wil. 'In fact, as they haven't had their breakfast yet, *we* don't know either! You're just going to have to come down and take your chance!'

'Well, in that case I'll stay up here, thanks!'

'What's going on?' asked Gisella as Seth steered Rhoani carefully through the knot of trees. Farrow padded behind them. Mortimer beamed.

'Seth! You got your bow handy?'

Seth took a wary glance around the gnarled trunks.

'Er, yer. Why?' He swept the tree with a wary glance.

'Well, it seems,' said Mortimer jabbing his finger towards the spiky canopy above their heads, 'that the *pest* that *stung* us has settled in this pine tree and I was wondering if you could get rid of it?'

With eyes full of mischief Mortimer waved the whistle and the slingshot for Seth to see. For a moment Seth looked completely baffled then a wicked smile erupted on his face.

'Ohhh! Right! Yer, no problem,' he said yanking a bolt from his jacket which he nestled into his bow with a deft click. 'One bolt should be enough, Mort, I'm pretty sure I can see a pair of legs up there. D'you want me to wing it,' he closed one eye and aimed up into the tree, 'or kill it?'

'*NO!*'

The branch bounced again – this time much more violently. There was a terrified shout and twigs, pine needles and cones cascaded down over their heads.

'I'll come down. Don't shoot! I... I was only messing around!'

Seth kept the bow trained into the tree. They waited. After a lot more falling leaves, pine cones and twigs, a body, dressed entirely in black, crashed through the lower branches and landed with a dull thud between Wil and Mortimer – the body was followed almost immediately by a black hat.

'Elegant!' observed Mortimer.

First to approach the crumpled heap now lying on the ground with his hands over his head was Phinn. Wil opened his mouth to call the hound back but Mortimer held up his palm and Wil stayed quiet. The heap let out a pathetic cry.

'Oowee! Nooo, don't let it eat me!' it squealed. 'Please! I gave you my stuff. Pleeeease… call it off!'

But before Wil even contemplated saying anything, Phinn lost interest. He padded over to the crumpled hat, sniffed it and gave it an experimental nudge with his huge nose. The hat rolled away in a half-circle on its brim. Phinn took a surprised step back and stretched his head as far forward as he could without moving his feet. He sniffed again and opened his mouth to investigate further.

'Leave it!'

The sharpness of Mortimer's voice made the hound look up. The boy on the ground hugged his head and whimpered. Seth lowered his bow.

'Down!' ordered Mortimer. To Wil's absolute amazement, Phinn obeyed immediately – so did Farrow and Mia. Wil felt a twinge of envy; Mortimer was just so good with the hounds – he could make them do just about anything – even Phinn!

Clearly not quite as impressed, the boy started to sob.

'For goodness sake, stop that whingeing and get up,' said Mortimer. 'But be warned – there's still a bolt and a knife aimed directly at your heart!'

The boy sobbed louder than ever.

CHAPTER TWELVE

The Jackal

'Right, my friends here and I are in a hurry and you are seriously holding us up, so shut up,' said Mortimer, not even trying to hide his exasperation. 'I'm going to ask you some questions and it's my advice that your answers are brief and truthful – if I like what I hear I *won't* give my friends permission to kill you. OK?'

The sobbing stopped. The boy rolled over and raised his filthy hands, showing equally grubby palms. His pinched face was also filthy except where his tears had carved clean rivers down both cheeks. He fixed Mortimer with a wary stare.

Mortimer smiled dangerously and Seth took aim again. Wil echoed the gesture by flicking his thumb across the point of his blade. Gisella stood a little way off with the horses and rolled her eyes skywards.

Taking slow, deliberate steps, Mortimer strode around the quaking boy.

'Who are you?'

The boy looked barely as old as Seth. He took a deep shuddering breath and swallowed.

'I…I'm the… I'm The Jackal.'

'Really!' said Mortimer raising an eyebrow. Wil saw the corner of his mouth twitch.

'Yer!' said the boy, shoulders back and chin set. But then his shoulders dropped slightly. 'Er... but, well, er, my real name's Colin.'

His eyes flashed quickly to Seth's bow, 'I prefer The Jackal though!'

'Is that what your friends call you?' asked Mortimer. 'And what about your parents – I bet your mother just loves shouting, "Come on, *The Jackal*, your supper's ready"!'

Seth chuckled.

'I don't have any parents.'

Seth stopped chuckling.

Mortimer frowned.

'Oh, what, er... what happened to them?'

'Dunno. I... um... well, apparently the cook, y'know, at the castle – the old one – she died last year – she found me among some sacks of flour when I was a baby. She called me Colin... Colin Miller.' The Jackal nodded then frowned and added. 'Don't know why though?' Then he shook his head as if to dismiss the question and went on. 'Anyway, I grew up in the castle – scavenging, y'know, in the kitchens. Oh, and I helped with the pigs, too, y'know, for my keep.'

'Oh!' exclaimed Gisella. 'That's terrible. Didn't anyone come forward to claim you?'

'Why should they? You know what it's like in the city!'

'No, not really,' said Gisella quietly.

'Oh, well, y'know, it's bad enough trying to feed yourself – impossible if you're poor! Reckon I was lucky – least I never went hungry! There's always stuff to steal, y'know, in the castle kitchen and the staff hardly *ever* notice!'

Gisella looked aghast. She stepped in front of Mortimer who had just opened his mouth and then seemed to think better of it.

'What! You mean no one actually looked after you there?'

The Jackal sat up. He tucked his skinny knees under his chin and hugged his long shins. His once black, pointed boots were scuffed and grey from lack of polish. Wil could see a hole in one of the soles.

'Well, no – I mean, yer! Y'know, they taught me right an' wrong. They cared about me… I mean, cook used to hit me with a wooden spoon, y'know, if she caught me stealing stuff… and, er… the baker clipped me round the ear once 'cos I nicked a bowl of raisins that were supposed to go in some cake he was making!'

He smiled at the memory and hugged his knees closer.

'How does being beaten show that someone cares about you?' asked Gisella.

The Jackal looked surprised.

''Cos if they hadn't cared they would have sent me to Rexmoore. And he would have flogged me for stealing and then, y' know, he… he would have thrown me out on the street!'

He gave a definite nod to confirm this fact and then reached into his long, grubby jacket. In one sweeping move-ment Mortimer drew his sword; Seth, who had lowered his bow, took direct aim again and Wil raked back his arm ready to throw his knife. All eyes were fixed on the boy's concealed hand. The Jackal froze.

'What!' he said, wide-eyed, and very slowly drew a golden pear from his tattered pocket. 'Oh, sorry, I've only got this. Never take more than you can eat in one go. Y'know, small amounts – less likely to be noticed. Then, if you do get caught, running away's easier!'

With another sage-like nod The Jackal bit the top off the fruit, complete with stalk and munched. Without needing to be told, Seth lowered his bow and Wil slid his knife back into his boot.

'Yes, Wil, but he's a half-starved urchin from the kitchen of that castle,' said Gisella. 'Did you see the way he put away the piece of pie I gave him!'

Mortimer had quizzed The Jackal while they all tucked into huge slices of chicken pie, once again supplied by Martha, and now he, Wil and Gisella were standing at the edge of the copse in whispered debate about what to do with the boy.

Seth meanwhile had found the slingshot. He had already smacked Phinn on the bottom with a lump of mud – Phinn, clearly deeply offended, was now at a safe distance with his bottom firmly on the floor.

'Well, I'm not sure I believe that story,' said Wil in a low voice. 'I mean, if he'd stolen a horse to come up here surely someone would have come after him?'

'Well, he did say that it ran away when he climbed the tree, Wil,' said Gisella, her face full of sympathy. 'He's stranded – we can't just leave him here!'

'And he could prove useful if he knows his way around the castle, Wil,' said Mortimer. Wil couldn't disagree but he couldn't shake the unease that tickled at the back of his mind. He was also deeply concerned that the moons were once again on the rise and they still hadn't reached Armelia.

'Look, I don't know why, but I just don't think we should trust him,' he argued, absently watching Seth rake the slingshot back. It was loaded with another lump of dry earth. 'I just don't understand what's he doing this far out of Armelia – and as for that horse – has anyone spotted it wandering anywhere?'

He turned and peered through the trees as if to emphasise his point. Seth glanced around, too. The loaded sling slipped out of his fingers and thwacked its missile into a branch above their heads. Soil rained down on them.

'Oops!' said Seth and surreptitiously pushed the sling into his boot.

'Well, I think we should give him a chance,' said Gisella combing earth out of her hair with her fingers. 'We certainly can't just leave him here. After all, Wil, we've got the hounds, the horses *and* the weapons. And I've got a feeling that getting into the city might be a challenge – let alone the castle. At least if he's with us, we can keep an eye on him!'

'You've got to admit it, Wil,' added Mortimer. 'He might have a stupid name but he could be pretty handy if he knows his way around Armelia! Might even know where they're keeping Tally.'

'I just think it's all a bit too convenient,' admitted Wil. 'What if it's some sort of trap?'

'Na,' said Mortimer flicking a tiny fragment of Seth's missile back at him. Seth raised his arm and batted it away. 'We could have killed that boy in a second – Rexmoore would know that.' He looked around at The Jackal, who seemed to have overcome his fear of the Fellhounds and was nestled against Farrow's back – both were dozing peacefully. 'Na, he's just a kid with a tin whistle and a slingshot. Probably comes up here to hide the stuff he's stolen and to keep away from that cook's wooden spoon! I bet he knows the Fells – and the city – like the back of his hand.'

So, Wil was outvoted. They had, however, agreed that The Jackal would not be told about their need to get into the castle until they had no other option. After all, as Mortimer had pointed out, they didn't yet know if Tally was there.

What The Jackal was told was that as long as he got them into Armelia, Mortimer would hold back on the order for the Fellhounds to rip him apart.

'But that's right *into* the city, mind,' warned Mortimer in a voice that would have chilled ice.

'Well that's not going to be too difficult,' called Seth before The Jackal could speak. 'I think there's a gate, look, over there!'

Mortimer had sent him to keep a look-out – in case anyone did come searching for a stolen horse. Seth had stationed himself on top of a stack of huge oval stones on the edge of the trees. He seemed oblivious that the stones were balanced precariously one on top of the other – Wil counted seven in all. The stack marked the tip of a sweeping valley through which was etched the road to Armelia. The only thing between them and the city was a solid wall, behind which a great heap of buildings rose above the parapet as if clawing their way to freedom. In the middle of the wall, almost taunting the attempt to escape, Wil could see the outline of a huge gate.

'Wonder if that's to keep people out?' said Gisella.

'Or in!' said Mortimer.

Armelia didn't get any more appealing as they got closer – and the road didn't get any easier. The stark drift of the Fells gave way to the craggy valley, riven between equally craggy hills that seemed to tumble towards Mort Craggs like desperate infants following an older sibling. Old snow lurked in crevices. Odd-shaped boulders sat abandoned in the path casting weird shapes that made Wil feel like they were being watched. As the group picked their way along the base of yet another unkempt gully, smaller rocks embedded in the frozen ground made the horses stumble.

Mortimer had insisted that The Jackal ride with him.

'Best place to keep an eye on him,' he had said. So Gisella volunteered to walk with Wil – a proposition that Wil had certainly not objected to. But when Shadow lost his footing and slid down a bank on his rump, Mortimer insisted that they all walk – a proposition that Seth certainly did object to.

The going was hard and slow and they made their way in silence. Taking care where he put his feet at every step, Wil wondered how Tally and Tanith had coped over this terrible terrain. Bryn had told Wil before the Moon Chase that Tally had the makings of a good Fellman; but he had also told Wil that Lady Élanor would never allow her to try, fearing that something terrible would happen. Did that mean that Tally had never ridden out on the Fells before? And what if she'd never been this far north? Thesker Fell was one thing but the ragged terrain of Tel Harion was a challenge all of its own.

Another nagging thought – louder than the other ones – was also tapping at Wil's brain; if The Jackal hadn't known what Fellhounds were, well, did that mean that Armelia didn't have them? After all, Wil hadn't seen them before the Moon Chase – Mistlegard was just too poor and Peachley Hills didn't have too many Wraithe Wolves to worry about. And if Armelia didn't have Fellhounds, Wil's thoughts followed, how were they going to get into the city without attracting too much attention with three enormous hounds that each stood shoulder high to a grown man?... And gates meant gate keepers – surely that meant awkward questions–

'Wil, are you okay?'

Gisella's voice interrupted his trail of worry.

'Er, yer, I'm fine.' He slowed his pace. Gisella slowed, too.

On their left the granite rocks of Mort Craggs were now towering over them like rows of crooked teeth grinning down on them – and certainly impassable to anything without wings. Way off – much further to the right – the peaks of the

Eiye Mountains rammed through a huddle of clouds in the ice-blue sky. The only sound was of boots, hooves and paws crunching, slipping and tripping over the frozen ground. Despite being in the company of friends, the whole oppressive scene made Wil feel isolated and inadequate.

As was Phinn's practice when he and Wil walked out on Peachley Hills, he meandered along, barely two paces ahead of Wil as if forcing his master to slow to a pace that suited him; soon Wil and Gisella were quite some distance from the others. Wil lowered his voice.

'I was wondering about Tally. Rexmoore's bound to have her by now. I mean, look at it down there.'

'Yes, I know what you mean. It isn't what I expected at all,' Gisella replied as quietly. Mortimer looked over his shoulder. He halted Shadow and waved for them to catch up.

When Gisella next spoke her voice was its normal volume, for everyone to hear.

'I don't know if the light's playing tricks on my eyes,' she said squinting into the distance, 'but as we're getting closer that tower looks like it's actually made of gold!'

The Jackal's face broke into a bright smile.

'Oh! That's because it is! Been building it for years! It's for his wife – she just loves the stuff, y' know – Imelda's Golden Tower, that's what he calls it – Lord Rexmoore, y'know. You should see the rest of the castle – falling down! All the gold that's collected, y' know, in taxes – they melt it down for bricks – every scrap!'

'What?' gasped Gisella. 'You mean all the gold our parents hand over to Rexmoore's henchmen… it's used for building that!'

Wil suddenly felt quite sick.

'So what did they do with my father? He couldn't pay them,' he said almost to himself.

'Prob'ly made him work up there,' answered The Jackal in a matter-of-fact voice. 'Yer. They bring them in all the time, y'know – the ones who can't – or won't pay.' He smirked. 'Make them work, y'know until, well, until they drop dead… or fall off the wall, y'know.'

'Oh!' breathed Gisella.

Wil's windpipe was suddenly tight. It was all he could do to drag in enough air to stay conscious – his world went red. He grabbed The Jackal and threw him to the ground.

'No, actually I don't know.' Wil's jaws were so tightly clenched his teeth went numb. 'But what I do want to know is *exactly* what they do to them.'

'Take it easy, Wil,' said Mortimer carefully. He, Seth and Gisella knew about Wil's father being taken away by Rexmoore's men; they also knew that Wil had been told that his father was dead.

Consumed by anger, Wil pressed down on the boy's throat.

Frantic, The Jackal clawed at Wil's arm.

'Gurnnn!'

'Come on, you streak of nothing! Tell me! What do they do to them?'

Gisella grabbed Wil's shoulder.

'Wil, he's certainly not going to tell you if you kill him!'

Beside her, Phinn towered over the two boys. The huge hound was barking loudly but Wil was too angry to notice – or care. He put all of his weight on his elbow. Phinn dropped low, ready to spring.

'No, Phinn, leave!' shrieked Gisella.

'No!'

The shout that came from Seth, Mortimer and Gisella echoed around the valley. Phinn opened his huge jaws and lunged.

Wil was never sure what brought him to his senses – it could have been the chorus of three alarmed voices yelling in unison; or it could have been Phinn's misjudged dive that sent him rolling and winded away from The Jackal – but either way, before Phinn could get his bearings and go in for what undoubtedly would have been a fatal attack, the word, *'Leave!'* exploded in Wil's head. Phinn stopped in his tracks.

Once again The Jackal lay whimpering in the dirt.

Phinn stood, poised, his tail wagging to and fro in great sweeps – waiting for his master's order.

Wil crouched on all fours, trying to catch his breath. His heart was racing.

The others watched – no one moved.

Eventually Wil broke the silence.

'Just tell me,' he panted, without raising his head. 'Just tell me… What happens at the tower?'

The Jackal shuffled awkwardly. He threw Mortimer a pleading glance.

'Tell him,' ordered Mortimer.

Fixing his eyes on Mortimer, The Jackal spoke.

'Well, from what I've seen, y'kn-,' Mortimer raised a warning eyebrow. 'Er, yer… well, er, they bring them in and set them to work. Some go straight up to the wall and some go to the foundry, y'–, er, that's where they make the bricks.'

He stopped.

'That can't be all,' said Gisella looking appalled. 'Where do they sleep? What do they eat?'

'Oh, yer. Er, well, they sleep in the tower and, y'know, Cook makes them porridge and …' He swallowed; his wary eyes did not stray from Mortimer's face. 'And... er… they take the bodies to a field on the edge of the city…'

'Go on,' said Mortimer.

Reluctantly, The Jackal picked up where he had left off.

'There's a man, y'know, up there. He, er, carves their name on a stone – with the words 'Taxes paid' underneath. They put the stones, y'know, on the, er… graves…' He tailed off, leaving a shocked silence hanging in the air.

After a long time, it was Seth who spoke.

'How does he know their names?'

'They tattoo each man's name on his arm when he's brought in – just the last name, y'know… to save ink.'

Wil lifted his head. He could have sworn he saw a flash of something bordering on humour cross the boy's face again, but this time he was far too shocked to react.

Wil was eleven years old when Rexmoore's men had taken his father. As he crouched there on the frozen ground, Wil could almost hear his mother. She had wept and begged them not to take him but they pushed her away and she had fallen into the mud. Wil's father had struggled to get to her, to help her up, but they wouldn't let him; one of the men had hit his father with the hilt of his sword before another had dragged him, semi-conscious, and thrown him onto the back of the wagon. Wil had desperately wanted to help but he was too scared – there had been blood on the man's sword *before* it had struck his father's cheek.

That day, they took Wil's father and two other men from the village; afterwards, Wil's mother told him time and again that if they earned enough to pay the tax then Lord Rexmoore would let Wil's father come home. She always maintained that Rexmoore was a fair man. But no matter how much they handed over every time Rexmoore's men came calling, Wil's father was never with them. Wil's only really vivid memory of the man was his frightened, blood-streaked face as the wagon rattled and squeaked its way out of Mistlegard – out of Wil's life forever.

It was Wil's father who had taught Wil how to handle a knife. They used to practice after Wil had done his chores – much to his mother's horror. From that day, Wil was allowed to practice his throwing to his heart's content – now, he was very good.

As The Jackal's words sank in, it occurred to Wil that he had never really thought about what happened to the gold that his family had paid. Something inside Wil went very cold. Wil and his mother had done everything they could to raise enough to pay Rexmoore's tax and eke out a living; from growing beetroot and turnips in their tiny field, to sweeping floors in the local inn, to raising chickens to sell at the local markets – well, the ones that the foxes didn't eat anyway. All that and Wil's father had died working on a tower that was being built with that same gold – and hoards more, collected from people like Wil and his mother all over Thesk. *Surely there was someone who could stop this,* he thought. Out loud, he asked, 'What about the people who live in Armelia.' He struggled to keep his voice level. 'Do they know what happens to their gold?'

Wil's face was ash-white. His eyes were red. Phinn stood panting, poised as if he was taking in every word.

The Jackal shrugged.

'Dunno. Some work for Rexmoore anyway. I guess most people just ignore what's happening or they're too scared to do anything about it.'

'And which one are you then, hey?' asked Wil, but he was on his feet before the boy could open his mouth. 'Don't bother,' he added walking away. 'Just get us into Armelia.'

CHAPTER THIRTEEN

Plan B

'Blimey, Cecil, you seen these!' called a voice from high above their heads. It was now very late in the afternoon; they were tired and hungry and the gate into Armelia looked depressingly solid close up. Wil's feet were numb from hours walking over snow-coated rocks; and Gisella, normally nimble over even the most challenging terrain, had slipped down a treacherous section of scree and was now sporting a badly grazed elbow and a cut lip.

A few seconds later another voice replied from the other side of the gate.

'Seen wha'?'

'Tell you what, boys,' the first voice called down, 'You should stick a saddle on them an' ride 'em over the Fells!' The voice exploded into a roar of laughter and a face appeared over the top of the gate.

'By the moons, Alg, now that's what I call a dog!'

Mortimer stepped forward with a patient expression on his face and nodded up at the two moons rising from behind Mort Craggs.

'Good evening, gentlemen. Would it be possible for you to open the gate and let us in?'

'You 'ere for the Alcama Fest?' called a voice from lower down behind the gate.

'Er, yes,' said Mortimer throwing The Jackal a quizzical look. But The Jackal didn't respond. The face peered down at them.

'You got gold?'

'Er, no,' answered Mortimer. He turned to the others – they all shook their heads. Wil felt his pulse quicken at the question – gold now held an entirely new meaning for him.

'Well, unless you got gold we can't let you in – orders see.'

The Jackal had not spoken since Wil's outburst. Now Gisella gave him a gentle nudge. He stepped forward and doffed his hat.

'Hi Algernon. It's me, The Ja-, Colin,' he called. 'Look, this lot are my friends. They've come for the Fest. Just met up over at Thesker Pyke – I forgot about the gold thing. Can you just let us in anyway?' He flapped his arms at his side and bounced on his toes.

'Colin? Colin Miller? They been looking for you all day, you little–. Said you nicked Lady Imelda's quail's eggs. Mhaddphat's gonna string you up when she finds you! If I were you I'd stay out there with yer mates!'

'Quail's eggs?' said Gisella in an enquiring whisper.

'Long story,' returned The Jackal out of the corner of his mouth.

'And who's Mhaddphat?' whispered Seth.

'The cook – she's a bit weird,' hissed The Jackal.

A second face appeared at the parapet above them.

'You discussin' how you're gonna get those eggs back to her ladyship?'

'Er, well, yes actually,' answered The Jackal with a bold voice. 'I've got them here in my pocket – all twelve of them.' He cupped his pocket for effect. 'Just let us in and I'll go straight up to the castle to return them.'

The two faces ducked back behind the wall.

'Weird, how?' asked Mortimer in a low voice, his own face still turned up towards the gap where the gate-keepers' faces had just been.

'Weird. In a, y'know, dangerous kind of way,' answered The Jackal, also looking up.

The face of Algernon re-appeared.

'I 'eard you're gonna need a lot more than twelve. You sure you got no gold? What about on those dogs? Those collars – they gold?'

'Oh, no,' Seth piped up cheerfully. Wil was nearest but he had no way of shutting Seth up without attracting attention. Seth carried on. 'It's wrought iron. Gold's not nearly strong enough to hold a Fellhound!'

He shook his head proudly and patted Farrow hard on the shoulder. Mortimer looked skywards.

'Seth!' hissed Gisella.

'What?'

But it was the man on the gate who spoke next.

'Sorry, no gold, no entry. Shame actually – I reckon those dogs would stand a good chance in the Unexpected Pets contest, 'ey, Royston.'

'Wha',' called Royston, from lower down, clearly no longer next to Algernon.

'These dogs – Unexpected Pets – would have given that dragon a run for its money.'

'Dragon?' called the muffled voice.

'You know – that noisy little thing we let in earlier. A Lesser Crested Ridge Creeper, if I'm not very much mistaken – it's the call you know – very distinctive.' Algernon let out three shrill squawks and nodded in an "I know my dragons" kind of way.

'So can we come in then?' asked Seth brightly. 'You know, for the contest?'

'If it was up to me boys, I'd open the gate now, but its orders, see – more 'un my job's worth to go against orders.' And with another shake of his head he disappeared. This time neither face re-appeared.

From behind the gate Wil heard a disembodied voice. 'Bloody big dogs, mind! Bet they take some feedin!'

Mortimer stood looking up at the solid oak gate as if willing it to open. But as the voices of the two men faded into the distance, it was obvious that an alternative route into Armelia had to be found. After several more minutes, Mortimer turned to The Jackal.

'Well, the deal was that you would get us into the city – not just outside the gate! So I'm hoping that you have a Plan B here?'

'Plan B?' The Jackal looked genuinely confused.

'Yer, you know, Plan A didn't work, so now we go to Plan B – and the moons help you if we have to go to Plan C!'

Realization dawned.

'Oh, you mean like another way in!' For some reason The Jackal's sudden smile did not fill Wil with any confidence. 'Round the back, y'know, er, by the market – that's were I usually get in and out.'

'So why didn't you take us that way in the first place?' asked Wil. Unable to shake the feeling that they were being watched, Wil was very keen to get off the Fell – they might have been at the end of the valley but Tel Harion was still far too close for comfort.

'You didn't ask,' said The Jackal. 'You all just headed for the gate, so I thought you, y'know, had gold with you. I mean, everyone around here knows about the toll to get into the city!'

'Well we aren't from around here, in case you hadn't realised by now,' replied Mortimer pithily.

'Oh, well, n..no… course. Should have guessed after that thing, y'know, about the tower.. and the..er, gold… er,' stammered The Jackal. The look on Mortimer's face suggested that he was seriously contemplating shooting The Jackal where he stood; and Wil was sorely tempted to let him. But the rising moons were marking the beginning of the third night since Tally was taken and they were no nearer finding her. For the moment at least, Wil was forced to admit they needed help… and The Jackal was the only one offering.

'Look, we need to get into Armelia tonight. We don't have any gold but we, the horses *and* the hounds really need to be on the other side of this wall. Can you help us?'

The Jackal pursed his lips, walked a few paces forward and studied the lack of gap between the two huge gates. He turned back to face them.

'You know Plan B?'

'Yeess,' replied Mortimer, clearly running short of patience.

'Well, er, there's good news and bad news.'

'I think we'd better have the bad news first,' said Mortimer with a quick glance towards Wil.

The Jackal increased the distance between them with another step and said simply, 'Plan B won't work.' He attempted a further retreat and pressed his back hard against the gate, 'It's the animals. They'd never, y'know, climb the wall.'

'Climb what wall?' asked Seth from behind Mortimer. He was standing with Rhoani and Shadow. All three Fellhounds had long since got bored and were lying on their haunches waiting for orders. The Jackal looked at them as if they had only appeared that minute.

'Well, you never said anything about the animals! Get us into Armelia, you said. Get us in and we won't shoot you, you said!' The Jackal waved his arms up at the gate as he spoke. 'Now you tell me you don't have any gold to get through the gate but you want to get two horses and three of the biggest dogs I've ever seen in my life into the city.'

The Jackal closed his eyes tightly.

'And what's the good news,' asked Gisella. 'You did say there was good news.'

The Jackal didn't open his eyes.

'I was really hoping that you'd just shoot me after the bad news,' he said, bracing himself flat against the gate, eyes still pressed shut.

'Why?' asked Gisella sounding horrified.

'Because there is no... hang on,' The Jackal opened his eyes wide and beamed, 'Can you swim?'

CHAPTER FOURTEEN

Troubled Waters

Seth peered down into the canal.

'Oh, great!'

A few feet below, the dark water flowed with treacly slowness under the city wall through a low culvert.

'The *last* time I came out with you lot I nearly drowned!' Mortimer frowned down into the murky blackness.

'Mmm, but luckily for you Wil was there!' He turned to The Jackal.

'And the plan is?'

'Well, the river goes under the wall here so we can swim into the city,' said The Jackal. 'It flows right round the city – well, y'know, under it actually. There are loads of wells, y'know, where it's deep. It leads to the foundry – the mill wheels, y'know, there's two – we can get out just before the first one.'

'And what happens if we don't, *you know*, get out?' asked Wil, with a suspicion that he wasn't going to like the answer.

'Oh, don't worry, you'll get out. It gets really shallow – I fell in there once – only went up to my bu- ackside.' He threw Gisella a furtive glance.

'Yes, but what happens if you *don't* get out?' said Gisella.

'Weell, y'know, the wheel…chguh,' The Jackal coughed and said no more.

'Great!' muttered Mortimer.

'Are you sure this is the only way in?' asked Wil. He cast a hopeful glance at the huge slabs of masonry that towered over them. The city wall butted right up against Mort Craggs; reaching skywards, the sheer rock glistened wet where the peaks way above were finally giving up the last remnants of winter.

'Well, like I said y'know, I normally climb – over there,' answered the boy and he waved his fingers towards the tops of a clump of trees that look like they were peeping over the wall. 'But there's quite a big drop on the other side into the kitchen garden. I twisted my ankle once, y'know. And at least this way, y'know, you can take your dogs!'

Wil studied the gap between the water and the roof of the culvert. Pretty sure he would be able to keep his own head above the water he wasn't at all convinced about Phinn. True, the hound liked paddling, but back home Wil couldn't persuade Phinn to go over his knees into East Lake. In fact, it had proved so difficult that he had wondered if this might be normal for Fellhounds. He was just about to ask when Mortimer plonked down on the grass and eased off his boots.

'Right, Wil. You and I'll go with The Jackal,' he said, folding his cloak. 'We'll take Mia and Phinn. Seth, Gisella; take Farrow and the horses and go back around to the gate. Once we get out at the mill we'll try to find a way to get you in without having to get our hands on any gold. At least with dragons around I don't think we'll have to worry about the Fellhounds attracting too much attention!'

Wil sat on the bank in just his shirt and breeches – the evening cold was already creeping into his bones and he was not looking forward to his imminent swim. Almost as an afterthought Mortimer had agreed to Gisella's suggestion that their cloaks and boots could be thrown over the wall in order that they had something dry on the other side. Although he was concerned that searching for clothes would delay them even further.

'Yes, but getting pneumonia isn't going to make you any quicker either!' was Gisella's rather testy response.

Taking the bundles that Mortimer and Wil had rolled and bound with their belts, she peered along the bank.

'So where's the bridge?'

'Oh, there isn't one,' replied The Jackal. Once again Wil had visions of Seth getting very wet. Fortunately Mortimer already had a solution.

'Gisella, take Shadow – you'll be fine. Just point him in the right direction and he'll do the rest.'

Gisella beamed. Mortimer turned to The Jackal who had insisted on keeping every stitch on, including his hat.

'Right, before we get in – where's the best place for Gisella to chuck our stuff over?'

The Jackal waved his hand vaguely again.

'Oh, it's only a little way. You'll see the top of a big tree just up there – y'know, a plum. There's a bit of a hump on this side. If you stand on that you should, y'know, be able to get the stuff over. Er, you can throw, can't you?'

'What?' said Gisella, her voice suddenly rather high.

'Er, nothing, y'know, it's just that you're a…, y'know, girl.' He wrinkled his nose and looked suddenly awkward. Gisella froze.

'Look, I really think we should be going now,' interrupted Wil – he'd seen that expression on Gisella's face before and it never ended well. Mortimer came to The Jackal's rescue.

'Right, are we sorted? In you go… Jackal,' he said with a glimmer of a grin.

The Jackal lowered himself carefully into the water. Wil could hear the sound of teeth chattering before the boy was up to his knees.

'Right, Wil, go on, you next. Just get in and call Phinn. He'll come in after you. If not, start swimming away – he'll definitely get in then.'

Unconvinced, Wil slid down the bank and... immediately regretted it. The water was beyond freezing. It was so cold he was astonished that it was actually flowing. Within seconds he couldn't feel his hands or feet; his heart beat as if it was about to pump itself out of his body.

Gisella called from the bank, 'What's it like, Wil?'

He took a deep breath, 'F-Fine,' he said, only just managing to control his shivering limbs. 'B-but I'm not sure I want to stay in l-long! Ph-Phinn, come on.'

Phinn stood on the bank above and peered down at him – as Wil's body temperature plummeted there was no way he could focus on the hound's mind but he was pretty sure Phinn's expression was not one of admiration.

'Phinn, c-come on!' Wil called again. But Phinn simply sprang over the canal on to the other bank, barking loudly. Mortimer frowned.

'Tell you what, Wil. I'll get in with Mia. Once he sees what she's doing he'll get the idea.'

Mortimer plopped into the freezing water beside Wil and called to Mia. Without hesitating, Mia trotted a little further down the bank, found a gentler slope and splashed in. Within seconds she was happily swimming around Wil and Mortimer.

Phinn stayed on the bank.

'I don't like to c-complain guys, b-but I'm f-freezing my b-backside off here!' called The Jackal. He was already swimming towards the gap under the wall. With wide powerful strokes, Mortimer set off in the same direction – Mia followed.

'It's OK, Wil,' Mortimer called over his shoulder. 'Just follow us, he'll come.'

Unconvinced, Wil kicked his legs hard and followed. The Jackal was now at the wall, with Mortimer and Mia not far behind. Thanks to the many stolen hours swimming and playing with his friends over on East Lake, Wil was a strong swimmer and he was at Mia's heels in a few powerful strokes.

The silence from behind him was embarrassing.

'Don't worry Wil, he'll come,' shouted Mortimer. Wil swam on.

Almost at the culvert Wil could feel the current getting stronger. He grabbed at the slimy stone of the wall to let Mortimer and Mia go through first.

Suddenly something on the other bank caught Wil's eye – a movement in the shadows. An image flashed across his brain and his blood ran even colder. But then it was gone. Was it an image or a feeling? And what about Gisella and Seth – there on the bank, exposed to… what? It had been so quick Wil wasn't entirely sure it had been there at all. Treading water, he scoured the hills but in the fading light all he could see was shadows – shadows everywhere. Then came the sound of pounding paws… a very brief silence… then a huge splash. Ice-cold water surged over Wil's head and into his mouth – his eyeballs felt as though they were going to freeze in the cold.

When he surfaced, Phinn's nose was the first thing Wil saw – only inches away – and a huge tongue as Phinn gave him a warm lick. On the bank, Gisella and Seth looked like they were trying extremely hard not to laugh.

'See, I said he could swim,' said Mortimer and he ducked down and swam under the city wall.

The journey was longer than Wil had expected; although as they progressed he was sure the water was getting warmer. His racing heart slowed and his lungs relaxed, which made breathing a lot easier. It was pitch-black. A long way ahead Wil could see a shaft of light. He fixed his eyes on it and ploughed through the blackness in slow sweeping strokes. Phinn stayed close, moving through the water as if he'd been born to it. The strange feeling that Wil had just before they went into the tunnel was gone completely and Wil quickly persuaded himself that what he must have felt was Phinn's trepidation as he worked up to getting wet. After all it made sense; Phinn had never swum before, and therefore Wil had never sensed Phinn like that. He certainly knew when the young hound was excited, or cross, or sulking – as that happened nearly every day – but nervous was new. Now all Wil could feel was the serene calm of Phinn's steady heartbeat and the power of his huge paws pulling through the water. Wil hooked his fingers under Phinn's iron collar.

'So, you like swimming after all then, hey?'

Without missing a beat, the huge Fellhound continued to plough through the blackness gently pulling his master in his wake as he swam.

'You OK, Wil?' Mortimer called-out in the dark. Wil could see his friend's bobbing head silhouetted against the little strip of light way off down the tunnel. 'If you grab Phinn's neck–'

'Already worked that one out, Mort. The water's not as cold now.'

The Jackal's voice echoed off the walls from somewhere ahead of them.

'Oh yer, I forgot to say, keep your mouth shut!'

'Why?' called Wil.

'Let's just say, not everyone uses this water for drinking!'

'But you said there were wells,' said Wil, with a sudden and very deep desire not to be in that water any more.

'Mmm. Well, they're also used for y' know, disposal, as well as collection,' said The Jackal's disembodied voice.

After that piece of news it was a while before they spoke again. Wil kept his lips pressed firmly together and hoped that no one would be disposing of anything as they neared the light patch which was obviously a 'well'. But they passed by unscathed and swam on.

With the light from the well behind them, in the distance Wil spotted another source of light – an opening, this time. He also felt the water slow, as if it was suddenly much deeper below them. Wil suddenly felt very vulnerable. His fingers tingled and his legs felt as if they were on fire as he tried to control the fear surging through his body. He could hear every drip, sense every trickle and – unfortunately for Wil – he could feel every heart that beat, fluttered or pounded in the darkness.

'Er, how much further, d'you think?' he called as he heard a slithering sound across the tunnel above his head.

'Not far now, we've ju–'

Silence.

'Sorry, didn't catch that,' Wil called. Phinn and Wil suddenly collided with Mia. 'What the–'

'That you, Wil? Can you see The Jackal? He was there.'

Wil guessed that Mortimer was pointing towards the light. There was no sign of The Jackal. Mortimer called out, 'Hey, Jackal … Colin, hey!'

Still silence.

'I think it's time we got out of here, Mortimer.'

Something slid between Wil's feet – something quite large, cold and very slimy.

'Yep, Phinn, we *really* need to get out of here.'

Most likely, it was the tone in Wil's voice rather than the words, but Phinn and Mia suddenly picked up the pace. Feeling very exposed and scared as Wil was, the tunnel was definitely getting lighter, which he hoped meant that they were getting closer to the mill.

They had just passed under the second well hole when, without any warning, something smashed into the water behind them.

'Whoa!' shouted Wil before he could stop himself.

The illuminated well dimmed slightly and a voice from above said, 'D'yer hear that, Ivy. Told you there were ghosts down there – I heard they've run out of room behind the tower and they's just chuckin' the dead in the canal now.'

The hounds swam on, taking Wil and Mortimer out of earshot – they were long past when the bucket was hoist back out of the well.

Just before the mouth of the tunnel, Wil's feet hit thick, slimy ground. Goo squeezed between his toes. Within seconds Phinn and Mia were powering through shallower but much faster flowing water. Both Wil and Mortimer clung to the hounds' collars as they fought against the current to stay on their feet.

'I think we're getting near the mill,' called Mortimer, now wading chest deep. 'Keep your eyes open for somewhere to get out.'

'Still looks pretty steep to me,' Wil called back. They might have been out of the tunnel but the sheer canal walls were narrowing and certainly weren't offering any way up and out of the water.

'That's got to be the mill, look, there.'

Mortimer was pointing towards a huge tower – and attached to it was a mill wheel – a *spinning* mill wheel.

The sound of crashing water was almost overwhelming now. The wheel squeaked and groaned; its battered buckets seemed to hurl more water back than they carried. Wil could really feel the power of the water. Frantically he scoured the canal sides for a way out. Even Phinn lost his footing. Then Wil noticed something that almost robbed him of what little breath he had left – the wheel was in a vast trough *behind* the millrace. The water was gathering speed because it was falling.

'We've got to get out of this now,' he shouted.

'Yer, I know,' Mortimer yelled back. He was jabbing his finger towards the narrowing channel. 'That gap – over there – I think it's an overflow. That's our best bet.'

But they were all caught up in the unstoppable flow. Wil grabbed at the stones that lined the canal but his nails just found thick green slime and slid off. Desperately kicking against the current he slipped and slid in his effort to avoid another crash that might cost them all their lives. It was impossible to concentrate on Phinn and try to communicate with Mia, but to Wil's relief Mia seemed to have cottoned on to the plan and expertly negotiated the slim gap dragging Mortimer, still clinging to her collar. Once Phinn saw his sister's manoeuvre, he too headed for the tiny opening. But just as the Fellhound surged through the heavy flow Wil lost his footing. His frozen fingers slipped from Phinn's collar. Phinn went one way – to join Mortimer and his sister – and Wil went the other, towards the drop at the end of the millrace.

Frantic now, he clawed at the low wall between him and safety, desperately trying to stop himself being dragged over the edge. The rhythmic pound of the rolling wheel filled his ears, water filled his mouth… *this was not how it was meant to be!*

Lying on the bank of the still pool, Wil forgave Phinn the few tooth marks across his back.

'Well, *now* do you see how useful a Fellhound can be, Wil?' panted Mortimer. 'Thank the moons that wall was low enough for him to reach! I really thought we were going to be picking bits of you out of that wheel.'

'Thanks Mortimer – I'm gonna have nightmares as it is!'

Seemingly unperturbed, Phinn was up to his knees, taking great gulps and blubbing water through his nose.

'You'd think he'd have had enough of that stuff for a while,' said Wil with an exhausted laugh. He sat up. Away from the boiling mill water, bobbing at the edge in the reeds below Wil spotted a dark shape. A horrible thought crept into his mind.

'D'you think that's what happened to The Jackal – look, isn't that his hat… down there?'

'Look Wil, he told us he'd come that way before and he seemed pretty confident that we'd get out. We must have just missed a gap earlier that he knew about,' said Mortimer. 'I bet you we bump into him again. I bet he'll be at the gate – probably got the others in already!'

With that Mortimer jumped to his feet and wound the ends of his wet shirt into a tight twist until they stopped dripping.

'Right, let's go and find our stuff – we're not going to have to worry about Mia and Phinn drawing anyone's attention; people are going to wonder what the hell we're doing soaking wet in this freezing cold!'

Wading through the crowded streets of Armelia, it very quickly became apparent that Mortimer and Wil had no reason to worry about the Fellhounds *or* being wet. The Alcama might be a night away but it seemed that the festivities started early in the city.

Everywhere Wil looked there were people dressed – or nearly dressed – in the most outlandish costumes. Bright orange and purple silk seemed to be a recurring theme, as did strange people and even stranger animals; he even spotted a troll drinking in one of the many bars that lined the shabby streets – only the second he'd ever seen in his whole life.

Despite the evening cold, groups were spilling out of dark doorways and gathering around makeshift tables. At one point Wil knocked over a chair. Bending to set it upright, something hissed at him from under the table; a pair of scarlet eyes blinked slowly out of the gloom. Then a bright green forked tongue unfurled and wound around the chair leg. Wil jumped back and banged his head on the table.

'I do hope you aren't trying to steal Sebastian?' asked a velvet voice.

The abandoned chair rose and righted itself.

'Er, no. No!' said Wil backing away another step. 'What is it – he?'

'Oh, I won't trouble you with the detail,' said a woman wrapped from head to toe in orange silk. She flashed him a serene smile. Whatever Sebastian was, he stayed hidden under the table. 'If you stick around for the competition tomorrow, you might just find out. Are you entering that?'

'Sorry?' said Wil. Then he realised that Phinn was standing just behind him. 'Er.. yer, probably. I, er, haven't decided yet.'

'Well, I hope he does tricks then,' said the woman, casting a disparaging eye over Wil's shoulder. 'I mean – a Fellhound... hardly unexpected, even for Armelia.'

Taken aback, Wil was desperately trying to think of a trick that might impress the woman when Mortimer re-appeared in the crowd and gave the woman a stiff smile.

'Today, Wil!'

Not wanting to seem rude, Wil opened his mouth to wish the woman luck for the competition but the gap between them had already been filled by a couple having a row.

Up ahead, Wil could see a crooked sign hanging from a single hook. The sign read *The Olde Mule*. Again the doorway to the little inn was spewing people out onto the street. As they got closer a man charged out of the crowd. He ran right up to them and yelled something completely incoherent right into Mortimer's face. Mortimer stopped but did not react and the man, covered from head to toe in orange and purple tattoos, stuck out his tongue then sprinted back into a cheering group, where, as one, they drained huge jugs of frothy black ale – goblets stood unused and seemingly forgotten on a nearby table.

'What do you think they're drinking?' asked Wil. He was fascinated and horrified at the same time. In Mistlegard, Wil worked in the tiny inn where he swept the floors and occasionally served behind the bar if they were shorthanded. Everyone there drank mead or barley beer, neither of which were anything like the colour of the brew in those jugs – they also drank out of goblets.

'That'll be Rat Beer,' said Mortimer with a knowing grin. 'Makes you mad and keeps you *bad*!'

'Rat Beer! Please tell me it's not made out of real rats!'

'They've got to do something with them, Wil. Flying rodents – the city'd be over-run otherwise!'

'*Flying* – ohh, I've heard of them! When I was young my father used to say that if I didn't go to bed, rats would fly into my room and eat my mattress. I've never seen one though and I never thought they made beer out of them – *erch!* I bet it's disgusting!'

'The Fellmen from Little Thesk bring it when they come for the Moon Chases. I tried it once – made me want to fight with everyone,' said Mortimer with a grimace. 'You're right – give me barley beer any day – or Lady Élanor's elder wine!'

Back at the bar, the orange and purple man had taken delivery of a long pitcher that he was now clutching in both hands. While his companions sang a very rude song he stood swaying – allowing whatever was in the pitcher to slop over the sides; the song came to a raucous end and the tattooed man downed the contents of the pitcher in one. His friends roared and clapped; he ran down the alley at the side of the bar and vomited over his feet.

'Let's get out of here, Wil, just in case you're tempted!'

They walked away from *The Olde Mule* just as a fight broke out behind them.

CHAPTER FIFTEEN

Plan 'D'

The two moons were high by the time Wil put his hand on one of the cloth bundles – it was Mortimer's. They had found the castle's kitchen garden surprisingly easily – largely because it was the only place around that seemed to have any trees. In the silver moonlight, their silhouettes were easy to spot even from some distance; although, of course, the fact that the garden was below the castle was another giveaway, as Mortimer had been quick to point out.

It was also fortunate that they had found the gate into the garden unlocked. It had creaked loudly when Wil tried it, but when no one came to investigate he had pushed it wide and they had simply walked in.

As they searched for their belongings, the massive, part-built tower above them glistened in the light of hundreds of torches that were now burning across the entire city. The smell of smouldering tallow drifted through the evening air. Higher up, the serene reflection of the converging moons glowed gold – a stark contrast to the dancing torchlight.

'D'you think Tally's in that tower?' Wil whispered, still searching for his own clothes. A moment later he spotted Phinn, his head in an apple tree, nudging a tightly wrapped bundle with his huge nose. Grateful for the help, as he was now very cold, Wil stretched up and retrieved his cloak and boots. It was then he noticed that despite the lingering winter chill, all of the fruit trees in the garden were laden with blossom. The garden seemed oddly warm, too, and was filled with the gentle hum of bees – again very odd so soon after what had been a very hard winter quarter across the whole of Thesk. The bees were calm but busy – Wil could feel them; for them, here, this day was like all others – it was as though they were telling him – here it was always warm and there was always blossom.

But even in this tranquil garden Wil also knew that there was no point trying to reach Tally with his mind – she had been the one to work out that his mindreading abilities, useful as they were, only extended to animals; and remembering the searing pain that always resulted in Tally's attempts to read Wil's mind, he hoped that she wasn't going to try to reach him! But Wil was sure that Mortimer had no idea about his, or Tally's, telepathic skills, so he thought it best to keep both his observations and his thoughts to himself.

Hauling on his boots, Mortimer scoured the part-built tower and the crumbling walls that made up the rest of the castle and finally answered Wil's question.

'Well, she's bound to be in there somewhere, Wil,' he said wrapping his cloak around his shoulders. 'But with The Jackal gone I haven't had a chance to come up with a Plan D yet. Look, let's go find Gisella and Seth. I can't work out anything until I've had something to eat!'

The journey through the city was trying; they had to fend off numerous offers of beer, two attempted fights and a very friendly young lady who took an instant shine to Mortimer. By the time they got to the gate both Wil and Mortimer were hot and very hungry – although they were almost dry.

As Mortimer guessed, Mia and Phinn hadn't attracted nearly as much attention as Wil had feared – although a group of overly friendly travellers had tried very hard to swap them for two rather tired-looking Bragghounds.

'Honest, mate, they're tidy fighters, they are!' insisted one of the travellers, pressing the chain leash of his own hound into Wil's hand while he attempted to walk away with Phinn. Fortunately, by way of objecting, Phinn had sat down – and once a Fellhound decides he's not moving, he is definitely *not* going anywhere! So, as politely as he could, Wil had pressed the lead back into the man's hand and set a slow but determined course away towards the gate. Phinn followed.

'What did you say they were again?' the man had called after them, amiably waving a tankard of ale.

'Fellhounds!' Mortimer and Wil had chimed – and not for the first time during that walk.

'Big, mind! Gor, bet they can sh–'

But the man's voice was drowned by a sudden commotion up ahead.

'Great!' said Mortimer. 'That's all we need – a fight right at the gate. There'll be guards down here in no time if this gets out of hand!'

Then several people in the crowd nearest to them stepped back looking slightly scared and Wil caught the sound of a familiar, though slightly odd sounding, voice.

'Get your handsh off me, you… you oaf! I could knock you down with one punsch… and don't try and stop me!'

A tall, blonde boy put both his hands up and retreated muttering something about a tambourine.

'Gisella?' said Wil not quite able to believe the scene in front of him.

Seth's voice called from somewhere among a sea of people and horses – all swathed in orange and purple.

'Wil, Mortimer! At last!'

Behind him, a young man who looked a little older than Mortimer was playing a flute – the tune wound through the wandering horde like a playful puppy. Two others plucked at small harps, although their valiant efforts demonstrated more enthusiasm than musical skill; overall, however, the sound was not unpleasant and fitted the chaotic spectacle of the drifting group.

Suddenly Gisella's eyes found Wil. She shrieked.

'Wil!'

Seemingly oblivious of all around her, she charged towards him, waving with both hands as if fearing he might not spot her.

'Wil, Wil, Wil! I'm sooo glad you've come! Oh, and Phinney too. Phinney, oooh, look. Theshe are my new friendshsh – well, mine and Seth'sss,' she slurred and held out her hand to Phinn who backed away. Unperturbed, Gisella twirled back to face Wil and beckoned him closer with a crooked finger. 'But to be honesht,' she whispered conspiratorially, 'he'sh being a big meanie. He took my drink and shaid I couldn't have any more!'

As she breathed over Wil, all became horribly clear – Gisella was drunk!

Seth forced his way between two harp pluckers, neither of whom took any notice of him, Farrow, or the two horses he was dragging in his wake.

'They were at the gate when we got back,' said Seth.

In one hand he held the horses' reins; in the other he was clutching a tambourine. Every time he waved his hand the tambourine jingled – and in his present agitated state it was jingling a lot.

'We tried to keep in the shadows like you said, Mortimer, but one of them, that guy over there – Jev – he saw Farrow and his father used to breed Fellhounds over in Grizzledale and he came over to talk to us and the guys on the gate weren't around so they well, Jev, invited us to join them while they waited to be let in and that's when they brought out the mead,' Seth finally took a breath and jingled again.

Gisella stood beside him smiling at anyone who passed and humming as tunelessly as the harpists.

'So why didn't you just say no, Seth?' asked Mortimer. Gisella meandered away, back towards her new friends.

'Gisella, no, stay here.'

Without taking his eyes off Seth, Mortimer reached for Gisella's arm and missed. She took the tambourine from Seth's hand as she went.

'I did!' Seth said in answer to Mortimer's question. 'But then Gisella said that if we didn't join in they would get suspicious.' He looked utterly mortified. 'So we had a goblet of mead and then Jev gave Gisella some of his drink – I think it was some sort of beer – very dark, smelt awful! And, well, she didn't seem to like it at first, but Jev kept talking to her and being really friendly–'

'How friendly?' demanded Wil. He was trying to keep an eye on Gisella and listen at the same time.

'Oh, *really* friendly – she kept giggling – I've never seen Gisella like that before – then she had more to drink and then…er, then she started dancing.'

'What!' said Mortimer. 'On her own?'

'Oh no, they were playing music – it was really good actually and Gisella and Jev were dancing. And then they fell over–'

'I don't think I want to hear any more,' said Wil.

'Oh no,' Seth insisted. 'Once she fell over I managed to get her to sit down with me. I gave her some water and a bit of food but then they opened the gates – just now. We've only just got in and … er… as you can see, she's … er… livened up again.'

Seth's voice trailed off. All around them people were laughing, singing, or shouting to one another; some were busy bartering with stall holders for bulging pies, or glistening slices of roast boar. The air was full of the smell of smouldering charcoal, burning meat fat and stale beer – Wil caught a whiff of another smell; two men were standing very close to the edge of one of the city wells. He turned away quickly. Gisella was now tottering among her new-found friends as they all headed off into the city. The tambourine had been replaced by a harp. Every now and then Gisella stopped, brushed her fingers over the strings and then tottered on. Wil watched. Jev sidled up and offered Gisella his flask. Beaming, she lifted it to her lips and took a greedy mouthful; at the same time Jev slid his arm around her waist – if Wil had had one last straw at that moment, it wouldn't have just snapped, he would have ripped it up into a hundred tiny pieces and stamped on it.

'Right, I've had enough of this!'

Wil waded into the crowd. Mortimer made a futile grab for Wil's arm although he did manage to stop Phinn from following.

Gisella's face lit up as Wil approached as if seeing him for the first time that evening.

'Wil! When did you get here? Thish is Jed, my er..'

She swayed slightly and Wil saw Jev tighten his hold.

'Jev, it's Jev,' corrected Jev quietly. He looked directly into Wil's eyes with an almost-smile, but Gisella gave him a dismissive wave and threw her arms around Wil's neck.

'Oh, I'm so happy to see you Wil! When did you get here? I've really, really, really, really missed you.'

Jev released his grip and stepped back. Gisella bounced on her toes.

'Did I ever tell you Wil, I really, really, reeeeeally like you. Did you know that?'

Much as it *really* was very nice to see the look on Jev's face and to have Gisella snuggled so close, the smell of beer was overpowering. Wil prized Gisella's arms from his neck and turned in search of Mortimer and Seth.

'Oh,' said Gisella. 'Wil, you don't like me!'

'Look, Giz, of course,' he turned back, 'I do.'

But Gisella's eyes gazed at him unseeing. She swayed again and flopped forwards. Wil bent before she hit the floor and hoisted her unceremoniously over his shoulder. Most of the travellers had moved on by now but a small group of stragglers around them cheered.

'Nice one!' said Jev. 'Was planning to have had a go at that one myself, but after all that rat beer – na, I'll leave her to you.' And with an admiring grin he patted Gisella's bottom. Wil hitched the unconscious Gisella up onto his shoulder, turned and turned back. He punched Jev in the ribs – just once – then waiting just long enough to see his drunken rival double-up and hit the floor, Wil marched out of the crowd into the nearest alley. The stragglers cheered again.

'Oh dear, this is all my fault,' wailed Seth. 'If only we hadn't spoken to those people. If only I'd stopped her from drinking that beer.'

'Much as I do hold you partly responsible, Seth Tanner, Gisella really should have known better,' said Mortimer, obviously livid.

They had found a quiet corner next to a blacksmith's forge – closed for the night. Wil had plonked Gisella unceremoniously down onto a pile of hay, where she had already been sick once. She was now fast asleep. Wil had hoped that the first aid bag would have come up with something to bring on instant sobriety but all it had offered was an empty bottle. A tiny label swung from the stopper. Wil's heart sank at its words:

> *For excess alcohol: Accompanied by sickness, headache and feeling like death – endure it and learn from the experience!*
>
> *Best before: If Nothing lasts Forever, this cure will last a very long time, though few will only use it once.*

Their second evening was rapidly running into their second night and they were no nearer finding Tally or Tanith; and now they had to sit and wait for Gisella to sober up. *And* Wil was trying very hard not to be cross with Gisella for allowing herself to be chatted up by that Jev bloke. Finding an apple and some cheese in his pack, he flopped down into a straw-filled corner and brooded over what Gisella had said – just before she had passed out. Maybe it was just the beer talking, he thought, or did she really care about him? Then he remembered their conversation in the river – she had told Wil that she was only being friendly with Mortimer because she wanted to be a Chaser – but was that really true? Maybe she was only telling Wil that so that he would help her to make up with Mortimer…

A voice as rough as a bucket of gravel rattled above the hubbub of the crowd, waking Wil from what had turned out to be a surprisingly comfortable night's sleep.

'NO! You thick or *what?* I said quail eggs – get them yer now!'

'I...I'm so sorry Ms Mhaddphat, they told me you would be here before sundown last evening. I, er, I thought you had changed your mind, or gone somewhere else...' said another, much smaller voice.

'What!' yelled Mhaddphat. 'A hundred and forty I ordered– DON'T tell me you sold 'em!'

A faint pink light in the east told Wil it was nearly dawn – already the city was humming and Wil was sure that unlike him, Mortimer, Seth and Gisella, *it* hadn't slept. Somewhere close by a small child started to snivel.

'An' you can be quiet,' she growled. The child continued to whine incoherently. 'SHUT UP!'

Mhaddphat's shout was so loud that Gisella jumped up and peered around through very bleary eyes. Mhaddphat continued to bellow.

'What am I gonna do now? YOU can tell her ladyship. *I* ordered them an' *YOU* let me down!'

'I... I can see if Cecil has some... over on Bell Street. If... if you'd like?' The voice was pleading now.

There was a moment of peace before the voice exploded again.

'Get over there then! Go on! NOW!'

The child whinged. The yelling did not falter.

'An' *when* you got em, bring 'em up the castle. I'm no' wasting any more of *my* time! *I* go' things to do!'

The child mumbled incoherently and then started to sob – the tone was much higher than Mhaddphat's low growl but no less determined. Mhaddphat was some distance away before she called to the child.

'Faerydae, GET 'ERE!'

And then all that remained was the crowd as before; singing, shouting, fighting and drinking. Gisella slumped back on to her makeshift bed and instantly went back to sleep. Mortimer's head popped up from a pile of hay at Wil's feet.

'That's it!'

'That's what?' said Seth, with a wide yawn.

'Plan D!' said Mortimer.

'Plan D?' echoed Seth, but Wil was catching up fast.

'We buy some quail eggs and deliver them to the castle?'

'Not quite, Wil – but not far off. We go find that guy and offer to *deliver* the quail eggs he's going to buy,' said Mortimer. 'I mean, he's hardly going to want to go himself, not after the pasting that woman's just given him!'

'And do delivery boys usually take their animals with them in the city?' Wil couldn't help asking.

Mortimer glanced over at Rhoani and Shadow happily munching on a mound of hay that Gisella hadn't been sick on.

'No, Wil. Seth can stay here with Gisella. Mia, Farrow and Phinn need to be fed anyway. We'll deliver the eggs, get into the castle and find Tally.'

Wil wasn't entirely convinced such a simple plan would work but, unable to think of anything better, he kept his mouth shut and nodded.

'And Seth,' Mortimer added looking at Gisella, 'If Gisella wakes up and can stop being sick for long enough, you need to find Tanith. You might want to start with the castle stables if you can find them.'

'And what happens if anyone asks any awkward questions?' asked Seth.

Mortimer studied Mia, Farrow and Phinn for a few seconds and then said, 'Tell them you're here for the competition. Tell them,' he nodded towards the Fellhounds, 'Tell them they're a herd!'

Chapter Sixteen

Special Delivery

Despite the early hour Bell Street was even busier than the market around the city gate. Rickety stalls selling honey, cheese and delicious smelling hams were jammed next to tables overflowing with jewellery made of anything from brightly coloured gem stones to carved bone. One table was groaning under the weight of sheep skulls, their hollow eyes staring out at all who passed.

'You want to buy a lantern, boy?' breathed a scruffy little man. 'Put one in your window tonight, boy. Keep the Alcama evils at bay when the moons cross.'

Behind the temporary stalls dowdy shops sat silent – their weather-beaten shutters framing empty windows. Except for the orange glow of illuminated bone, each one was as dark and gloomy as the next; it appeared that the Alcama came early in Armelia.

'Er, no thanks,' said Wil, wondering what Armelia looked like when it wasn't the Alcama. 'I, er, I haven't got a window.'

'Well, evil be upon your soul, boy!' hissed the man and turned away. Beside Wil, a woman picked up one of the skulls. 'You want to buy a lantern, lady?'

Wil moved on. The stall next door boasted the biggest selection of knives he had ever seen; and next to that was another very ornate display, this time of cream-coloured daggers. A glint of red caught Wil's eye. He leant forward. For a dagger, it was very odd. Like a stretched 'S', its rounded edges tapered to a deadly point. Mounted close to the tip Wil could see what looked remarkably like a drop of blood; although Wil had never seen one before, he assumed it to be a ruby.

'Dragon's tooth,' said a bright voice from behind the table. 'Giant Redback – left that in my Dad's favourite bull – absolutely no fear, your Redback. If you ever get chased by one, best thing to do – throw yourself off something high and hope you hit the ground before it plucks you out of the air. Once a Redback's got your scent, believe me, you're a goner!'

The girl pulled a knobbly woollen shawl around her shoulders and, with her bottom lip curled down, nodded. Another ruby sparkled in her nose – a similar, but much shorter tooth dangled from her left ear.

Wil picked up the tooth dagger and turned it over in his hand.

'So what happened to the bull?'

'Managed to stitch it up. It's fathered fifteen calves since!' she beamed proudly.

'Gosh, I bet your father's pleased!'

The tooth was easily twice the length of Wil's hand. It felt surprisingly rough – like it was covered in the tiniest of scales.

'Dunno,' said the girl, looking up into the night sky. 'Redback swallowed him in one. He's up there somewhere – the dragon, not my Dad.'

Wil hastily returned the tooth to its place in the fan-like display. 'Oh, I... I'm sorry,' he stammered and, lost for anything else to say, moved away from the table. Up ahead,

Mortimer was standing outside a shop – one of very few that was brightly lit and open for business – and if Wil's ears were not deceiving him, the shop was definitely clucking.

'…needs them urgently, you see,' Mortimer was saying to a tiny man as Wil joined them.

'W-well, yes, I could see that,' answered the man. As he spoke he jerked his head back and forth, eying the boys suspiciously. 'She really was very cross, wasn't she,' he added casting a nervous glance at their nearest neighbours.

'Yes,' said Mortimer, oozing a confidence that even drew in Wil – and he knew Mortimer was lying! 'She's making quail egg soufflé. Absolutely delicious. It's a new dish for the festival – a surprise for Lord and Lady Rexmoore. Cook really must have them as soon as possible.'

Mouse-like, the man twitched his head upwards.

'Oh, dear, this really is awful. I can only get eighty – they've gone off lay. It's the moons.' He seemed to be talking more to himself than to Mortimer. 'Everyone knows, quail go off lay when the moons cross – just like the cows won't give any milk. Even moonpig meat can be a bit iffy during Alcama. Oh dear!'

He ran a shaking hand through his thinning hair.

'Mmm, sounds like you've got a problem – and you know what Mhaddphat's like,' said Mortimer crossing his arms over his chest.

'Oh, don't,' said the little man covering his face with his hands. 'I just can't face her. She'll roast me alive!'

'Look, tell you what,' said Mortimer with a conspiratorial wink. 'How about we deliver them for you? We'll say that Wil here dropped some on the way.' He leant closer and whispered, 'She's got a bit of a soft spot for my friend,' Mortimer tapped his nose, 'treats him like the son she never had.' He winked again.

'Oh!' gasped the man. 'But what about Galorian? I know he's a little brat, but surely she hasn't given up on him already? He's only three!'

Mortimer didn't miss a beat.

'Older son, of course! I mean, a three-year-old's hardly going to be a help around the kitchen now is it? No, Wil here is her right-hand man.' Mortimer threw his arm around Wil's shoulder and drew him close, 'Fetching, carrying, peeling, plucking – she hates plucking, did you know that–'

'Mort!' interrupted Wil out of the corner of his mouth. Mortimer dropped his arm.

'Well, anyway,' he said, throwing his shoulders back so he looked even taller than usual. 'We are here offering to take those eggs up to the castle but if you want to do it yourself, we'll be off.'

And with that he turned, caught the edge of Wil's cloak and pulled Wil around with him.

'No, Wait! Yes, I mean – *please*,' begged the man.

'Keep walking,' whispered Mortimer.

The tiny man burst into tears. 'Please, s…stop. I beg you.'

Both Mortimer and Wil turned back towards the clucking, quacking and squawking shop. Without waiting to be asked, the little man grabbed the handle of a large wicker basket and scampered after them. Still sobbing, he handed the hamper to Wil and threw his arms around Mortimer's waist. Looking slightly embarrassed, Mortimer patted him on the shoulder. Then without another word, the man darted into the crowd weeping loudly as he disappeared.

Mortimer threw Wil a triumphant grin.

'Right, let's go deliver some eggs!'

The creaking gate that led into the castle's kitchen garden was wide open, hanging silent on its hinges. Gingerly stepping into the garden, Wil could see the dark shapes of bee skeps piled high against the wall; the heady aroma of rotting straw mixed with mature cow dung suggested that their honey-producing days were long gone. All around him, though, Wil could hear the soft hum of bees going about their business in the pink glow of the waking day.

'Watch you don't get stung, Wil,' said Mortimer, ducking under low-hanging branches of apple, plum, damson and cherry.

But Wil was confident that the bees meant no harm. He could feel their contentment so strongly that his mouth filled with the taste of Martha's delicious honey cake.

'Just be careful where you put your feet,' he replied in a whisper. 'They're a very close family and don't take kindly to having their relatives squashed!'

'Oh, right-oh!' laughed Mortimer. 'And what do you think they'd do then?'

'You really don't want to know, Mort. Just watch your feet!'

Picking their way up the garden, Wil spied a door in the old stone part of the castle; again wide open, the dingy entrance was a stark contrast to the glowing golden tower behind it. And the gravelly voice that bellowed from somewhere beyond the doorway was far from welcoming.

'I told you already, Galorian, I'm busy. I go' things to do, I 'aven't got time now!'

'But Faerydae took my barey sugar. She won't gi'e it to me,' replied a boy's familiar infantile, *very* whiney voice.

'No I didn't!' objected another voice – a girl – still young but older than Galorian. 'He said I could 'ave it!'

'I didn't gi' you my barey sugar! I never said nothin'!'

'Did too, you liar! Mmm, its reeeeally yummy! Baaaarley sugar, my favourite,' said the girl, exaggerating her own correct pronunciation of the word *barley* as if to taunt her brother all the more – it worked.

'Yaaarghhuhuh,' sobbed the boy. 'I want it. I want my barey sugar. Yhaaarghhuhh!'

'Right, that's it, ger out the two of you! Ger out and don't bother me 'til breakfast time! I said I'm BUSY!' Mhaddphat's voice echoed out over the garden. Wil felt a ripple of disquiet among the bees. He offered the hamper of eggs to Mortimer.

'Do you want to do this?'

'She'll be fine, Wil. You watch…and don't forget, we've got the solution to one of her problems – she's *bound* to be pleased!'

'Yes, but if you remember we've only got *part* of the solution!'

Another bee skep lay up-turned on the doorstep together with an old sheep's skull. The black tip of the cold candle was just visible through one of the eye sockets. Next to the skep was a water trough, brimming with thick, green water – above which hung a bell. Mortimer's fingers had just closed around the ringer when two tiny figures pelted out through the open door. With no sign of them stopping, Mortimer jumped out of the way – the skep and the skull went flying. One of the figures was waving a twist of barley sugar high in the air and the other was sobbing – very loudly. As they disappeared among the fruit trees, another, now familiar voice came after them.

'Oh my gaawwd! If I get my hands on you two – just SHUT UP, WILL YOU!'

Mhaddphat appeared in the doorway brandishing a rolling pin. Wil nearly dropped the hamper.

'Whoa, a hobgoblin!' he said before he could stop himself.

Mortimer didn't say anything – his expression, however, said plenty.

The tiny woman's chubby face folded into a grimace. Her top lip disappeared under her bulbous nose and her beady black eyes disappeared under bushy, equally black, eyebrows.

'Yer, and what of it!'

She raised the rolling pin higher above her head – waist-high to Wil and Mortimer. Wil lowered the basket for protection and Mortimer closed his hands across his breeches. The hobgoblin glanced at the basket, 'What you want?'

'Eighty! Oh my gaawwd! What I am supposed to do with eighty?'

Mhaddphat, now brandishing a carving knife, stomped around the great pine table in the middle of the vast kitchen – her huge bottom swinging from side to side with each heavy step. She had not stopped shouting. The kitchen, that moments ago had been full of bustling staff, was suddenly empty – with the exception of one very elderly-looking hobgoblin who seemed engrossed in the contents of a saucepan boiling over the fire.

'I said a hundred and twenty. *Eighty* – I can't believe it!' She stopped and pointed the knife at Wil and Mortimer. 'You sure there's eighty? You counted 'em?' She peered over the edge of the table suspiciously and then stuck her face into the hamper and started to count. The elderly hobgoblin muttered something about checking pickled onions and tottered out of the kitchen through a door at the far end of the room.

'I thought you were going to tell her I dropped some,' whispered Wil. 'She's going to kill that egg seller next time she sees him.'

'That did occur to me,' Mortimer whispered back, his lips barely moving. 'But which would you rather? She's armed with a knife. And that rolling pin's only over there.' He nodded to the end of the table. 'There are a lot of parts of me I'd rather stayed attached – it was an easy choice!'

'Seventy-six, seventy-seven, seventy-eight, sev-' Mhaddphat stopped counting. Her head popped up from behind the wicker lid of the hamper, 'Eighty! There's only eighty! Oh my gaawwd! What do you expect me to do with eighty?'

'I think its going to be a long night!' said Mortimer, but as he spoke there was a crash and a high-pitched squeal from the garden.

'Was that one of you?' demanded Mhaddphat with a glare brimful of accusation. With the quail eggs seemingly forgotten, she cocked her oval head to one side. Her pointed ears turned, seeking out the source of the disturbance.

'Wow,' breathed Wil. Of course, he had heard of hobgoblins before – every wealthy household in Thesk had at least one – but he had never actually seen one. They certainly didn't have any in Mistlegard, being such a poor village; but his mother had told him about an estate just the other side of Grizzledale that had three. Apparently hobgoblins were exceptional cooks, owing to their own voracious appetites; this also made them quite expensive to keep – and looking at Mhaddphat bent over the basket of quail eggs, Wil could certainly believe that! Male hobgoblins were also very useful during harvest; having long arms and being so low to the ground, they could pick whole estates of vegetables in just a few days without the backache that Wil had come to know so well during their own harvests.

The squealing outside was getting nearer to the inside – and much louder. There was another crash and then uproar.

'Ger them off, Faerydae. They's 'urtin me. Argh, i' urts! Mama, Argh! Mama!'

The cries were so high-pitched that Wil and Mortimer had to put their hands over their ears. On a shelf next to the fire a bottle of oily, yellow liquid exploded – its sticky contents splattered up the wall.

'Mama!'

Mhaddphat slammed the hamper lid down and waddled towards the kitchen door, her knuckles swinging only a hair's breadth from the floor. At the same moment, two terrified hobgoblets charged into the room – followed by a dark buzzing cloud.

'Run!' bellowed Mortimer. But Mhaddphat was in the way.

With her mouth wide open – easily the size of Wil's head – she was running back and forth scooping bees out of the air. Wil stood transfixed. She crunched down on a mouthful of buzzing bees – and Wil's world went mad. Buzzing filled his ears and closed around his brain like a veil – the noise made his teeth vibrate and his fingers tingle. Bees were dying – and not just in the kitchen.

Wil grabbed Faerydae by both arms, 'What did you do?' he yelled. She didn't answer.

'What did you do to the bees?' he repeated, forcing the words through his clenched teeth. Suddenly aware that he was shaking the speechless child, he stopped, but didn't let go. Her little face crumpled.

'It was Galorian. He started it. He lit the fire!' she howled.

Wil released the hobgoblet as if she had stung him, took a deep breath and charged straight through the angry swarm. Oblivious, Mhaddphat continued to swoop and chomp. Wil was vaguely aware that Mortimer was shouting something but he didn't hear the words – his only thought was of what he knew he would find out in the garden.

Sure enough, there in the middle of the little courtyard was a smouldering skep. The hum was deafening. Bees were streaming out of the tiny opening at the base of the basket. Next to it were two more skeps, not yet alight but clearly next in line. Wil swept up the smoking hive in both arms and ran to the trough but it was far too narrow to dunk the skep straight in and anyway, he didn't want to save the bees from burning only to drown them in the process! Frantic now, he looked around but there wasn't a bucket or even a cup in sight – nothing. Then he spotted the bell. With one hard tug he yanked it from the wall and dipped it into the water. At the first bell-full smoke and steam billowed up into Wil's face. He coughed and gagged but he kept going. The steam was scalding his hand but within a couple more scoops the skep stopped smoking, and within a couple more it stopped hissing. Only then did the buzzing in Wil's ears start to subside. Retrieving the two unmolested skeps, Wil then headed for the biggest apple tree he could see and set down all three under the drooping branches, alongside two others that were already there.

As he put the last skep into place a bee settled on Wil's hand – the badly scalded skin was starting to blister and peel. He felt absolutely no desire to brush the bee away. Another came, and then another. For a reason he could not explain he reached into one of the unharmed skeps and sank his hand into the waxy honey within. The relief from the pain was instant.

Behind him, what was left of the swarm in the kitchen billowed out into the courtyard like a puff of thick black smoke – followed by a very confused Mortimer. From inside the kitchen Wil could hear the two hobgoblets wailing loudly, and Mhaddphat shouting again. Mortimer strode down the garden brushing bees out of his hair and talking as he went.

'Right Wil, I'm not really sure what happened just now but, er, any time you want to join me?'

'Oh, yer, …er, right,' said Wil. The sound in his head had gone. With great reluctance he carefully withdrew his hand from the soothing honey. The bees had gone back to their business and Wil could feel them – once more, calm and safe.

'Uh, Wil, don't want to rush you here, but…' said Mortimer, nodding his head back towards the tower. 'I reckon we can still get in if we go back now.'

'EIGHTY!' The voice exploded from the door of the castle kitchen. 'HE'S ONLY GIVEN ME EIGHTY! WHAT AM I GOING TO DO WITH EIGHTY QUAIL EGGS? OH MY GAAWDD!'

Mortimer shrugged, 'Or perhaps not.'

CHAPTER SEVENTEEN

Unexpected Pets

Seth's face fell when Wil and Mortimer neared the city gate.

'No Tally, then' he said needlessly.

Mortimer cast a brief and rather disparaging glance towards Wil.

'No. Let's just say it didn't quite go to plan and leave it at that shall we. Please tell me you had more success, Seth. How's Gisella?'

Wil looked around – Gisella was nowhere in sight.

'Seth, you haven't let her wander off back to that Jev idiot, have you?' His hand felt much better after the honey and he was quite confident he was up to punching someone, if needed.

'No!' said Seth, with a smug look. 'No, I went off to find Tanith, which I did, and Gisella stayed here to watch our stuff. And while she was waiting, guess what?'

His eager expression suggested that he really did expect them to guess.

'She found Tally,' said Mortimer dryly. Seth beamed.

'Yes!'

'Where?' chorused Wil and Mortimer.

'Up there. Where you've just been!'

Seth pointed towards the golden tower.

'You see that balcony thing above those trees? She's in there. I really did think you'd find her.'

Wil squinted back towards the high wall of the castle garden with its blossom-coated fruit trees. The twin moons had given way to a bright morning and the tower shone like a beacon in the sunlight; Wil's stomach tightened – the likelihood of getting Tally back to Saran before the moon crossing that coming night was fast disappearing.

'How do you know she's there, Seth?' asked Mortimer.

'Because Gisella heard that egg seller talking to some woman when he got back to his stall– after you'd taken the eggs, we guessed. She – the woman – told the man that Tally was being a complete nightmare and she'd be glad when the Alcama came because at least she'd get some peace.'

Wil went cold.

'What did she mean by peace, Seth?'

'I don't know. Gisella said that another lady arrived and they started talking about something else – but not before the other woman told the egg man that she was surprised he couldn't hear Tally's language from here because her room overlooks the whole city. And as you can see,' Seth paused to survey the castle and then continued, 'that balcony is the only one that looks out over this part of the city. I don't know how big Armelia is though, so I couldn't say if it looks out over all of it – but I think it's a fair bet that's where she is.'

Wil thought back to the first time he had met Lady Élanor's feisty young sister – she had been covered in flour at the time and, yes, he would certainly agree she had a colourful turn of phrase when she was cross!

'Well, at least we know she's still alive then,' said Mortimer. Seth nodded, looking extremely pleased with himself. Mortimer shot another disparaging look in Wil's direction. 'It's just a shame that we were so close and didn't know it! So where's Gisella now?'

'Well, I found Tanith – I said I found him, didn't I? I told Gisella that they're keeping him with the other animals for the Unexpected Pets contest, on the other side of the main square – you should see it – its massive and they've got this huge–'.

'Seth!' snapped Mortimer. 'I'm not interested in sight-seeing – where are Gisella and Tanith?'

Unperturbed, Seth's eyes shone with excitement.

'Well, she said that we'd be less conspicuous if she took Phinn, Mia and Farrow there, too. So I stayed here with Rhoani and Shadow, to wait for you, and she's gone down to keep an eye on Tanith and to blend in. I can't wait to get back down there. Some of those creatures are awesome!'

'Well, I just hope Gisella has recovered from her earlier revelling and hasn't acquired a taste for rat beer!' said Mortimer.

'Oh, don't worry about that,' grinned Seth. 'Before she went I offered her a drink of elder wine and she was sick behind those bales again!'

Hardly able to contain his excitement, Seth led the way into yet another packed street. Ahead Wil could hear the sound of cooing birds and suddenly a cloud of doves exploded into the air. A shot of pure joy filled Wil's heart as, with slapping wings, the liberated birds flapped skywards. Everyone ducked for cover except for a small boy who very carefully lowered the lid of a huge and now completely empty basket and stole away into the crowd.

Behind the basket a shop window was stacked with cages of chickens, Fell hens, turkeys, pheasants, and Rockmoor quail – Wil realised that they were back on Bell Street.

Right in the middle of the square, standing above the crowd, Wil could see a huge stage. Thick metal bars like sentries marked its perimeter, broken only by a high gate in the middle of the side nearest to them. The square itself was edged by stalls selling anything from rat beer to boiled eggs; while others housed animals. The smell was bad enough, but the noise!... deep booming barks, yaps, caws, cries, mews, yowls and baying; all competing with music coming from every direction. There was also shouting – lots of shouting.

'What is that?' asked Wil. Just in front of them, a willowy woman dressed entirely in white was cradling something in her arms. Except for its childlike face, the creature was covered all over in silky, jet-black fur. A pair of huge green eyes turned on Wil. The woman followed the creature's gaze. Both she and her little companion had long, cat-like ears – one set, tipped white on black fur; the other, tipped black on pale skin – they looked as if they had been painted. The woman was wearing a delicate silver band on her slender wrist; from it swung a fine silver chain that was attached at the other end to an identical band around the animal's neck. She stroked the animal's head with fingers as white as snow and fingernails like daggers.

'We are Fayarie,' she said blinking slowly. She had the same startling green eyes as her pet. 'We can swap form but can never be the same.'

'What's its name?' asked Wil. He reached out to the little animal but pulled back when, with a spitting hiss, it lashed out with a needle claw. The woman laughed – the sound reminded Wil of a babbling brook.

'Take care, those claws can rip a man apart in the blink of an eye,' she answered and made to move on. 'Her name is Olan. I am Olath – we are sisters.'

'Wow!' said Seth, wide-eyed. 'What does it – you – eat?'

But the woman melted into the crowd, carrying the little Fayarie away without giving an answer. Two elderly men, deep in conversation, bustled through the gap she had left.

'Well, I'm sorry to argue, Twyford, but that cry was unmistakable. That cat-like caw – classic,' said one. 'And the livid underbelly – a mature male, I've no doubt.'

'Yes, Meldon, the Lesser Crested Ridge Creeper is ……'

They passed by and their voices drifted out of earshot.

A little further on, the produce stalls gave way to animal pens. Seth was already peering into the first pen. Wil caught up and looked over Seth's shoulder. Inside, half-buried under a mound of straw, he could see two dogs. They were munching on a long marrow bone and, by the size of their heads, Wil guessed that they were quite a lot smaller than Phinn.

'Well, I can't see anything unexpected about them,' he said. One of the dogs grabbed the bone from the other and started to growl. Two shabby men who stood at the edge of the stall stopped talking.

'Torris, be'ave! Share or I'll 'ave that orff you!' snarled the man nearest to Wil.

Torris abandoned the bone and got to his feet. Both heads rose together – attached to one muscle-packed body.

'Yep,' said Wil with a nod. 'That was definitely unexpected!'

'What's that?' Seth asked the men.

'A Drangfell Pinscher,' answered the man without looking round.

'How old is it?

'Three.'

'Are they easy to train?'

'No.'

'What do they eat?'

The man turned slowly and looked Seth up and down. 'Inquisitive boys,' he said and turned back to his friend. A little way ahead, Mortimer called out over the crowd.

'Wil, Seth! I can see Gisella. She's over there.'

Mortimer was jabbing his finger towards the corner of the square but all Wil could see was a long-legged animal with the head and horns of an antelope that was happily munching on a net stuffed with holly leaves.

Wil and Seth had a great deal of difficulty keeping up with Mortimer as he strode off in the direction he had just been pointing. There were people and animals everywhere.

''Scuse me,' said a dishevelled man. Wil stepped backwards and felt a painful jab in his back. Someone else stood on his toe.

'Don't these people sleep?'

Seth was oblivious. His wide eyes shone as he took in the sights around him.

'Wow! Did you see that?' he said pointing back over his shoulder as he battled towards Mortimer, who was waiting not very patiently. 'It was like a massive deer but with a bull's head. Did you see the sign? *Beware of the poo!*'

'A bonacuss!' exclaimed Mortimer with a look of genuine horror. 'Who thought it was a good idea to bring one of those? Everyone knows their dung is highly dangerous!'

'I didn't!' said Seth.

'Oh, I did,' said Wil. He stepped out of the way of a frazzled-looking woman who was trying very hard to keep control of two rodents, both the size of a Peachley sheep, that Wil recognised as pranxies. 'Bonacuss can shoot their dung quite long distances and it burns like fire if you get it on your skin. Apparently, it's really difficult to get off, too. So if you ever see a bonacuss lift its tail, run – and whatever you do, don't look back!'

'Blimey!' said Seth. 'And I thought some of Farrow's poo could be a bit unpleasant!'

The pranxies were now fighting and, spooked by the commotion, Rhoani lashed out with his back leg. One of the pranxies dropped to the ground.

'Oh, no! I'm so sorry,' exclaimed Seth.

The creature lay stone still but the weary woman beamed.

'No, really, thank you!' she said wiping a trickle of sweat from her forehead. 'They've been squabbling over that dead dwhykely for ages. It's the smell! I made the mistake of letting them have a run off their leads over there,' she pointed to the ruins of a building at the end of the street. 'But rather too late I realised it's infested and you know what dwhykelies are like – take over anything that's not been lived in for a full moon and wreck it in two. I should've known by the stink – they say their breath is the worst,' she wrinkled her nose in disgust. 'And judging by the smell of *that* thing, I hope I never get close enough to find out! Yech!'

'Yes, but is it alright – the pranxie, I mean?' asked Seth.

'Oh yes, dear,' said the woman with a dismissive wave. 'No sense, no feeling, pranxies. Love 'em dearly, but they do take some work.'

In the brief time they had been talking, the other pranxie had ripped the dead dwhykely in two. Wil just caught sight of a scaly tail dangling from its mouth before it swallowed and the tail disappeared. The woman scooped up the other half of the little corpse. The pranxie looked up at her expectantly.

'No, Sissey,' said the woman firmly. 'We'll save this for your sister.'

She dropped the end of the two chain leads she had been clutching and stuffed the ragged remains of the unfortunate dwhykely into a bag under her cloak. 'And it's no good giving me that hard done-by look. Kibbles will be very upset if you eat it all!'

She wrinkled her nose and gave a little shrug.

'Oh, aren't they just gorgeous. I'd have another in a heartbeat if I had the space. See, dear, Kibbles is back on her feet. Told you. No sense, no feeling!'

The woman chuckled affectionately.

'Have you seen the dragon yet?' she asked, watching the two pranxies – they were fighting again.

'Er, no, not yet. We knew there was one here though,' said Seth, eagerly looking about.

'Oh, you must go and see it. It's smaller than I would have expected – but then that's what makes it unexpected, I suppose! It really is very cute!'

Mortimer had pushed back again through a sea of now very familiar orange and purple and his expression did not suggest he was about to go and admire a dragon – cute or not.

'Wil, Seth! Get a move on!'

'Oops, looks like I've got you into trouble with your brother!' chuckled the woman. She gathered up the leads and dragged the squabbling pranxies off towards Bell Street. 'Right, come on Kibbles, give it a rest or I'll get that horse to shut you up again!'

Draped in an orange and purple tunic that was far too big for her, Gisella was standing in front of two stalls only a short distance from the fenced stage. Wil could see that her face was etched with worry. She spotted Wil, Seth and Mortimer elbowing their way past one of the many groups of tuneless musicians and waved frantically. Phinn's head appeared over the top of one of the stalls.

'Where did you get *that*, Giz?' asked Seth looking her up and down.

'It was all I could find – they'd sold out of my size. Anyway, I've just heard something terrible!'

'What?' demanded Mortimer.

Gisella shook her head and nodded towards an exceptionally tall woman standing in front of Phinn's stall. Wound around the woman's neck was a vivid-red scarf. With a polite nod Wil reached past and stroked Phinn's nose. The lady looked down and gave him a smile that didn't quite reach her eyes. The scarf hissed.

'Oh, don't mind Erena. She means no harm.'

Not convinced Wil took a step back.

Gisella and Mortimer ducked into the other stall, leaving Seth to hold the horses. Wil wasn't sure quite what to do. Head and shoulders above the crowd, the woman continued to smile down at him, the snake's head crooked in her hands.

'I think the pegalus has unnerved her. You don't see many about nowadays, do you?' she said in little more than a whisper.

Wil was just about to ask what a pegalus was when Mortimer called his name. The woman with the snake slid behind Shadow and drifted away into the throng.

'Wil!' Mortimer called again, more sharply this time.

Wil turned.

There, standing with Gisella and Mortimer was a beautiful golden horse. Its long mane swept down its thick neck in a curtain of silver and gold threads, all the way down to … a pair of wings.

'Now *that* really was unexpected,' breathed Wil.

A gentle whinny rippled Tanith's velvety nostrils and a wave of recognition drifted over Wil's mind.

'We need to get to Tally now, Mortimer,' Gisella was saying. 'Apparently they're going to be judging the contest first thing this afternoon and I just heard someone saying that Rexmoore's holding a young girl. They are accusing her of being a witch,' she looked directly at Wil. 'I don't know if they were talking about Tally, but whoever it is, Wil–'

Out in the square a bell chimed. A voice boomed out over the crowd.

'Oyez, Oyez!'

Whatever Gisella said next was drowned out by a deafening cheer that erupted from the square. Wil turned. A man swathed in a red and black cloak edged with gold braid was standing tall and proud, high above them in the centre of the stage. Behind him, Wil could see a thick wooden pillar surrounded by a mound of smaller logs. In one hand the man gripped a bell; in the other he held a tightly rolled scroll. He rang the bell again and with a well-practiced flourish, he unfurled the scroll and raised it. The square fell silent.

'Oyez, Oyez, Oyez,' he called again, his voice echoing off the buildings around the edge of the vast square.

'Hear ye all.
Lord Rexmoore greets you as his guests.
At noon,
This festival will commence with the Unexpected Pets contest.
A bar of purest gold will be the prize,
So come for the spectacle and feast your eyes.
Bragg hounds, marbussal and a dragon too,
But for those behind the bonacuss, mind that poo!'

The crowd roared with laughter. The town crier held up a finger and waited for quiet before he continued.

'But don't wander too far
After the award of the bar –
Lord Rexmoore has a treat in store.
As the moons cross, evil moves through the city this night
But we shall be saved by a fire burned bright –
Here be the pyre and see fingers twitch
When we light the fire for the burning of a… WITCH!'

Wil, Gisella and Mortimer stood as if rooted to the ground. The crowd around them erupted – the excitement in the air was almost palpable.

After a few moments, Seth's head poked into the silent stall.

'I'm guessing you heard that then?'

CHAPTER EIGHTEEN

The Golden Tower

Wil's mind raced. Was Tally *the* witch? Was Lady Élanor right – did Imelda really know that Tally had been born at the Alcama? It would certainly give Imelda an awfully good reason to put Tally on that stake – maybe, he thought, it was actually all part of Imelda's plan to lure Lady Élanor into Armelia as Morten Mortens had suggested? But one thing of which he was sure was that they – he – had to get Tally out of that tower – just in case. With so many people eagerly anticipating a burning, it would be impossible to rescue Tally up there on that stage. Even with a winged horse there were far too many weapons out there in the crowd to make a flight to freedom a realistic possibility.

No, much as Wil's whole body disagreed with him, their only real chance was to get Tally while she was still at the castle and go out of Armelia the way they had come in – through the gully under the wall – *before* too many people noticed that she'd gone!

'Yes, but if we go in right by the castle we won't have too far to swim,' argued Wil. Mortimer shook his head.

'It's just too risky, Wil. We haven't got a clue what happened to The Jackal, and when *he* disappeared we'd only just come under the wall!'

'But Wil's right, Mortimer,' said Gisella. 'We'll never get her out from down here – don't forget, we've got to get Tanith out too, and that'll be far easier if we can walk him out of the gate once the competition is over. I've heard that everyone's betting on the dragon now anyway, so we can just go as gracious losers – I bet no one will try to stop us!'

'And once they're both on the other side of that wall, they can fly back to Saran,' reasoned Wil. Having Gisella's support buoyed him up immensely. Above, the sky was clouding over but, by the height of the sun Wil could see that they were close to mid-day now. 'Look Mortimer, it's the only way they've got any hope of getting home before the moon crossing tonight!'

Chin in his hand, Mortimer strode across the stall and back again. Then he tapped a pile of straw with his toe, pinched his bottom lip between his thumb and forefinger and strode to the other side of the stall again. He stopped and faced them.

'Right, this is what we're going to do.'

'Yes, Seth, but this way makes sense!' Mortimer insisted.

Seth was sulking at the prospect of being left behind again and Mortimer's patience was wearing thin. He took a deep breath.

'Look Seth, I need you to stay here with Gisella, Rhoani and Farrow. Wil and I will get Tally then Wil can take Tally out of the city via the canal using Phinn and Mia, like we got in. As soon as they're safely away and *not* being swept back towards the mill,' he threw a worried glance at Wil, 'I'll meet you by the bonacuss stall with Rhoani. Gisella, you can take care of Tanith – get him out of the city as soon as the bonacuss is loose.'

Gisella nodded but Seth remained stubbornly resistant.

'But why can't *I* go with you to get Tally? Wil could stay here – with Gisella.' Wil bent to check that his knife was in his boot – Gisella went pink.

'Because, Seth, Wil can't ride! And *you* can't swim – or had you forgotten that minor detail!' snapped Mortimer.

'And anyway, Seth,' said Gisella. 'If you and Mortimer are going to let that bonacuss out, you're going to need a hound that knows what its doing – Mia and Phinn are just too inexperienced.'

Seth kicked the ground with the heel of his boot.

'Oh, okay, I suppose.'

'Right,' said Mortimer before Seth had a chance to change his mind. 'That's sorted then. As soon as I'm convinced Wil's in that water and going the right way, I'll be back. I'm pretty sure we won't have very much time before someone notices that Tally's missing, Seth, so we're going to have to move fast. I need you over at that bonacuss stall – I'll be there as soon as I can.'

Mortimer sat astride Shadow and offered his hand but Wil shook his head – there were bits of him that were surprisingly tender after the long ride across Tel Harion and he wasn't looking forward to the ride home already – especially if it meant riding *and* flying at the same time!

'Its okay, Mort, I'll walk, thanks.'

Tanith crooked his head over Gisella's shoulder. She shielded her eyes from the mid-day sun and looked up at Mortimer.

'Any suggestions if you get caught?'

'Get out of the city any way you can and get Tanith back to Saran before the moons cross tonight. You've both got your bows?'

Seth swung his bow over his shoulder and opened his jacket – he might still be sulking but by the number of bolts Wil could see, Seth was certainly ready for action. Gisella gave a brief nod towards their packs and her already loaded bow piled in the corner of the stall. Wil was struck by a sudden thought.

'Hang on a minute Mort.'

The rod that had fallen on his head at the Black Rock and a length of silk rope were still tucked under the now considerably smaller stock of pies at the bottom of his bag. Frowning, Mortimer studied both items.

'I can sort of see the rope, Wil, but the rod I'm still not getting.'

Then he turned Shadow and headed off out of the square back towards the golden tower.

Gisella watched Wil click the rod into one long length before he wound the rope around his waist.

'Where did you get *that*? And what is it?'

'Long story and a bit of a mystery,' answered Wil with a grin and he set off at a jog to catch up with Mortimer.

Away from the square the crowds were much thinner. At the far end of Bell Street Wil and Mortimer took a detour to avoid two shrieking women who were pulling great handfuls of hair from each other's heads – half empty jugs of black beer sat abandoned in the gutter beside them.

Two more turns and Wil and Mortimer found themselves in near enough silent and deserted streets. They rounded another corner and Wil stopped. In the distance he could hear the sound of running water.

'I think we must be getting near the mill.'

They headed towards the sound and with one more turn the cobbled road gave way to the grassy track. It ran along the edge of the canal, past the pool that had provided their escape from the mill wheel the previous morning. To Wil's left, the mill wheel was no longer turning. Wil could see now that it was mounted on the side of a vast stone building, behind which rose a huge chimney. On the far bank a little oval boat bobbed on the shoreline; there was no sign of anyone but a fishing line dangling from the stern suggested its owner may not be far away, and was intending to come back.

Beyond the little craft, heading up the hill towards the incomplete tower, two weary donkeys were hauling a cart up a rutted track. The cart was piled high with gold – *lots* of bars of gold. Mortimer gave a slow whistle and whispered.

'Hey Wil, I think we've just found where they make those gold bricks.'

The Jackal's words flooded back into Wil's ears. A crystal clear vision of a man's gnarled hand carving Wil's father's name onto a headstone crashed into Wil's mind. It hit him with such force that he nearly toppled into the canal. He saw Mortimer's arm reach to stop his fall. The image vanished. Then he heard – or felt – a scream. Was it pain... *fear*? No, it was laughter – cruel, shrieking laughter. It lasted only the briefest moment before the sound of gently trickling water once more filled the air.

'Wil, *Wil*, are you OK?' Mortimer was still gripping hold of Wil's arm. Leaning heavily on the staff, Wil shook his head and listened again. His hands were clammy and he felt sick.

'D-did you hear that?'

'Crronk!'

Bewildered, Wil searched for the source of this new noise. Pricilla was perched on the top bucket of the now motionless mill wheel. With a flap of her wings, she uttered another loud

'*Crronk! Prruk!*' and glided low over the water towards them. But just before she reached the bank, she swerved upstream and set down on a crumbling wall.

'That bird looks just like the one that hangs around Lovage Hall,' said Mortimer.

'*Crronk!*' said Pricilla indignantly.

'It is the one,' said Wil. As with Lady Élanor's unusual abilities to heal and Tally's ability to read minds, Wil wasn't sure how much Mortimer knew about Pricilla, so instead he repeated his question.

'Did you hear that noise just now, Mort? That laugh?'

Mortimer frowned, 'What laugh?'

Pricilla took off from her perch and soared towards them. Within a beak's length of Phinn, she changed course and with a single beat of her wings wheeled away towards the castle; rather belatedly Phinn took exception and snapped at the empty air. Wil listened for the sound again – whatever it was – but nothing came. All he could hear was the stubborn trickle of the water on the mill race. Pricilla came gliding back. Wil shrugged.

'Must have been a bird or something,' he said unconvinced. But Mortimer wasn't paying attention. He was watching Pricilla circling just above them, calling and then flapping back up river towards the tower. She repeated the move four times.

'I think she wants us to follow her,' said Wil eventually.

'*Crronk!*' called Pricilla, circling again.

Wil nodded.

'Yep, I definitely think she wants us to follow her!'

Minutes later they were at the base of the golden tower. Close up, its gleaming walls were surprisingly smooth and Mortimer gave up trying to find a foothold almost as soon as he started to look. Pricilla was nowhere to be seen.

'I just can't see what we are supposed to do, Wil,' said Mortimer, making no attempt to hide his scepticism. 'Are you sure that bird was trying to give us a message?'

Wil didn't answer. It was obvious that Mortimer was completely unconvinced.

'Look, Wil. You can stay here if you want and try to work out what that bird is trying to tell you but I think I'll head back to the castle garden. I reckon I can get in through that door at the back of the kitchen – did you see it? I spotted that Mhaddphat woman at the egg stall again just now so with any luck there won't be anyone to get in my way.'

Wil bit his lip. What was Pricilla trying to tell them? Ironically Wil's own rather haphazard ability to read the minds of animals was at that moment completely failing him – although he'd always had the feeling with Pricilla that it was up to her when Wil read her mind – *and* what he saw!

'OK, Mort,' he said. He knew Mortimer would be happier doing something and, on his own, Wil hoped that Pricilla might be a bit more forthcoming. 'Although the moons help you if Mhaddphat does catch you! And what about the hobgoblets? I bet she left them to torment the bees!'

'Oh, don't worry about them. Martha gave me a block of treacle toffee – goodness knows why! It'll glue their teeth together for weeks!' And with a laugh he kicked Shadow into a gallop and headed back towards the walled garden with Mia lopping easily behind him. Phinn took a long look at Wil and settled back on his haunches.

'Yep, that's right, boy – all I need to do now is figure out what on earth Pricilla was trying to get me to do!'

From where Wil stood, the golden tower seemed to stretch up into the clouds. He took a few steps back, put his hand on his hip and craned his neck to see if he could get a better view of the tiny balcony nestled halfway between him and the sky. As his hand rested on the silk rope around his waist the staff in Wil's other hand became strangely heavy. The hint of an idea crept like a shadow into the back of his mind. Not really knowing why, he let go. The staff clattered to the ground where it immediately broke into three to make a triangle. The idea got a little sharper.

'Crronk, crronk, prruk!'

Wil looked up. On the edge of the balcony he could see Pricilla's black shape. The idea crystalised.

'Ohh! Well come down here and give me a hand!'

'Crronk!' came the reply but when Wil looked again there was no sign of the raven. He sighed.

'Great! That bird is very useful when she wants to be,' he said to Phinn, 'But if she doesn't want to be…'

He reached for the triangle. With a snap, it once more became a rigid staff. He weighed it in his hand. Then he slid one of the bolts out from his boot and retreated a few more steps. He surveyed the tower again. The balcony was a long way up.

Wil's first three attempts to fire a bolt through the railing at the edge of the balcony resulted in both him and Phinn retreating at speed as the missile fell short and plummeted back to the ground. The fourth attempt, however, went straight over the ledge high above.

Sure now that he could make the distance, Wil tied the rope to another bolt, leaving enough of a tail to fasten to the rounded end of the staff. He loaded the bolt into his bow, took a step back and looked at Phinn. The hound's unblinking amber eyes studied him through a pair of straggly eyebrows.

'Yes, I know,' said Wil. 'I think this is what they call a long shot.'

He released the bolt.

To his utter amazement the bolt went straight through the balcony railings taking the staff with it. He heard a satisfying clatter.

'Well I'll be!' he breathed.

The silk rope dangled from the balcony falling just short of the ground – whether this was a sheer coincidence or design on someone's part, Wil had no time to contemplate. He gave the rope a sharp tug – it held. Then he wound the end around his hand and leant backwards – it still held. He took one last look around the skies for Pricilla – no sign and no sound.

'Right, Phinn. Wait here. I'll go and get Tally then we'll go and find Mortimer.' He looked at the balcony high above his head and back at Phinn. 'Unless he's up there already, of course!'

The climb up the sheer tower was challenging – especially as Wil had forgotten to take off his cloak. Luckily the rope held. It was also very easy to grip, and going hand over hand Wil found he could walk up the gold bricks fairly easily, although he couldn't help wondering why everything he did lately involved heights!

About halfway up, Wil was just starting to feel a bit more confident when a huge spider crawled out of a wide crack that was working its way from the balcony to the ground like a vein. Wil very nearly let go of the rope!

He reached the little balcony panting and sweating and was deeply relieved to see the triangular shape jammed against the other side of the railings, forming a perfect anchor. With one final effort, Wil hauled himself over the rail and flopped onto the balcony – to be greeted by a round of applause.

At the back of the balcony, a narrow door lay wide open into a dark room. The applause petered out and was replaced by the same shrieking laugh Wil had heard by the mill. Suddenly he felt very cold.

'Oh, do come and join us,' said a boy's voice. 'We were wondering how you'd get in – nice touch with the stick!'

Warily, Wil got to his feet using the rail for support but he caught the triangle with his foot in the process. It sprang back into a rigid length and gave in to the weight of the rope still dangling down the side of the tower. It slid through the bars. Wil just had time to see the staff plunge into the ground a few feet away from the dozing Phinn – the Fellhound did not stir. Both Phinn and the staff were an *awfully* long way down.

'Oops!' said the voice behind him. Wil turned. There in the doorway wearing a smug grin stood The Jackal; he was a lot cleaner than the last time they had met and his rags had been replaced by sleek purple velvet. 'Wil, come and meet Mother. Oh, and by the way, I'll take that bow... and the rest of those bolts.'

CHAPTER NINETEEN

Ŋats and Ŋorrors

In contrast to the gleam of the sunlit gold, the dark interior of the tower took Wil by surprise. Temporarily blind, he was aware of something fluttering and distressed to his right; he was also aware of something else – pain, hate, darkness – he wasn't sure, but it felt…. oddly familiar. His mouth went dry – with a huge effort he shut it out – it couldn't be; his imagination or the light, were obviously playing tricks on his mind.

'*Crrrronk!*'

Wil turned towards the sound, blinking desperately to clear his eyes. Somewhere else in the room a woman shrieked. Clapping, again. Wil's stomach wound into a double knot. There, pegged to a large wooden table by a bolt – *his* bolt – right through her wing, was Pricilla! She flapped, but her body contorted grotesquely as the bolt held her in place. Wil span back to face The Jackal who was looking extremely pleased with himself.

'Mother and I guessed she was a friend of yours by the din she was making,' he drawled, loading another of Wil's bolts into Wil's crossbow. 'She was a gift really. I couldn't believe my eyes when she flew in here… followed by your bolt. Nice bit of shooting by the way. I thought knives were your thing?'

Wil was struggling with the scene before him. Had he really shot Pricilla? And The Jackal was very different from the last time they had met; Tally was nowhere to be seen and… a strange darkness edged his mind again – there was something lurking in the corner behind the clapping woman and it smelt really bad!

The woman suddenly jumped up from the chair in which she had been sitting. 'A hat!' she exclaimed. Jammed down onto her head, almost covering her eyes was a beret covered with little oval strips of pink felt. 'It'll make a very nice hat. Those feathers – black. Lovely. I need a new hat.'

'Yes, mother,' the boy crooned. 'What an excellent idea. That's why I caught her… for you. For a new hat.'

Relief and hate coursed in parallel through Wil's veins. *He* hadn't speared Pricilla to the table – The Jackal had. And he'd done it for his mother's entertainment!

'You'll pay for that, Jackal… or whatever your name is!' hissed Wil.

'Oh, I thought The Jackal made me sound quite romantic. And anyway some of that was true… well, my name *is* Colin. The Miller bit – being found in the flour sacks and being called Miller – just my little joke. Ha, ha!'

He stopped laughing abruptly and aimed the bow at Wil's heart. 'Actually my name's Tinniswood. I believe you killed my father.'

The woman clapped again even more enthusiastically than before.

'Oh, you're so clever, Colin darling. My clever, funny Colin. A new hat for mommy. So clever and so kind!'

With his eye on his bow, realisation started to dawn. It had all been a trap – and Wil had walked right into it. He'd actually felt sorry for this boy; he'd trusted him! Wil felt like a complete fool.

Whatever was in the corner moved; excruciating pain shot though Wil's entire body. Beads of sweat erupted on his forehead.

'Where's Tally?' he demanded.

The same noxious stench wafted around his nose again, stronger this time.

'Poooohhh!' cried the woman waving her hand over her nose. 'Snuffy's made a smell! Make the smell go away Colin, make it go now!'

Colin reached for a scent bottle and sprinkled copious drops around his mother's head and shoulders. A strong smell of bergamot hit Wil's nostrils.

'Tally?' The boy frowned and his eyes searched the room as if he was trying to recall the name. 'Ooh, if you mean the headstrong, foul-mouthed harridan that we used to get you here…' He walked to the balcony and looked out towards the city square. 'I suspect Lord Rexmoore and his charming wife are *warming up* the crowd for her big moment, as we speak.'

'What?' choked Wil.

'Yeees,' said Colin. Wil could see he was enjoying this. He let the bow drop and held out his right hand to inspect his now pristine and beautifully manicured nails. 'You know, you were taking such a long time to find her that we had to give you the information in the end. I mean, it was getting painful!' He ran his thumbnail under the even longer nail on his middle finger and flicked it. 'And when it looked like you'd finally got the message I agreed to wait here with mother to see you tucked in, so to speak. They've gone down to judge the competition before lighting the bonfire. I think it's a marvellous idea, don't you – burning a witch for the Alcama.'

'Tally is not a witch!' Wil hissed through gritted teeth.

Colin wrinkled his nose. Wil's crossbow was now pointing at the floor.

'Weeell, I'm not sure that's strictly true, now is it, Wil? I mean, that temper of hers is pretty evil, for a start! Imelda tells me it's some sort of anniversary today too, now what was it?' He put his finger on his lips and studied the ceiling, 'Oh, that's it – the day she was born…and, well, she did arrive on a flying horse – pretty *unexpected*, wouldn't you say?'

'Flying horse! You have *seen* some of those pets down there, haven't you?'

'Yes, but no one else can speak to their pets!' retorted the boy.

'I speak to Phinn all the time!'

'Yes, but you don't have full-blown conversations with him. You know, full sentences – answering questions!'

'Answering questions!' echoed Colin's mother, with a theatrical nod.

Wil floundered. Fortunately – or not – the thing emitting the smell chose that moment to emerge from its corner.

'Snuffy-woo!' exclaimed the woman with her arms outstretched. Colin took a rapid step back towards a doorway on the other side of the room and raised the crossbow. But this time it wasn't pointing at Wil.

'No!' said Wil. Pain and rage washed over him. Suddenly he found it very difficult to breathe.

From out of the corner limped a black shape. Low to the ground and smaller than the others Wil had seen out on Tel Harion, but a Wraithe Wolf nonetheless. The Jackal laughed again.

'Well, how's that for unexpected, Wil Calloway?'

Wracked with pain now, Wil looked from the wolf to the boy and back again. Colin's mother cooed.

'So bootiful,' she whispered. 'Snuffy, come to mommy. Ooo, sooo cute.'

But Snuffy did not look remotely cute to Wil. As the wretched animal dragged its pain-wracked frame into the light, the reason they had not already been ripped apart became obvious. Around the wolf's neck was an iron collar bound so tightly that Wil could hear the animal's laboured breath; an iron muzzle had been fixed around its jaws – how, Wil did not even begin to try to imagine – and where there should have been a barbed, razorsharp claw on each of its front legs, Wil could see wounds crusted with dried blood that leaked afresh as the animal limped forward.

Colin's mother seemed completely oblivious to the animal's terrible condition. She bent to her knees, threw her arms around the wolf's neck and hugged it tightly. The wolf let out a low growl and tried to flick its head around to bite, but the collar and the muzzle rendered it helpless.

'Meet the winner of this year's Unexpected Pets competition, Wil,' said Colin with a callous smile. 'Mother wins every year. Last year I got her an albino sabre tooth – exceptionally rare, you know.'

'But I thought the competition wasn't until later – and this is hardly a pet!' exclaimed Wil, unable to take his eyes off the sorry creature as he shared its pain. With her arms tight around the wolf's neck, Colin's mother cooed and giggled. 'Weell, you know, bit of poetic licence, hey? She always wins because she gives the gold bar back to Imelda. Not remotely interested – no, hats are Mother's first and only love... Anyway,' he shrugged, 'Imelda asked me to wait for you first. This way Mother and I can make more of an entrance.' He didn't take his eyes off the Wraithe Wolf. 'Mother does like a bit of a do. She hasn't been too well for a while now. Doesn't get out much. The Unexpected Pets is her one big treat of the year.'

'So what happened to the sabre tooth tiger,' asked Wil, doubting that the pathetic animal in front of him considered this to be any form of treat.

'Oh, it was marvellous. We got enough fur to make two hats *and* a cloak,' answered Colin. 'I wasn't too keen on the cloak, white is so difficult to keep clean, but the hats were a triumph – winter wear only, of course. We had one each.'

Wil felt sick.

'And what will you do with Snuffy-woo?'

'Another hat, of course! They're all unique, you know. She's got quite a collection; although the dwhykely turban smells appalling when it gets warm. We've got the claws from this one already, as you can see. We're planning to use the teeth too. I mean – two sets from one mouth – I think this one'll be an absolute classic!'

'So what about me?' asked Wil, unable to avoid the question any longer, and needing to take his eyes away from the suffering wolf even if he still shared every painful breath.

'You?' said Colin in mock surprise. 'Oh, yes. Um, you're going to stay here so that Imelda can ask you about Lady Élanor's legacy later. She's a pretty good inquisitor too, you know.'

'And how are you going to stop me from escaping once you've gone off to the competition,' asked Wil, making no attempt to hide his contempt for this cruel, arrogant boy. Colin slowly turned and took aim with Wil's crossbow.

'I've got to shoot you in the leg to stop you running awa-'

The tower door exploded off its hinges. Wil's bow flew out of Colin's hands and Phinn bounded into the room, pinning the door with Colin under it to the floor. Wil heard the bow skitter across the floor but couldn't see where it went. Colin's mother shrieked and released the wolf to clap wildly.

'Oh, Colin. A door – a dog – a new hat!'

Her shrieking laugh echoed around the bare room and she continued her insane applause.

Still on top of the door, Phinn swept his huge tail across the floor boards and gave one deep bark; a moment later Mia, followed by Mortimer, appeared in the doorway at the head of a golden staircase. Mortimer looked from Wil to Pricilla, to the clapping woman, to the pathetic Wraithe Wolf – one of its wounds was now pumping with blood.

'Can I borrow your bow, Mort?' said Wil quietly. He was feeling faint now and it was taking all his strength to stay conscious.

Without a word Mortimer threw the loaded bow to Wil and in a blink the wolf lay dead. The pain raking through Wil's body lifted immediately.

Under the door Colin lay motionless. Mortimer put a hand to his neck. 'Still alive,' he said abruptly. It sounded to Wil like a question. He shook his head.

'No, leave him.' Wil glanced back at the mutilated wolf. 'Although I'm not sure why,' he added bitterly.

Then the wailing began.

'Nooo. Snuffy-woo, my Snuffy-woos. No prize for mommy. Nooooooo.'

Wil yelled over the din.

'We need to get back to the square, Mort.'

He grabbed the Wraithe Wolf's back legs and hauled it onto the flattened door. A groan came from underneath.

'With any luck we've just bought ourselves some time,' he said, running to the table.

Pricilla kept still while, with shaking hands, Wil eased the bolt out of the wood as carefully as he could.

'We'll have to leave the bolt in her wing until I can get to my bag,' he said and tucked the raven under his arm. 'Right, let's go!'

Pricilla gave a forlorn '*Prruk*'.

Mortimer grabbed Wil's bow from the edge of the balcony.

'You might find this useful then,' he grinned. 'Can I have mine back now?'

Colin's mother was lying across the door with her arms wrapped around the wolf. She was wailing again. Another low groan came from underneath the door.

'Ooooh, why isn't Snuffy-woo playing with mommy?' She kissed Snuffy-woo's head, 'Snuffy-woo loves mommy.' She kissed the animal again and Wil caught a closer glimpse of her beret – the pink strips weren't felt at all, they were little furry ears. A thought struck him: Colin had said they were going to use the Wraithe Wolf's teeth – razor sharp needles. Easy to nick yourself, thought Wil, recalling Giles Savidge's fate on Tel Harion Fell. He looked at Mortimer.

'Right, this time we really are going to get Tally!'

And stepping over Colin's mother and the wolf, Wil stamped very heavily across the door before he and Mortimer broke into a run.

'Snuffy-woo's not playing with mommy…what's mommy going to do now?' wailed the woman.

'Make a new hat!' called Wil over his shoulder.

They charged down the golden steps two at a time. At the bottom a long stone corridor led them back through the now bustling kitchen. Being considerably taller than the half-dozen hobgoblins that were stirring, kneeding and rolling, Wil doubted that their appearance would go unnoticed, but he didn't care. He and Mortimer hit fresh air and took off towards the square. Behind them a voice boomed out of the kitchen doorway.

'WHERE'S MY QUAIL EGGS? I ORDERED A 'UNDRED AND TWENTY AND YOU GI' ME EIGHTY. I DON' 'AVE TIME FOR THIS. OH MY GAAAWDD!'

CHAPTER TWENTY

Lord Rexmoore

Mortimer gathered up Shadow's reins.

'I'll go on, Wil. Seth'll be waiting by now so I'd better get there before he does anything foolish – there's no way we can release that bonacuss until we've got Tally. Keep Mia with you and just for a change can you try to keep your crossbow with you!'

'Okay, okay!' said Wil, hitching the bow over his shoulder. 'But how are we going to get Tally and Tanith out now? We're going to be right in the middle of the competition!'

As if to endorse Wil's statement, a cheer erupted from the square. Mortimer jumped into Shadow's saddle in one clean spring.

'Dunno yet. But I'll think of something. See you back at Tanith's stall,' he said and kicked Shadow into a gallop from a standing start.

Then a thought struck Wil.

'But what if Tanith's *in* the competition?' he called.

But Mortimer was too far off and didn't hear him.

It was difficult to know if the competition was, in fact, under way as Wil headed back towards the square. There were still an awful lot of people milling around and the market stalls on Bell Street were now doing brisk business despite the crush;

carrying a raven with a bolt through her wing certainly proved challenging with everyone competing for what little space there was.

But what to do?

Wil stood brooding for a moment. He had no doubt that his first aid bag would have something to help Pricilla but there was still the problem of how to keep her safe while he went to help the others rescue Tally.

'Hi again,' said a cheery voice.

Dragged from his thoughts, Wil didn't recognise the smiling girl sitting behind one of the stalls, but then the ruby in her earring caught the sunlight and the tale about the dragon's tooth and the bull came flooding back.

'Have you come back for the dagger? I knew you would! Hey, what've you got there?'

Before he could stop her, the girl reached over and drew back the edge of Wil's cloak.

'Oh, wow, a raven,' she whispered. 'They are so intelligent. I had one once – Caroline. Is this your pet? Have you just bought it?'

'Er, no,' said Wil. Pricilla was so still he wasn't entirely convinced she wasn't dead. 'She's mine, er, from before. She followed me here and then got injured.'

'Oh, that's terrible!' said the girl, looking appalled. 'Did someone hurt her? Some people! They can be so cruel. Here, let me see.'

She held out her hands.

'*Prruk!*' said Pricilla, but she made no effort to escape the girl's fingers. Wil's mind raced. The raven trusted this girl, he could feel it … and anyway he really didn't know what else to do … maybe if she could just mind Pricilla for a while…

'Does he... she have a name?' asked the girl, carefully unfolding Pricilla's injured wing. A small boy pushed in beside Wil and reached out to touch the bird. The girl rounded on him, 'There's nothing for you to see here so go away!'

With a pout, the boy ducked under Wil's arm and scuttled into the crowd. Pricilla winked.

'Her name's Pricilla,' said Wil. 'So, er, so you know a bit about ravens then?'

He crossed his fingers.

'Well, I didn't have Caroline for very long – the Red Back... you know,' said the girl. She wrinkled her nose. 'But she was a great bird. When I first found her she had a broken leg. I fixed that... hmm, this bolt though, wouldn't know where to start.'

Wil took a deep breath.

'Look, I've got to find my friends in there,' he jabbed his thumb towards the square. 'And... well, I just can't take Pricilla with me – it wouldn't be fair, she'd get crushed in no time. I don't suppose you could, er...'

The girl's mouth broke into a resigned grin.

'So you don't want to buy the dagger then?'

'If I had the money...' said Wil truthfully – it really was a handsome knife.

The girl stroked Pricilla's head gently while she thought. After a moment she nodded.

'Okay. I'll watch her for you. But I do want to see the moons cross so make sure you're back here in plenty of time!'

'Oh, believe me, I'll be back long before then,' said Wil, thinking of his promise to Lady Élanor. *Not* being back in plenty of time wasn't an option!

Another roar rolled around the ramshackle buildings that lined Bell Street – followed by rapturous applause. The square was now jam-packed. Everyone was wearing some sort of orange and purple costume: capes, dresses, robes, trousers with one orange leg and one purple leg; one man towered above the crowd on orange and purple stilts; and almost everyone wore some sort of orange and purple hat. Almost as soon as Wil walked into the knot of colourful revellers pushing and shoving, his sense of direction completely deserted him.

Phinn and Mia stayed close while Wil searched for something familiar. The whole area was littered with people, stalls, wagons and campfires; even the weird and wonderful – although sometimes appalling – smells that had caught his attention previously, this time made no impression. Wil couldn't get the smell of the putrefying Wraithe Wolf out of his nostrils.

Beside him, Phinn's hot breath warmed his arm through his cloak.

'*Hey, Phinn,*' he thought, fondling the hound's ear as he tried to concentrate. '*Can you sniff out Gisella? I haven't got a clue where we are.*'

Phinn raised his head and sniffed the air – whether this was more to do with the wild boar spit roast to their left or because he had heard his master's words, Wil wasn't entirely sure but he decided to give the hound the benefit of the doubt. Wil needed to get the idea of Gisella into Phinn's mind. But what to think of? Almost immediately the vision of Gisella washing in the river came to him and he tried to push the image towards Phinn. And it really was a very pleasant image – Gisella's long, athletic legs; her gentle laugh; she looked pretty, even when she was cross...

A gruff voice jolted Wil out of his memory.

'You gonna stand there all day?' growled the man behind the spit roast. Phinn's interest had turned to the wild boar.

'Oh, no... sorry,' said Wil. He moved Phinn and Mia on a few stalls and tried again but Phinn didn't respond.

Somewhere in the middle of the arena a band struck up with a very lively rendition of something Wil's father used to play on the flute. Nearby, a young girl's eyes flicked from Phinn to Wil but, ignoring her wide-eyed interest, Wil fixed his gaze on the plainest, least distracting thing he could see – the brown woollen cloak of the man in front of him.

'*Find Gisella, Phinn. Find Gisella.*'

Wil made the image in his mind so big that he felt he could reach out and touch it. But Phinn didn't budge – in fact this time he didn't even do Wil the courtesy of looking interested. It occurred to Wil that perhaps a more recent image might be more helpful. He thought again and after one more very enjoyable moment, he abandoned the splendid memory of Gisella in the river and thought instead of Gisella with Tanith, here in Armelia. He tried to make both Gisella *and* the winged horse as clear as he could. He pictured Tanith's mane of fine golden strands, his kind brown eyes and his inquisitive velvety muzzle; then Wil thought again about Gisella; her tanned face, her soft hand resting in his. Almost immediately Phinn raised his head, sniffed the air and set off around the edge of the crowd. Wil moved to follow – so, too, did the curious girl. Wil's concentration broke. He stopped abruptly, surveyed the row of stalls with a frown and then looked down at the girl as if noticing her for the first time.

'Er, someone told me there was a dragon around here. Can you point me in the right direction?' he said, not having to try very hard to look lost.

The girl's eyebrows rose almost into her hairline.

'Oh, you mean the Ridge Creeper? Oh, it's so cute. But you're going in completely the wrong direction – it's over there, next to the pork pie wagon,' she said, pointing back past the end of Bell Street to the other side of the square. 'I'll show you if you like. Are these your dogs?'

'Er, yer. Er, it's OK. I'm sure I'll find it,' said Wil, thrown by the girl's suggested change of direction. Waiting, Phinn turned his head just enough to keep one eye on Wil.

'Phinn, come, *this* way,' said Wil. But Phinn stubbornly held his ground and took one step forward. Mia was now alongside him. A man behind them tutted and a woman shook her head.

'You'd think 'e could take 'em round the back. I can't see anything with them in the way!'

Another woman pursed her lips and nodded in silent agreement. Wil turned back to the girl.

'Think I'll give the dragon a miss. Don't want to cause any trouble,' he said with an apologetic grin and ducked into the crowd, thinking very hard, '*Go! Phinn, Mia. Find Gisella!*'

Despite the very large number of unusual animals in the square, two determined Fellhounds weaving through the sea of purple and orange at shoulder height to most people had the effect of making even the burliest drunk step to one side. The trouble was, no one linked Wil to the hounds and as soon as they passed by the sea closed in again. Everywhere people were talking, eating, playing music or drinking; others were fighting or dancing – although in some cases it was actually very difficult to tell the difference.

The noises and the smells were overwhelming and, struggling to keep up, it was only then that Wil started to wonder whether Phinn and Mia really would be able to find Gisella: after all Phinn hardly knew Gisella, and Wil had no idea how long she had been working with Mia before the misunderstanding with Mortimer. With every step, Wil was becoming more convinced that they were going the wrong way. A snarling, gnashing dog fight broke out in the pen he had just elbowed his way past.

'Right, that's it. Give me that bone, Torris!'

With surprising agility, the owner of the Drangfell Pinscher vaulted over the rail into the animal's pen. More shouting followed, 'And this time you ain't 'avin' it back!' Then the man vaulted back out of the pen gripping a huge bone in his thick fist. 'Bloody dogs!'

Despite a rather tatty green rosette hanging limp from the corner of the stall that certainly hadn't been there earlier, Wil recognised Torris's owner... and the enormous bone. They *were* on the right path.

He was just feeling guilty for doubting Phinn when a bell chimed. The entire square seemed to take a sharp breath in.

Another voice Wil had heard before boomed out over the square, now tightly packed with upturned faces.

'Oyez, Oyez, Oyez.
Hear ye all.
You've heard the bands and laughed at the jokes,
But before the witch goes up in smoke,
There's gold to be won and animals galore,
So without further ado let's close our hands
And welcome fair Imelda and Lord Rexmoore.'

The town crier's announcement was met with very little applause but on cue owners and animals erupted from every stall. There was a loud crash and a shout and a wagon was upturned. Lifted off his feet in the surge, Wil was swept forward by the flow of people converging on the arena. Tall as he was, the crush of bodies made breathing extremely difficult and he thanked the moons that Pricilla wasn't still tucked in his jacket.

With what felt like the weight of the entire crowd behind him, Wil's crossbow dug painfully into his back.

'Mind what you're doing with that thing!' growled a man's voice behind him.

'I wish I could!' wheezed Wil.

Whatever the man said next was completely lost. Somewhere overhead a canon exploded. Everyone stopped dead as the deafening boom bounced between the castle walls and the golden tower, and before the echo stopped another voice called out over the hundreds of heads.

'Riiiight, now I've got your attention, I think we could do with a bit of order round here, don't you think?'

The pressure on Wil's chest eased very slightly.

Standing on the stage, high above the crowd, a spindly man was beaming.

'Riiight,' he repeated in a harsh, nasally tone, rubbing his hands together as he spoke. 'First of all, all those without animals take three steps back.' He flicked his long fingers as if ushering away children. A few people around Wil shuffled; some took a few tiny steps back but most only managed one. The man raised his eyebrows and cocked his head to one side, 'Now come along, I'm sure we can do better than that! One more step, Thaaat's it. Good!'

He clapped twice then pressed his hands together again.

'Now, all those people with green rosettes move back, too.'

He wagged his finger at someone near the front.

'Yeees, madam. That includes you. Naughty, naughty! *Everybody else* knows that runners-up are not allowed into the main competition.'

There was an almost universal groan. The man on the stage held up his palms.

'Sorry, but those *are* the rules.' His smile almost cut his sharp face in half.

A few people retreated another inch; several people around Wil swore and a lady to his right burst into tears.

'We were counting on that prize. There's tax due. How am I going to feed the children now?' she sobbed. The speaker on the stage seemed oblivious to the building tension and continued to beam.

'Oh, and by the way,' he said, raising his voice slightly. 'For those who haven't met me before, I'm Lord Rexmoore.'

No one cheered. Wil ducked down behind the very short person in front of him – suddenly, not wearing anything purple and orange felt like a distinct disadvantage. To his right, a man put his arm around the sobbing woman, muttered something too quiet for Wil to hear, and then gently guided her away. Wil made an attempt to follow. Perched on the woman's shoulder was a bright green bird with one orange eye and one purple eye – as it shifted its weight Wil could see it had two sets of wings.

Above him, Rexmoore surveyed the scene with an open-mouthed beam.

'Well, I'm not sure if you heard me there but,' he called with a slow nod; wiry arms wide, palms upturned, '*I'm* Lord Rexmoore.'

Half-hearted applause rippled through the crowd. One lone soul clapped. Rexmoore turned to a sour-faced woman behind him.

'Well, well, dear. We've got a deaf old bunch here today, haven't we?'

Without waiting for an answer he turned back, his smile fixed. Behind him, the woman's malevolent eyes bore into his back.

'We'll give it another go, shall we? I mean, there's always room on the pyre for one more up here,' Rexmoore gestured extravagantly towards the stacked bonfire – Wil wasn't sure if it was a good thing or not, but there was no sign of Tally. The woman – Imelda, Wil guessed – allowed a glimmer of a cruel smile to cross her face. Rexmoore opened his arms once more.

'*I'm* Lord Rexmoooooore.'

The crowd gave in. An exaggerated cheer rang out around the square – although Wil, now carefully edging backwards, was sure he could hear people booing, too.

Seemingly satisfied, however, Rexmoore continued to organise – and patronise – the crowd, which gave Wil the opportunity to retreat. By the time he reached Mia and Phinn the number of entrants waiting at the gate to the arena had been greatly reduced.

Scanning the row of animal pens behind him in the hope of seeing Tanith, or Gisella, Wil could see that almost all were adorned with limp, green rosettes.

'*Find Gisella. Find Gisella.*'

The words rolled around in his head but neither Phinn nor Mia seemed to be getting his message. They had stopped, their amber eyes fixed on the arena. Wil cursed under his breath. He was much further back now and from this distance it was very difficult to see – let alone hear – what was now being said up on the stage. One thing was obvious, though; there were a lot of very unhappy people between him and Lord Rexmoore.

'You watch,' said a man to whoever was listening, 'It'll be that Tinniswood woman again. It's the same every year. All those gold bars she's won – reckon she could build her own tower by now.'

A few people around him nodded. A boy about the same age as Wil put his hand on the shoulder of the girl next to him and stood on his tiptoes.

'You know, I don't think she's there,' he said, craning his neck for a better look. Wil breathed a sigh of relief and prayed that The Jackal and his mother were still in the tower where he had left them.

'I bet that's why Rexmoore's faffing about,' said the man who had spoken before. 'The old girl's late.'

'Prob'ly got something so dangerous this year that they can't bring it up 'til the last minute!' said another voice. 'Remember that sabre tooth tiger. I nearly wet myself when they brought that thing in last year!'

'Yer,' said the boy, still peering over the crowd. 'And two years ago, d'you remember those dwhykely things? Gor, that smell! Let them loose once she'd got the gold, too – worse'n rabbits, dwhytelies! They're all over the place now – took over my gran's house the day she died!'

'Yer?' said the man. 'Wonder what happened to that tiger.'

'Dunno. Oh, hang on. Something's happening … I think they're bringing the finalists up onto the stage. Gor, this is gonna take ages!'

Suddenly a cheer went up – a *very* enthusiastic cheer. Wil tried to get a better view but stopped short of leaning on the girl's other shoulder.

'What's happening?' someone asked. 'That woman arrived, has she? Come on, tell us what she's got.'

The boy leaned harder on the girl, who didn't seem to mind.

'No!' he said. He dropped back down. His eyes were shining with excitement. 'It's the witch. They've just brought on the witch!' Then he was back up on his toes again. 'Ooh, I bet that hurt,' the boy cringed, 'Blimey, she looks a right handful!'

Unable to contain himself any longer, Wil put his hand on the girl's shoulder and was just in time to see Tally kicking wildly. Two men were dragging her backwards towards the bonfire; Wil could just make out another man doubled up on the floor. Rexmoore and the entrants to the Unexpected Pets competition, now whittled down to about twenty, had backed to the edge of the arena including – Wil's heart almost stopped – Tanith and Gisella!

The wave of rage that hit Wil's mind was like nothing he had ever experienced before – even his collision with the eagard was like the gentle breath of a summer breeze by comparison. Burning anger seared through his limbs; his eyes were blind and his brain screamed. Pain burned into every pore of his body like it would never stop. Somewhere, in the red-hot mist, he could hear barking. He tried to focus on it, to will it nearer. But in a flash it vanished. The hissing mist consumed him completely.

CHAPTER TWENTY-ONE

The Ties that Bind

'Wil, *Wil!* Can you hear me? Wil, *please* wake up!'

Tally's voice tickled the edges of Wil's bruised brain. But it couldn't be Tally's voice; she was in Armelia. He – Wil – was at home in Mistleguard and when he opened his eyes he would see his mother's face and smell the bread she made in the dark hours of every morning. He loved his mother's bread. When he was little she used to tell him that it was an extra large spoonful of love that made it so delicious – sweet and warm. She would carve him a thick slice fresh from the oven and spread it with oozing butter that would drip over his fingers as he ate. His father had–

'Wil, *wake up!* Oh, I'm so sorry. Oh, Wil!' said Tally's voice again.

But Wil knew it wasn't Tally's voice – how could it be? He breathed deeply trying to detect any hint of yeasty sweetness… He breathed in as far as his lungs would let him… and out; in… and out. But no smell came.

'Wil, *pleeease,* can you hear me?'

…still nothing but that annoying voice.

'Wil, *for goodness sake*, wake up!'

Oh, that voice. It certainly wasn't his mother – she never sounded that cross! Wil felt his forehead furrow into a frown... odd – there was something tight around his head…

and it hurt. He tried to rub his brow but his arms wouldn't move – neither would his legs. Was that music? He tried to move again – something cold and hard bit into his arm. What on earth–

'*Wil!*' said the voice – very sharp now – definitely not his mother's.

Reluctantly, Wil opened his eyes. Utter confusion! Why were his arms and legs shackled with chains? And why was Lord Rexmoore here – dancing with that woman?

Twirling the woman in a wide expanse of arms, Lord Rexmoore caught Wil's eye. The man's lips mouthed the words, 'Ah! At last,' then he bent and said something into the woman's ear. She dropped his hand and the dance stopped. The music, too, came to a faltering halt. Behind the couple, Wil could see a mass of purple and orange stretching as far as his eyes could see. Some people at the front clapped briefly. Most didn't clap at all. The woman bowed her head and glided backwards; with three broad strides Lord Rexmoore was at the front of the stage.

'Ladies and Gentlemen... *friends*,' he called out. And slowly turning towards Wil, he raised his arm. 'This was as much a surprise to me as it is to you now. Please, let me introduce... our witch's best friend... I give you... Master Wil Calloway!'

The crowd near the stage clapped politely, although Wil could see a few people exchange confused glances; some shook their heads and a few shrugged their shoulders. Further back, people seemed to have already lost interest.

Unperturbed, Rexmoore gave Wil a sly smile.

'Welcome back to the land of the living!'

Behind him someone in the crowd shouted, 'Burn them – just get on with it!'

With a delighted grin Rexmoore added, 'Well, for the moment at least!'

Then, with a beaming nod to the musicians, Rexmoore once again took centre stage and beckoned the woman. Poker-faced, she took hold of his outstretched hand and they resumed their dance. Below them, the people returned to their own revelry. Some danced; a few clapped in time to the tune. Everyone it seemed, other than Wil and the dancing woman, were having a wonderful time.

Like some very weird jigsaw, the scene in front of Wil began to slot together; although some pieces didn't seem to fit. For instance, Wil had no idea why he was tied to a pole; or who the witch was and why he was her best friend. Just below the stage Wil could see a fenced corral – there were quite a few people in there, together with a collection of really strange looking animals, some of which Wil recognised – others, no. And… he squinted in an attempt to find something that might give him some clues… there, among them was... Gisella… with a beautiful winged horse: *Tanith* – the name came to him in a flash. Next to Gisella, Wil could see his Fellhound, Phinn… and Mia. Both had thick ropes like halters tied around their heads. So if Mia was here, where was Mortimer?… and Seth? Had they come too, or was it just him – Wil – and Gisella? Then a big piece of the jigsaw fell into place.

'Tally!'

'Well, it's about time!'

There was no mistaking that acid response but the binding around Wil's head prevented him from investigating further.

'I've been trying to get you to wake up for ages!'

'Tally! But…how?'

Completely confused now, Wil didn't know what to ask next.

The music changed and the woman – *Imelda*, Wil's mind said – dropped Rexmoore's hand like a stone, leaving his lordship to twirl alone, apparently blissfully happy in his own company.

Imelda crossed the stage towards Wil. Where Lady Élanor was slender, Imelda was skeletal. She had the same shape eyes as Lady Élanor and Tally, but hers were set in a gaunt face; they were blue, too, but a cold and grey, not the pale, cornflower blue of her brother's daughters.

'It appears that my niece has proved useful after all,' she said with a smile that showed not a hint of kindness. 'I was starting to fear she would go to her death having had no purpose in life. At least with you finally here, that will not be the case.'

With a final, extravagant twirl, Rexmoore came to a halt behind his wife and embraced her bony shoulders. Revulsion flitted across Imelda's face. Behind them, the musicians continued to play.

'Now, my love,' said Rexmoore – sweat trickling down his temple. 'As I promised, we have the seer. *And,*' he turned to acknowledge Gisella, Tanith and the Fellhounds down in the corral, 'it looks like we've got more prizes than we'd expected. Yes, I think I'm safe in saying, my own one, that your brother's legacy will very soon be ours!'

He bent and kissed his wife's neck leaving a sweep of sweat across her cheek; Imelda's spidery frame shuddered. Seemingly oblivious, Rexmoore performed an extravagant pirouette and waltzed alone back towards the crowd. Imelda wiped away her husband's damp trail with the back of her hand. The music stopped again.

Lord Rexmoore was once more at the front of the stage, waiting for silence. Above his head the sun was sliding down the late afternoon sky on a collision course with the golden tower.

'Right,' said Rexmoore eventually, 'well I hope you've all calmed down after the excitement of the Unexpected Pets contest? What a result, hey! I bet you weren't expecting that one?' He raised his arms, palms up and nodded slowly; an expectant beam splitting his face. A ripple of polite applause petered out quickly. 'And I'm sure you're all looking forward to the highlight of this year's Alcama festival?'

The cheer this time was far more enthusiastic.

'Get on with it!' called a voice somewhere to Wil's right.

Rexmoore's smile got even broader.

'Well, just before we...' he acknowledged the heckler with a wagging index finger, '"Get on with it", as you say, The Hemlock Quartet are going to *warm* us up.' He chuckled at his little joke. 'So there's still time to get a lantern – only one gold schilling. And, for those who think they can't afford it – think again! Can *you* afford seven years of Alcama luck?'

He cast his face skywards with an expression of mock fear and clasped his cheeks. His knees buckled slightly. At the same moment, hundreds of pairs of empty eyes glowed gold as sheep skulls, laid cheekbone to cheekbone, lit up the edge of the stage. From somewhere below, a band struck up. Rexmoore, barely able to contain his excitement, skipped across to his wife and swept her back into the soft light. Imelda neither resisted nor smiled – she just danced.

From somewhere beside Wil a voice he now knew to be Tally's spoke just loudly enough to be heard over the music.

'Oh, Wil, I'm so sorry.'

From the direction, and the fear in her tone, Wil guessed she was probably already tied to the bonfire. But he didn't ask.

She went on.

'I didn't know what else to do. I've waited and waited in that tower – it was freezing! That Tinniswood boy...he's been so horrid. And my aunt...' she stifled a sob, 'she says that if you refuse to tell her where she can find the legacy, she'll burn me, and then Tanith, *and* Gisella as well.'

'But I don't know where – *or what* – the legacy is!' exclaimed Wil.

'I know,' said Tally's frightened voice. 'But she won't believe me. I've tried and tried to tell them.'

'I heard,' muttered Wil.

'Tinniswood told me about the trap… after he found you all out on the Fell – about getting you to the tower. But I couldn't warn you, I didn't dare try, you know, because of last time. Then when they brought me up here I saw Phinn and Mia. There was no sign of Tinniswood so I thought they were still waiting for you… and I… well, oh, I'm so sorry, Wil. I just had to try to warn you. But I honestly didn't think you'd react like that.'

'Like what?' said Wil – the red mist and the excruciating pain were lingering.

Tally was crying now.

'Oh, Wil, it was terrible. I thought I'd killed you – or that you'd gone mad! Everyone did.'

'What do you mean, Tally? What did I do?' asked Wil, only half wanting to know.

'You were screaming, Wil – Mia was barking and Phinn started howling. I mean, you didn't do that in the court… at the moon chase hearing. It was terrible. You just kept screaming and…oh, dear…'

'Oh, dear, what?'

'I couldn't stop myself. I was so worried – I… I called out your name.'

Wil closed his eyes. Tally kept talking.

'If only I'd kept my mouth shut. Gisella stayed where she was. *She* didn't say a thing,' she said with a very slight barb in her voice that Wil chose to ignore.

'Don't worry, Tally. We'd already met up with Tinniswood anyway. Did his mother make it to the competition?'

'No,' said Tally, sounding thoroughly miserable. 'Imelda was furious. They had to give the prize to that dragon down there.'

Wil scanned the corral. Gisella, flanked by two very large guards, was looking up at the stage; it was difficult to see her properly in the packed space but even from this distance Wil could see that her face was as pale as a cloud.

'Where? I can't see...' then, nearer the stage, Wil spotted an ugly lizard-like creature with a red bloom on its chest and a pair of wings that looked far too small for its body.

'That!'

The dragon hardly looked *unexpected* – well, unless you were going on size – it was a small dragon, a *very* small Lesser Crested Ridge Creeper. Anyone who had spent an afternoon at the foot of the Eiye Mountains – as Wil had done many times – would have seen Ridge Creepers far bigger than that roosting around Ewes Seat; although Wil had never heard of anyone having one as a pet.

The tiny dragon extended its neck and let out a pitiful yowl. Its long teeth hung like s-shaped tusks. It was wearing a gold rosette. Like some kind of scaly overgrown cat – its mournful cry all but drowned out the singers. They raised their voices but the dragon only cried louder until Wil could hear little else. Those closest to the din clamped their hands over their ears. The light around Wil's eyes dimmed and red mist fogged the edges of his vision again. With a huge effort he called out.

'Tally, stop it!'

'Stop what?'

'Trying to get into my head. I told you, I don't know anything about the legacy and as you've already nearly driven me mad once – don't try it again!'

'But I'm not doing anything!'

The red mist swirled. Wil's arms and legs burned.

'Tally, I'm warning you,' he said gritting his teeth in an effort to banish the pain. 'If you don't stop now *I'm* going to set that bonfire alight!'

'I am *not-*'

But Rexmoore had also had enough. With a petulant stamp, he stopped dancing; the singers closed their mouths and the music died. Mercifully, the dragon went quiet too. Wil's sight cleared and his limbs cooled. He could see a man clutching a length of chain that seemed to be attached to the dragon's collar. In the man's other hand was a large gold bar. He looked thoroughly miserable.

'Will you shut that thing up or it will lose its head!' hissed Rexmoore. The man gave a hesitant bow.

'Sorry, m'Lord. I think it's hungry. They… it… likes fresh meat – bonacuss normally – but no-one's got change for a gold bar.'

Imelda turned on her heels. Drawn to something on the floor next to Wil, a cruel smile crept across her thin lips.

In half a dozen strides she returned to her husband's side holding Wil's loaded bow. In a blink, she aimed and fired down into the corral. Several people screamed; Wil held his breath – so, he could hear, did Tally.

'There,' said Imelda without a hint of emotion in her voice. 'Fresh marbussal – not quite bonacuss but I'm sure it will do!' She lowered the bow, 'Oh, and by the way, that'll cost you half a gold bar, plus taxes. Guards, take that gold bar off that gentleman as payment in full and give him his change – unless he wants to buy a lantern!'

Other than his scaly pet, the man was now standing quite alone, giving Wil a proper view of Gisella. He almost forgot to start breathing again. Gisella's wrists and ankles bore the same shackles as Wil's, and Tanith's front hooves were bound to his back legs with a thick chain. He could hardly walk – taking flight would certainly have been impossible. Tally's choked voice was barely audible, 'Oh, no! Tanith!'

Wil searched the vast crowd in the forlorn hope that he might spot Mortimer or Seth. The light in the sky told him they were running out of time. Then something bright danced at the edge of Wil's vision. He tried again to turn his head but the bindings were no looser. A sudden cramp in his neck made him gasp. At the same moment the source of the new light became clear.

Tinniswood – The Jackal – holding a burning torch high above his head, came running onto the stage; the furious expression on his face made all the more alarming by a very swollen and *very* black eye.

'Colin!' said Imelda in a silky voice. She still held Wil's crossbow. 'So good of you to join us. Is your mother in good health? She was missed earlier; she will be disappointed not to have taken the prize again this year. We had such high hopes.'

Her mouth smiled but her eyes blazed.

'I am sorry, my lady,' said The Jackal, with a curt bow. 'Mother is extremely upset.' He threw Wil a look of deepest loathing, 'Snuffy met with an unfortunate accident earlier which forced my mother to withdraw from the competition.'

'Oh, I'm sorry to hear that. Accident?' asked Imelda, her whole being void of emotion. She ignored the black eye.

'Master Calloway killed him!' said The Jackal simply. 'Mother is not happy!'

'And it has taken until *now* to console her? Did you not think to inform us sooner?' Imelda's eyes flashed to her husband, who hastily nodded his agreement. She flicked the trigger on Wil's bow.

The Jackal looked suddenly uncomfortable.

'I… er, I was… er… held up,' he said at last.

'Yer,' said Wil, unable to contain himself. 'A *pressing* matter!'

'Colin?' said Imelda, raising her eyebrows.

'They took me by surprise!' Colin burst out. 'That dog down there. They knocked me out! They killed Snuffy, knocked me out and left me for dead. And mother missed the competition, and… and..' The Jackal whirled around and pointed first at Tally and then Wil, 'And *she* isn't going to tell us where the legacy is, so I've come here to help make sure *he* does!'

Rexmoore's face lit up, but Imelda was less convinced.

'And *what* makes you think you can be any more effective than *me*? After all Colin, it has not gone unnoticed that you have so far completely failed to get any information out of my niece, and, correct me if I'm wrong,' she said in a voice that warned that any attempt to correct her would be a very big mistake, 'your father *completely failed* to get any information about the legacy despite his rather lengthy stay in Saran some time ago!'

The expression of triumph on The Jackal's face threw Wil completely.

'Because,' he said, '*I* know where Master Calloway can find his father!'

'What!' gasped Wil. 'You mean you knew he was alive and you didn't say anything!'

Wil wriggled frantically, desperate to get his hands around The Jackal's throat, but the knife-like shackles cut deep into his arm. The Jackal chuckled. His confidence seemed to be growing with every word now.

'Well… you know… didn't seem particularly useful at the time! So, let's see… we've got your father, the lovely

Gisella,' he waved his fingers towards the corral while, in his other hand, he used the burning torch as a pointer, 'that flying nag, *both* your dogs, am I forgetting anyone... oh, yes, and Tally here.'

He walked to the front of the stage and pretended to search the crowd that almost to a man had completely lost interest by now. Then he returned to stand right in front of Wil.

'And, Wil, I know that Seth and Mortimer are out there too. But, well, as they won't want anything to happen to any of you, wherever they are, I'm sure they won't do anything foolish.'

The town crier edged onto the stage.

'Ah, hem.' He bowed and, with his hand in his bell to keep it silent, spoke in little more than a whisper as he addressed Lord Rexmoore directly. 'My lord, with all due respect these people all wait, as was promised on this due date. The burning of the witch the party will make, but I fear more delay a foul mood they will take.'

The crier finished his rather hasty rhyme and gave an apologetic bow.

'*Bell*...' thought Wil; the hint of an idea danced on the very edge of his powers of reason...

Rexmoore frowned.

'Yes, but the moons are nowhere near to rising,' he said searching the cloud-dotted sky with a frown. 'They're just going to have to wait. Bring on the jugglers and drop the price of rat beer by a groat, that'll keep them happy!'

The town crier looked as though he was going to speak again, but he backed away in silence.

'So, what d'you think, Wil,' snarled Tinniswood. 'Your father – in exchange for the location of the legacy? Oh, and we might even let your friends *and* your pets live!'

Unable to do what he really wanted to do at that moment, Wil didn't know whether to cry or laugh.

'But I don't know where, or even what, the legacy is!'

Imelda laughed.

'Oh, but you do, Wil Calloway. I know you do. You see, Sir Jerad sent word. I know you are a seer and you *will* lead us to the legacy whether you want to or not.'

'And to make sure you do,' Imelda added in a honeyed voice 'we will kill each of those you hold dear, one by one, and *not* terribly quickly… until you see that, no matter how long it takes, really, the only way that you will be able to stop the killing… is to do as we ask.'

Listening to her words, it dawned on Wil that Imelda and Rexmoore had no idea that the legacy was linked to the Alcama… neither did Tally.

The Jackal danced inches from Wil's face.

'So, Calloway, what's it to be?'

'You know, Colin,' interrupted Imelda, her tone still sugary. 'As we have the lovely Tally all ready and waiting… and a crowd *dying* to see Armelia's first witch burning in… ooh, quite a long time.' She turned defiantly towards her husband but the band had started to play again and, tapping his feet to another tune, he didn't seem to notice. She turned back – her expression impossible to read. 'Let's keep Master Calloway in the wings, as it were, and see if the smell of smoke will make him talk.'

The Jackal bowed so low his nose almost touched his knees.

'Be my guest, my lady. I am sure Wil's father, at least, can wait a *little* longer.'

The anger that Wil was trying so hard to fight down flared at these words and it took a supreme effort to hold his tongue; the idea he was formulating was just starting to take shape and he needed a clear head if he was to have even the slightest chance of making it work.

CHAPTER TWENTY-TWO

The Burning of the Witch

'No! I'm sorry my love but I absolutely forbid it!' said Rexmoore with a little stamp of his foot. 'It's not even dark! We won't get the full effect – I mean, people at the back won't see the flames!'

'Or hear the screaming,' sneered The Jackal.

'I can see that, my Lord,' said Imelda in the same patient tone that Wil had heard Lady Élanor use when Tally was being difficult, 'But the crowd is getting restless. Once they're occupied we can take the others back to the tower for a bit of peace… and *persuasion!*'

The Jackal surveyed the mass of purple and orange below them and added, 'They'll all be running around scaring each other to death once the moons cross anyway, my Lord, so we don't want to leave the burning until too late. It'll spoil the impact,'

But Rexmoore was adamant.

'Now look here,' he said, puffing out his chest. 'I don't ask for much all year Imelda, but this is *my* festival…'

…as the debate warmed up Wil turned his mind to Phinn. He looked at the darkening sky – time was not on his side. If he could get a message to the Fellhound his plan might just have a bit more of a chance. *Timing* was everything. He closed his eyes.

'*Phinn, when I say... find Mortimer.*'

'Well, *I* don't get much the *rest* of the year,' retorted Imelda.

'*Get ready, Phinn. Get ready.*'

'Agh! I can't believe you said that. I give you everything! Why do you think the castle is a hovel – to pay for your precious golden tower!'

'*Get ready, Phinn. Get ready.*'

'What, that half built effort! You told me it would be ready by this Alcama – just like you did last Alcama *and* the Alcama before that!'

'*Get ready, Phinn*'

'I think you'll find, if you *think* for a moment – you can do that, can't you? – that it wasn't even started then!' blustered Rexmoore.

The effort to concentrate through the blazing row was making Wil feel physically sick. He swallowed hard and opened his eyes. In the corral below, Phinn was rubbing his head up and down Gisella's back – and by the look of it, he was pushing quite hard. In an effort not to fall over, Gisella leant against the Fellhound's weight. Phinn pushed back. Wil watched – of course! Phinn was trying to get the halter off!

Gisella, trying her best to stay on her feet, threw Wil a questioning glance. He'd managed to work his hand free just enough to straighten his fingers with his palm down praying that she would understand and stay still. But poor Gisella was really getting pushed about and didn't look at all happy; even so, when two guards moved forward she gave an apologetic shake of her head and whatever she said prompted a hasty retreat.

On the stage Rexmoore planted his hands on his hips.

'Me! *Selfish!* For all these months I've had to put up with that cousin of yours… and her hats! Eccentric, you said! I can think of at least one other name for it!'

'That is my family you are insulting!' hissed Imelda. 'Colin, light the bonfire!'

The Jackal disappeared out of Wil's line of vision and Tally shrieked.

'NO! Get that thing away from me. You… NO! I will rip your entrails out with my teeth when I get free!'

The Jackal's spiteful giggle rang out over the now rapt audience. All eyes were on the bonfire – '*Perfect,*' thought Wil.

Below him, Phinn was still battling with the halter but it refused to budge.

'*Phinn, let Gisella help.*'

Phinn lowered his head immediately. Gisella hooked her finger into the rope and very slowly the Fellhound backed away. The rope slid over Phinn's ears.

'*Wait!*' thought Wil.

Phinn stood and watched.

Although Wil could not see her, Tally's language suggested things were not going well. Smoke was now billowing across the stage. The crowd were a haze of frenzied excitement and amidst the chaos Imelda and Colin were dancing and laughing like children. He couldn't see Rexmoore but, by the shouting, Wil could tell his Lordship was absolutely furious. It was time.

'*Phinn, find Mortimer. Release the bonacuss!*'

The words had hardly left Wil's mind when, in one arcing bound, Phinn leapt over the corral fence scattering unsuspecting revellers as he landed and sped away. But to Wil's amazement the crowd simply closed back in; no one gave chase. One of the guards pointed up at the fire and several people laughed; the action was on the stage – the witch was burning!

With Phinn on his way, Wil had to move fast. He tried to block out the sound of Tally, still screaming obscenities –

which at least meant she was still alive – and tried to fix another image in his mind–

'So Calloway, any *ideas* yet?' Imelda's voice broke his concentration. She and The Jackal glided past.

'Yer, untie me and I'll show you!' snarled Wil.

'Now, now, boy, there's no need for threats,' said Rexmoore, his eyes following his dancing wife. 'You could help yourself – and your friends – by telling us where the legacy– oh no, oh, goodness...'

Mid-spin, The Jackal stopped dancing.

'Mother!'

Imelda tripped over The Jackal's booted foot.

From behind Wil a childlike voice drifted through the smoke.

'A hat! Look Colin, Mommy's got a new hat. Ooh, so warm. A pretty new hat for Mommy…'

Someone in the front of the crowd screamed and The Jackal, Imelda and Rexmoore all charged out of Wil's very restricted line of sight. A woman – The Jackal's mother, Wil guessed – started shrieking, 'No, not my hat. You can't have it! Get your own. No! Don't do that! Aarrgh!'

Doing his best to ignore the unseen commotion, Wil shut his eyes tight and made one final effort.

'Wil, do something,' yelled Tally. 'This wood's wet but it's drying fast. Wil, please, you've got to do something!'

But it was no good, he couldn't to it. He couldn't get them to come.

Desperate now, Wil tried to drag his hands through the shackles, ignoring the razor edges that cut deep into his wrists with every move. Behind him, over Tally's frantic pleas for help, Wil could hear The Jackal's mother – whatever was going on back there, she was not happy!

Then another noise – a faint buzzing... the chains around Wil's hands and feet sprang apart. He clawed at the binding around his head. In seconds he was free. The buzzing got louder. Something tickled his hand – he looked down. The healing burn was covered with bees; bees were crawling across the padlock at his feet and out of the key hole of the lock that had fallen from his wrists.

'Wil, bees! There's a swarm of *bees!*' yelled Tally.

But Wil grinned. '*Thank you*'.

It took him a moment to locate Gisella through the haze of smoke. As his eyes finally picked her out, the little dragon once more found its voice. Wil pictured the chains around Gisella's wrists. A black buzzing cloud trailed down into the corral.

'Wil, anytime today!' yelled the voice behind him.

Bright orange flames were licking around Tally's feet. Wil plunged his hand into his boot – to his amazement his knife was still there. He began to hack at ropes that held Tally to the stake–

'Look, he's freeing the witch,' called a voice from the crowd.

'Stop 'im,' cried another.

'Call this a burning?'

People started to boo and something soft and squidgy hit Wil on the back of the head. A rotten tomato plopped to the floor.

'Oh, no you don't!' The Jackal came from nowhere – and with such force that he took Wil clean off his feet and away from the bonfire.

Tally screamed. The crowd roared. Shouts of encouragement boomed from everywhere. The little dragon wailed.

'This is more like it!'

'Go, my son!'

'Let her burn, let her burn, let her bu-urn,' they sang.

Wil and The Jackal crashed to the floor. Wil's hand hit a stray log and his knife disappeared.

'Guards!' yelled The Jackal. 'Guards!'

Wil punched out and caught the boy hard across the cheek, just missing his black eye; but for all Wil was the bigger of the two, The Jackal was on top, with his knee planted firmly on Wil's other arm.

'Guards!' screamed the boy. 'Can I have a hand up here!'

But no one came. The Jackal punched and punched. Wil felt his cheekbone crack. There was uproar all around them. Then suddenly – a blur of grey; the sound of air being knocked out of a pair of lungs and The Jackal flew high into the air. He landed somewhere past the edge of the stage. Phinn followed.

'Phinn, No!' yelled Wil. If Phinn caught The Jackal now he was sure to finish him off and Wil needed the boy alive – Wil needed to find his father.

On all fours, Wil fought to catch his breath. The fire crackled greedily; the crowd were beyond frenzy. An acrid smell filled his nose and with a deafening crack, the stake collapsed and gave in to the flames.

Wil sank into a crouch and wept – it had all been for nothing. Tally was dead.

How was he going to tell Lady Élanor? In a flash Wil's grief turned to rage. He had come all this way and risked so much, and she was gone. He had tried *so hard*… and failed … well, maybe there was still time to honour half of his promise. If he could just get Tanith home, back to Lovage Hall. Of course Lady Élanor would never forgive him, but–

'Are you going to stay there all night,' asked a cross voice. 'I mean, it wasn't even a real fight, Phinn saved you almost as soon as it started. Ooh, that cheek looks a bit painful mind–'

'Tally!' Wil was on his feet before she'd finished speaking. 'How?'

Tally grinned.

'You forget that I brought those hounds into this world, Wil. I was the first person they saw and I made sure their mother didn't crush them to death when they suckled. If I was in trouble, do you honestly think they'd just sit there panting?'

'But what did he do – Phinn – to get you out of the fire?'

'He's a Fellhound, Wil – what do you think he did! He's a bit singed though, but nothing that won't grow back!'

'Oh, so that's what I can smell – burning hair,' said Wil. Phinn certainly was looking a bit sizzled around the eyebrows.

'Er, no actually,' Tally walked to the edge of the deserted stage. Beyond her, the square was half-full and emptying rapidly. There were overturned carts, wrecked stalls and the smouldering remains of campfires everywhere. The little Ridge Creeper was wandering loose, abandoned and by the sound of it, deeply unhappy. 'Someone let a bonacuss loose.'

Despite the fact that Tally was alive and that his plan for Phinn to find Mortimer must have worked, Wil felt an odd sadness wash over him; it was exactly like the day Rexmoore's men had taken his father, and the pitiful cry of the Ridge Creeper wasn't helping one bit!

'So where are they – Gisella, Mortimer and Seth?' Wil said, trying to ignore his sinking mood.

'Well, Tanith is down there with Mia and... Oh... oh, dear. That looks like Gisella.'

Tally stared down into the demolished corral with wide, unblinking eyes.

'Wil,...it was the bonacuss... she couldn't get out of the way...No... Imelda... Imelda grabbed her...Wil, Imelda used Gisella as a shield!'

CHAPTER TWENTY-THREE

Bonacuss Poo

Without stopping to consider the height of the stage, Wil kicked the macabre skull lanterns out of the way and jumped. Phinn followed in an easy leap.

'Don't worry,' Tally called after him. 'I'll find my own way down.'

But her pithy tone went unnoticed.

Gisella was lying face down; Mia was nudging her with her huge nose but despite the Fellhound's best efforts, Gisella didn't move a muscle. Wil's throat was so tight speech failed him and unsure of what to do – but knowing he needed to do something – he gently lifted her hair from her face. Her normally tanned cheek was pale as stone but her neck was spattered with green liquid. Carefully lifting her shoulder, Wil could see that Gisella's orange and purple tunic was green with thick slime. The smell was overpowering.

'No, don't!' shouted Tally. She was scrambling over broken planks and struts that had not that long before been the steps onto the stage. 'Wil, don't turn her over! If that stuff gets any more air she'll lose her skin!'

Wil let go as if he'd been stung and Gisella slumped back into the dirt.

Tally hopped over the only remaining step.

'Oh, dear! Orange really isn't her colour is it?' said Tally. She patted Mia's flank as the forlorn hound plodded over to greet her. 'It's bonacuss dung, Wil. Eli has told me about it. They farm bonacuss on Rockmoor Downs – dangerous but delicious, apparently. Anyway, one of the young farmhands got in the way of a young bull – you know – behind it… and… anyway there's only one cure for bonacuss poo burns.'

She stopped abruptly, her gaze following the wandering dragon on the other side of the square – it was eating something and had at least for the moment stopped that mournful cat call.

'Well?' prompted Wil. Gisella remained stubbornly still and he was getting more anxious by the moment.

'Dragon urine,' said Tally.

'What! They've got dragons on Rockmoor Downs? How… where…?'

'Brom's Lair – it's the breeding ground for the Giant Redback, Eli told me that, too.'

'Well, I'm not even going to try to guess how that all works,' said Wil, recalling the size of the tooth he'd seen earlier. 'So, how do we get a sample from our little friend over there?'

Tally cast a quick look around the wreckage of wagons and stalls and headed for an upturned wagon a little way off. She disappeared into the debris that had once been the stallholder's wares and emerged holding up three dead hares. She looked very pleased with herself.

'With fresh meat and a little patience!'

As it was, the dragon proved to be extremely easy to catch and Wil felt what he could almost have described as a hug of comforted gratitude as he watched it gobble down two of the hares in quick succession.

'It's really small for a Ridge Creeper, isn't it?' he said throwing the remaining hare into the air. The dragon – not much bigger than a small, albeit very fat, pony – snatched at the offering just before it hit the ground and crunched happily.

'Well, maybe it's only young,' said Tally. Her arms were full of jugs that she had just found in a deserted bar nearby.

'We can't use those, Tally, they stink!'

The jugs did indeed reek of rat beer. Tally breathed a long suffering sigh.

'Honestly Wil, it's not as if we've got much choice. And anyway, once that dragon's done his bit the rat beer, I can assure you, will be a mere memory.'

'But will she be okay?'

Wil bent to make sure Gisella was still breathing.

'Why is she unconscious? Is it the fumes?'

'Na,' answered Tally. 'Tinniswood's mother hit her with a Wraithe Wolf's head – she was yelling something about Gisella trying to steal her hat.'

'Ooh,' said Wil, with a hollow laugh. 'I think that's my fault.'

The green slime was oozing into the dust where Gisella lay.

'Won't it get worse the longer that stuff's on her?'

'She'll be fine for the time being as long as we can keep the air off. As she's lying in it, that's about the best place for her right now,' said Tally, sounding oddly hard-hearted.

'But it's all up her neck – where it splashed,' said Wil.

'Mm, I'm pretty sure it's only the dung that's the problem; you know, the slime. I'm sure Eli said that the splashes just make the skin peel. It'll heal,' said Tally. She was poised ready to catch anything that the dragon produced but the dragon was not procuring *anything*.

'Well, maybe we could get this thing to hurry up if you're only "pretty sure"?' said Wil. He was frustrated by the dragon's lack of co-operation and by Tally's lack of compassion. It also hadn't escaped his notice that the silver light from the twin moons was brimming over the city walls like an over full cup. Trying to match Tally's tone, he added, 'I was supposed to get you and Tanith back to Lovage Hall tonight. Lady Élanor made me promise that I'd get you back before the moons crossed.'

One of the jugs slipped from Tally's grasp but she managed to grab it before it hit the ground.

'What? Why didn't you mention this earlier, Wil? What *exactly* did she make you promise?'

'Er, I can't...I can't really remember,' said Wil, thrown by her sudden alarm. 'Try!'

With a pitiful yowl, the little dragon waddled over to the upturned wagon and nudged the pile of splintered wood. Wil kept his eyes on the dragon.

'Um, she said,' he started – sadness was consuming him again. 'Well, she said something about only being sure you and Tanith are safe if you are at home with her – at Lovage Hall... er, Tally, I think you might need that jug!'

By the time the dragon had finished all three jugs were brimful with plenty to spare. All the time its doleful whine quavered through the empty square. Phinn and Mia lay with their chins on the dirt – their eyebrows flicking as they watched and waited.

'Right,' said Tally, setting down the jugs one by one next to Gisella. 'It's quite easy – all you have to do is pour the urine on every bit of green. I'd do it myself but if my sister wants Tanith and I back at the Hall before the moons cross, we *really* need to be there.'

'But it took us a day and a half to get here,' said Wil, his heart now in his boots – he suddenly felt desperately lonely. 'How will you get back in time?'

'Wil, don't you know anything about pegalus – they are capable of covering great distances *very* quickly – as the raven flies, you could say!'

The word *raven* hit Wil like a bolt.

'Oh no! Pricilla – Tally, Pricilla got injured. I left her with someone.'

'Who? Where is she?'

'I... I don't know?'

'What? *Who* you left her with? Or *where* she is?'

The dragon stuck its snout into the wreckage of another wagon a little further away. Wil's mind cleared a little in the sudden hush.

'Er, well both really.'

Tally looked appalled.

'You mean to say that you gave my sister's precious raven to a stranger so that you could rescue your girlfriend?'

'Now hang on, Tally! Actually I came to rescue you, remember!'

'You say!' retorted Tally.

'Blimey, you two make any more noise and Rexmoore's men will be back down here in a flash – loose bonacuss or not!'

A huge timber prop under the stage cracked and toppled to one side; Mortimer emerged, followed by Farrow who appeared to have a green stain across her rump; and then Seth.

'Hi Tally,' said Seth, before Mortimer could speak. 'You okay?'

'Oh yer, I'm great thanks,' answered Tally, her voice dangerously pleasant. 'Been holed up for days in a freezing tower made of gold with – for most of the time – no one to

talk to except a nutty woman with an obsession for hats!'
Seth threw Wil a slightly unnerved glance but Tally was in
full flow. '*Then* I got tied to a stake while nutty woman's son
tried to burn me alive! Gisella's rather inconveniently
got herself plastered in bonacuss dung; Wil's *lost* my sister's
raven and... *and* I've just been told I'm due home before the
moons cross. Me? I'm good *thanks!*'

'Oh,' said Seth in a very quiet voice. 'That's alright then.'

Mortimer stepped out from the debris holding out Wil's
hunting knife.

'Hey, Wil, I found this under the stage, thought you might
need it. What's happened to Gisella?'

'The bonacuss – Imelda used her as a shield.' Wil took the
knife and slid it back into its familiar home in his boot. 'But
it's okay because Tally said that all we need to do is pour
dragon wee over her and she'll be fine.'

Tally snorted.

'I did *not* say she'd be fine. I said she wouldn't lose all
her skin – well, not permanently. She was, after all, also
smacked across the face with a hat made out of a Wraithe
Wolf's head.'

'What?' chorused Mortimer and Seth.

'The Jackal's mother,' said Wil by way of an explanation.

'Ah!' said Mortimer. 'Right, well... er... shall I give you
a hand then. I'm guessing she won't need these just yet,
then?' He held up Gisella's crossbow and a handful of silver-
tipped bolts.

'Er, no,' said Wil, somewhat distracted. 'Apparently we
have to be quick. You hold, I'll pour.'

Stowing the bow behind the nearest up-turned stall,
Mortimer carefully rolled Gisella over. With a brief glance at
Tally, who ignored him, Wil trickled the pale yellow liquid
over Gisella's neck and tunic. The slime turned pale pink

almost immediately and little ribbons of steam drifted from the rosy goo.

'Goodness me, you'll have to be quicker than that, Wil. You're saving her skin – not getting her ready to meet your mother! Give it all a good splosh!'

Not convinced that Tally's intentions were entirely to the benefit of Gisella's health, Wil tipped each jug in quick succession. The steam rose now in clouds and, for the first time since they'd found her, Gisella stirred and opened her eyes. Tally put her hands on her hips.

'There, see. I would say she'll be as pretty as before but–'

'The moons are coming up fast now, Tally,' said Mortimer quickly. 'If you want to make it back to Lovage hall, you're cutting it a bit fine, even with Tanith.'

'Is Wil going to come with me?' said Tally, not moving an inch. 'After all, he did *promise* to get me back to my sister.'

'Er, no, Tally. I've got to help Gisella – my first aid bag, you know – if she needs anything else.' It wasn't the best excuse but Wil was so angry with Tally right now that the temptation to throw her off Tanith somewhere over Tel Harion might just have been too great – moons crossing or not! In fact, Wil was feeling angrier by the minute.

Mortimer came to the rescue.

'Seth'll go with you, Tally. He's lighter than Wil. Tanith will be able to go faster.'

Wil was struggling now to keep up. Rage was building inside him. White hot fury was flooding through his veins; red mist was clouding the edges of his vision again – something was closing in… and whatever it was, it was very angry. He shook his head, struggling to find even simple words.

'Does anyone know… what… er, happened… to the… er… bonacuss?'

Tally ignored him and folded her arms.

'I don't want *him* to come! I want Wil to come or I'm not going!'

Mortimer took a step towards her.

'Seth, get on Tanith. Tally, I'm only going to ask you this once and then if you don't co-operate I will personally lift you onto that pegalus!' Behind him, two silver orbs were now sitting on the battlements. 'Will you get on Tanith and get going for Saran!'

His tone left no doubt. It was not a question, it was an order. Tally twisted her toe into the ground as if daring to consider arguing and threw Wil a hurt look.

But Wil didn't notice.

Several very bad things happened all at once.

CHAPTER TWENTY-FOUR

Out of the Sky

'Get them!' shouted Imelda. 'Kill the hounds if you have to! Kill them all except the seer!'

Something whistled past Wil's ear and thunked into the ground behind Farrow. Phinn was on his feet in an instant – a second later his heart rending howl split the air.

'NO!' yelled Wil. But the ground under his feet began to tremble and out of the shadows, firing green slime in its wake, thundered the bonacuss. Mortimer skipped backwards, firing bolts as he went.

'Get behind that wagon! Seth, get Tanith over there – NOW!'

'Phinn! Phinn's been hit!' shouted Wil.

'I know, but he's on his feet.'

Wil scooped Gisella up in his arms and hurtled towards the wrecked stall – bonacuss dung was spraying everywhere. He ducked down to avoid getting plastered. Seth was already astride Tanith; the pegalus reared – just in time. Green slime splattered over a huge pile of sheep skulls on an abandoned stall behind them.

'Just give me a bow, Wil,' whispered Gisella. Wil nearly dropped her in surprise.

'Giz, you're–'

'A bow, Wil! And get Tally on that horse!'

Not sure whether to thank Mortimer or to curse him, Wil thrust her own bow and the bolts towards her and poked his head out from behind the flimsy barricade. Imelda had Tally by the hair – and by the look of things Tally was giving as good as she was getting. The Jackal, meanwhile, was loading his catapult with whatever was near, firing with surprising accuracy. Something hard smacked against Wil's temple.

'Ow! Giz, can you hit The Jackal from here?'

Gisella took aim.

'Which Jackal do you want me to hit?' she said and fired. There was a howl.

'Good enough,' said Wil. 'Well, it was the right one at least, but only got his arm from what I can see.'

'I'll try harder next time,' said Gisella with a slightly cross-eyed grin. 'Now go and get Tally!'

On the far side of the square, with nowhere else to run, the bonacuss was spinning on its haunches for another charge. The little dragon was standing right in the way. Imelda was still struggling to get the better of Tally; and Mortimer was grappling with one of Rexmoore's guards who seemed to be getting the upper hand. Amid the chaos, Wil could see all three Fellhounds. They were simply standing around the dragon.

'What the–' Wil was interrupted by Gisella's shrill voice.

'Wil, *get Tally,* I've hit Imelda. Get Tally on Tanith!'

Wil scrambled out from his cover but Tally was already on her way – she was pelting towards them, pointing up at the sky. Imelda, The Jackal and the guards left standing were all running too – in the other direction.

The bonacuss charged.

'Wil, *DUCK!'* screamed Mortimer and, arms over his head, threw himself across the guard he had just managed to overpower.

From out of the black sky plunged a dragon – a huge and very angry dragon.

But Wil didn't duck. It would be OK. Phinn, Mia and Farrow knew it, too – unfortunately for the bonacuss, it didn't know very much at all.

As the massive dragon swept skywards, the light of the moons blazed red across the crimson scales of its vast chest. In the square the little dragon stood, quite unharmed, surrounded by the three Fellhounds. The bonacuss lay dead, its great hulk smouldering; the sweet smell of roasting beef filled the square.

'Gosh, that smell's making me hungry. Have we got time for dinner?' said Seth brightly.

'No!' answered Wil, Mortimer and Gisella.

'Tally, get on that pegalus,' ordered Mortimer. 'I haven't got a clue what's going on but you and Seth are going – *now!*' And with that, he picked Tally up, all but threw her onto Tanith's back behind Seth, and slapped Tanith hard on the rump. 'Lovage Hall, Seth, and don't stop *til you see Lady Élanor!'

Wil didn't think he'd ever seen anything as beautiful in his life as Tanith spreading his huge, golden wings – with one graceful beat, the pegalus was in the air and in three more he was high over the city, silhouetted against one of the luminescent moons.

'If they get back in time I'll eat my boots,' said Mortimer.

'But I thought Tally said–' began Wil.

'Yes, but Wil, it's freezing; there are hungry eagards out there; Tanith has been cooped up goodness knows where for days and, in case it's slipped your notice – a dragon in the mood for a barbecue has just turned up!'

In the black sky above them, Wil knew that the huge dragon was circling, although, to his relief, it didn't seem in the least bit interested in Tanith.

'It's a Redback,' said a voice.

Out of the shadows at the edge of the square, stepped the dragon tooth girl – and under her arm, quite content, was Pricilla.

'I know,' said Wil.

Mortimer looked from the girl to Pricilla and then to Wil.

'She'll be back,' said the girl.

'I know,' said Wil again.

'It was the call, wasn't it?'

'Something like that.'

'The red chest was a bit confusing – they normally get red as they get older. I think it's stressed. But those teeth – way too big for a Ridge Creeper.'

'Er, excuse me butting in, but could someone tell me what you're talking about?' said Mortimer.

'The dragon, it's a Giant Redback – a baby,' said Wil, nodding over at the little dragon. 'The hounds must have realised it was an infant just as the bonacuss attacked. They surrounded it to protect it – I... I've only just realised.'

Then a whole range of emotions swept over him; thankfully, the white rage had gone. It had been replaced by confusion and anger, mixed with relief. There was something else too that Wil couldn't quite put his finger on. He wanted – no, *needed* – to protect that little dragon. Despite knowing that the Fellhounds would help, every sound, movement and smell around him felt like a threat; if anyone attempted to harm the baby dragon at that moment Wil knew he would kill them – no matter who it was.

Wil also knew that the Redback was close and low but she was not going to attack – not yet. She wanted her baby back. So why didn't he just call the hounds away? Because at the moment the Redback understood that her baby was safe; she trusted the hounds. Tally was on her way back to Saran but Wil knew that they couldn't just leave the little dragon. He'd seen the cruelty in Imelda's eyes and he knew that if – *when* she came back, she would give the order to kill.

There was something else nagging at Wil – a dull ache; Phinn's amber eyes were fixed on his master – an arrow was still sticking out of his shoulder. Wil could see that the Fellhound's front leg was wet but in the darkness he hadn't realised until now that it was wet with blood. Phinn swayed but held his position.

'Is that dog alright?' asked the dragon tooth girl.

'No, it's been shot' said Wil simply.

Gisella frowned.

'Wil?'

'It's Phinn, Giz. He's okay for a minute.'

Wil knew that any attempt to move the hounds away from the dragon now would worry the mother and put them all in danger. So, much as it tore at Wil's heart to watch Phinn suffer, it would probably be a lot worse if he didn't bide his time.

As if reading Wil's mind, the Redback swooped again, incinerating the remains of the stage on her way past. There was a loud scream and three of Rexmoore's men appeared, tumbling over each other to escape the burning timber. Behind the wagon Wil knelt on something unpleasantly limp and fury – another dead hare.

'Well, I don't think we're too safe here,' said Mortimer over the crackle of the fire. He watched the guards fleeing across the square – taking care to give a wide birth to the hounds and their charge. 'I've got the distinct feeling we're about to have company again and I've only got four bolts left.'

'There's more in Tanith's stall with the rest of our things,' whispered Gisella.

'Does this mean that I'm going to miss the moon crossing?' asked the girl.

Imelda's voice came from nowhere and everywhere at the same time.

'Oh, no! My dear, on the contrary, you'll be one of the stars of the show!'

Wil span around. Bobbing lanterns swung from unseen supports among the dark buildings on the edge of the square – the low glow making a perfect hiding place of the ink-black shadows.

Another voice echoed out of the golden gloom.

'Right, men. The next time that overgrown bird comes down, shoot it with everything you've got – shoot everything!' cried Rexmoore. 'Just don't hit the seer!'

'*So, Imelda's getting impatient,*' thought Wil. He caught sight of the silhouette of a spear standing needle sharp against the moonlight – the battlements were now manned.

Keeping his voice as low as he could, Wil murmured, 'Mort, where did you leave the horses?'

'By the main gate – where we found Gisella and Seth. Why?'

'Watch… and no, I'm not going mad,' said Wil. Then, without another word he scooped up the dead hare and stepped out from behind the overturned wagon. All around the edge of the square sheep's head lanterns seemed to be floating in the darkness – golden light waking their dead eyes. Wil's mouth went dry.

'Okay,' he called out. 'Let my friends go and I'll come quietly. I know where the legacy is – I'll tell you when they're safely out of the city.'

'No! Wil-' squeaked Gisella, but Wil heard a muffled whisper from Mortimer and she said no more.

'I also want to see my father,' Wil continued loudly. 'That's the deal. My friends go free and I see my father.'

'Your friends?' called The Jackal. 'What about your *precious* dogs?'

'They can fend for themselves,' said Wil. His matter-of-fact voice generated another unintelligible squeak from Gisella. Wil gripped the limp hare.

'*Pricilla, can you make a noise? Can you set the baby dragon off... please?*'

Apart from a very reluctant *Prrukk!* Pricilla remained silent.

'So, do we have a bargain?' Wil called. Still swinging the hare, he tried again.

'*Please Pricilla – oh, and sorry I left you but you wouldn't have been safe with us! If we're all going to get out of this, we really need your help. Pleeeaase.*'

'I don't think you are in a position to make deals, Wil Calloway. And as one of the people with you is *my* daughter, I am sure, when she knows that I am here and safe, she will not want to go *anywhere!*' Fermina Fairfax's voice cut through the air like ice.

'Mother!' called Gisella. Wil heard what sounded like a muffled 'No' from Mortimer but Gisella pulled herself to her feet and stepped out from behind the debris of the wagon.

'Daaarling!' purred Fermina. 'Have you missed Mummy? We really must have a little chat about your choice of friends, my dear, now that we will be living here... in the castle.'

'What!' gasped Gisella.

'Prrukk!'

'*Not yet!*'

'Yes, dear. And we've got so much to catch up on. In a way I must offer my thanks to young Calloway here – I mean, he may have taken away the only person I ever loved–'

'What!' said Gisella, for the second time. 'But my father–'

'Look, these reunions are all very heart-warming, but really,' interrupted Imelda with an impatient sigh. 'Look, dear, your mother met my cousin, Sir Jerad Tinniswood, and fell in love with him so she killed your father. Unfortunately his mother didn't like your mother so no wedding bells there. Sir Jerad heard about Wil's talent in Saran prison and told your mother, and then Wil killed him. So your mother told me and, well, here we are. Okay, that's sorted – guards, get him, kill them!'

'Now Pricilla! Please!'

To her credit, the din Pricilla made could have easily been attributable to a whole flock of ravens. Within seconds the baby dragon, confused by the sudden noise, started to yowl like never before. Arrows rained down but in the dark, with the lanterns, the smouldering stage and the moonlight creating a chaotic mix of long shadows and dark corners, mercifully none of the arrows found their mark. It was then that Wil gave the order.

'Phinn, Mia – get the dragon to the tower – as close as you can! Farrow, follow!'

High above, the Redback felt the change. She flapped her leathery wings to keep herself still while she listened. Then she dived.

Wil could feel her panic.

'He's OK. They will keep him safe.'

From the number and direction of the falling arrows, Wil got the distinct impression that Rexmoore had brought more guards, and they were advancing fast.

'Mortimer, get to the horses. Take the girls and meet me up by the kitchen garden. Try to draw off some of Rexmore's men,' Wil's mouth shouted, while in his brain he kept repeating, '*They will keep him safe. They will keep him safe.*'

This time, the Redback came in so low that Wil felt a claw comb the top of his head. Arrows ricocheted off her scaly belly like matchsticks. Oblivious of the onslaught, she soared over the body of the charred bonacuss, flexed her long talons and snatched up two screaming guards. With one beat of her massive wings, all of the lanterns went out and she skimmed over the city wall knocking another body off the ramparts as she passed. She let go. The screaming ended abruptly with two loud splashes. The dragon wheeled around for another pass; Rexmoore and Imelda were the first to turn and run. The guards took their lead, falling over each other in their haste to avoid incineration.

In the chaos Mortimer, Gisella and the dragon tooth girl stole away into the shadows with Pricilla, quiet once more; her job was done – the baby dragon had found its voice again and this time it didn't sound like anything would shut it up.

Wil fixed his eyes on the black shape circling high above Mort Craggs.

'*Right. Now, trust me and follow your baby.*'

Swinging the dead hare around his head, Wil led the strange little group away from the square and towards the castle. The Redback caught on quickly. Every time any of Rexmoore's men got within shooting distance, she swooped and unleashed a bolt of fire. Soon a river of flames cut the city in two.

Unnerved at first, Wil had seriously doubted his chances of reaching the golden tower without being burned to a crisp. But after the dragon's third well-aimed salvo he decided that she really did know what she was doing.

With its aim not quite as accurate as its mother's, the baby dragon repeatedly tried but failed to catch the swinging hare. This kept it moving but as it got more frustrated it also got louder. All the while Phinn, Mia and Farrow covered both sides and the rear. In the starry sky the moons moved inexorably closer.

The noise was almost overwhelming. Buildings all around crackled; glass shattered in the intense heat; the dragon above roared and the dragon on the ground wailed. Yet, the streets that only a few hours earlier had been packed were now strangely deserted and from every window the unseeing stare of glowing sheep skulls haunted Wil's lonely advance.

Behind him, Phinn stumbled. An arrow bounced off the cobbles and the roof of the building behind burst into flames. Overhead, the Redback roared.

Wil searched the dark sky but the blackness gave nothing away.

'*Just a bit further, I promise. Just follow me and you'll get him back.*'

CHAPTER TWENTY-FIVE

Wil's Plan

The castle cowered under Mort Craggs, storey after stone
storey clawing up the cliff face, all precariously balanced and
looking tired enough to topple towards the city at any
moment. Wil led the way across the great sweep of green that
marked the boundary between the city and the castle.
Goosebumps prickled on his neck – the sudden space made
him feel even more vulnerable. But the attacks had stopped.
Rexmoore and his men were also strangely absent. All Wil
could feel was the Redback's mounting impatience; her baby
was hungry and she needed to get to him. But they were
inching closer to Wil's goal with every step.

Amid the sound of the burning city Wil could hear
something else – a fight, or was it even a battle? But he dare
not give the noise any attention for fear of losing the fretting
dragon above him.

Up ahead, reflecting the flames, Imelda's precious tower
stood shining like a blood red beacon. Very soon they would
be right under the tower – but as Wil whirled the hare over his
head an echo of Phinn's pain ripped into his own shoulder.
The Fellhound couldn't go on much longer.

'Wil, *Wil!*'

It was difficult to hear anything with the cacophony
around him, even so Wil was sure he'd just heard Gisella.

'Wil. Over here!'

Wil could just make out Gisella's willowy shape, crouching in the shadow of the castle wall.

'How– What are you doing here?' asked Wil. As he spoke freezing air bit into his lungs – the Redback was somewhere high above Tel Harion. 'Where's Mortimer and that girl?'

All the time, Wil kept swinging the hare and moving towards the tower.

'I don't know,' whispered Gisella, stumbling over unseen stones to keep up. 'I went to get our – ouch! – stuff… couldn't carry that much but, ooh, ow… got your bag and a load more bolts.'

'Any idea where Rexmoore and Imelda are?' asked Wil. He thought it best not to mention Gisella's mother.

'They've gone to th–,' Gisella said but the baby dragon drowned her out with a heart-rending wail. Round and round went the hare – Wil moved closer to the wall. His ears picked up her voice again.

'… but The Jackal's around somewhere,' she was saying in a forced whisper. 'I nearly bumped into him back there. Luckily your large friend – ouch! – set fire to the roof above us and he made a run for it.'

'So whatever Imelda's doing, she must be expecting The Jackal to bring me in then,' said Wil, more to himself than anyone else. Gisella gave a contemptuous snort.

'Maybe. But if I find him again, believe me, he won't be able to!'

Wil grinned. Spoken like a true Fellman.

'Look, Giz,' he said. 'Phinn's not going to be able to walk for much longer but I've got a plan for the Redback… and, er… I need to find my father. Can you get Phinn out of here? Keep the bag – it hasn't let us down yet. I'll find you when we're ready to go.'

'Well, I can't say I'll be going to look for my dear mother anytime soon,' said Gisella in a passable effort of sounding like she didn't care. 'But sure, I'll help with Phinn – although he probably won't come without you, Wil. Fellhounds stick to their masters at the best of times – if either's injured they're usually inseparable!'

For a split second Wil lost the rhythm of his swing and the little dragon snatched the hare out of his hand. Wil cursed.

'Oh, Wil, I'm so sorry, that was my fault,' said Gisella stepping out into the light.

Wil had no idea where the bolt came from because it smacked into Gisella with such force that she span away before she hit the floor.

'YES!'

Wil didn't need to turn around. The voice told him who was standing at the balcony above him. His own bow was still somewhere among the smouldering timbers of the wrecked stage and although his knife was in his boot, by the time he reached down for it, The Jackal would get a bolt into his back, for sure. A faint moan from the shadows told Wil that Gisella was alive. He put his hands in the air and turned.

'Well, Wil Calloway, that's the first sensible thing you've done since I met you!'

Moonlight filtered through frothy cloud, illuminating the bow in The Jackal's hands – it was Wil's bow!

'I must get one of these, they really are quite effective, aren't they – y'know, *deadly*.'

Behind him, Wil could hear bones crunching – the baby dragon was enjoying every last scrap of that hare. The Jackal dropped another bolt into the bow and aimed it past Wil.

'Right, well, we'll start with that whinging reptile – Mother, how do you fancy a brand new trophy for your collection? A dragon skin hat – now you haven't got any dragon's have you?'

'I hope your aim's good then?' called Wil.

The Jackal held the bow in place but didn't fire.

'And why might that be?'

'Because dragons are notoriously hard to kill with a bolt – very deep hearts,' said Wil, his mind racing.

Behind him, he could hear the infant snuffling in the damp grass for more food; Phinn, Mia and Farrow were still standing guard. The sound of fighting drifted over the grass again from the brick mill.

'Sounds like they're having fun down there,' said Wil – more to buy time than for information.

The Jackal allowed himself a brief glance in the same direction.

'Oh, it's the peasants – some sort of revolt. Whining about taxes *again* – it's just so dull. I offered to come and find you while Lord Rexmoore sorts it all out,' he said in a bored drawl. 'I mean, these people, they live in the city for practically nothing, have a festival laid on *every* year... and when they're asked to contribute... you should hear the moaning. Oh, well, we're short on labourers for the tower anyway so it's a case of pay up or... oh yes, I forgot, you're well aware of the rules, aren't you, Calloway!'

Making a huge effort not to rise to the bait, Wil changed the subject – anything to keep the boy talking while he worked out what to do.

'So where's Imelda?' he demanded.

In the damp darkness, Gisella groaned again then she coughed – it was a bubbly, liquid-filled cough that made Wil's stomach twist into a tight knot.

'Ooh, that doesn't sound too healthy, does it?' said The Jackal. 'Listening to that cough anyone would think that girl

has just been shot in the chest… they'd be right of course!'
His cruel laugh rang out over the empty green.

In desperation, Wil took his eyes off the balcony. There
had to be something he could use – a rock or a stone –
something that would distract the boy just long enough for
Wil to get up there and…

There it was, right in front of him. The moonlight glinted
down its polished length – the staff! It was sticking point
down into the soft ground where it had landed earlier –
absolutely straight… *spear-straight*, thought Wil. And next
to it, in a perfect coil, was the silk rope. For the first time in
quite a while, Wil's spirits lifted.

The Jackal was oblivious.

'Anyway,' he said taking aim again. 'It really is lovely to
catch up Wil, but I'm busy. Mmm, dragon first, then your
dogs, then… well…' He leaned over the balcony and cocked
his palm behind his ear, 'I think it's fair to say she's a goner
anyway. So what's it to be, Wil the Seer – talk now, or I'll
shoot first and you can talk later.'

Wil had run out of time. He snatched the staff out of the
ground and hurled it up at the balcony. He heard the click of
a trigger and a dull grunt. Wil's bow thunked into the soft
ground just in front of him – the bolt hadn't fired.

Then something very heavy rammed into Wil's back and
his world went black.

Face down in the wet grass, Wil could feel hot air blowing
over him – not constant like a gentle spring breeze. No, this
air was blowing out – then in – then back out again. It wasn't
any sort of wind at all – it was breath.

'Dragon! Did you say dragon, Colin?' The Jackal's
mother's voice drifted down from the balcony above. 'Has

that nasty boy got a dragon? Oh Colin, you are sooo clever – another hat for Mommy!'

Keeping his face in the cool dew, Wil opened his mind – after all, he thought, if he was going to be eaten by a Giant Redback, he might as well know what she was thinking at the time! But the dragon wasn't thinking about him at all. All Wil could feel was relief and a very, *very* strong sense of warm love – the Redback and her baby were reunited and *she* really didn't care about anything else.

Wil lifted his head.

The Redback was feeding her baby. Nestled right up against the old castle wall, her enormous hulk dwarfed the Fellhounds; she even made the golden tower look pretty small. She gave a contented groan – almost a purr – while her baby flapped its tiny wings and butted against her, eagerly gulping down its long-awaited tea.

Somewhere in the distance the riot was still raging and a lot more of the city was now ablaze. The light of the fire masked the dragon's real colour but her iridescent scales grabbed what little light there was and threw just enough back to illuminate the ground around her.

But where was Gisella? On his hands and knees, and desperately hoping that her body wasn't lying crushed underneath the scaly giant, Wil blindly inched forward, patting the soaking grass. Then he heard a gasp followed by a weak gurgling cough – she was further away – not flattened but, by the sound of it, in a very bad way.

Wil crawled towards the sound. Phinn was there too, lying with his long back pressed firmly against Gisella's body from head to toe, keeping her warm. He was panting hard. With a stab of guilt Wil felt the arrow sticking out of the hound's shoulder; not deep but by the hound's sticky matted coat Wil guessed that Phinn had lost quite a lot of blood.

Wil's guilt bit harder when he knelt to look at Gisella. He didn't need to turn her over to see where she had been hit – the bolt had gone right through her chest; its silver tip sticking out of her back.

'Don't die,' he whispered. 'Don't die, either of you.'

A salty tear trickled down his nose and dripped onto Gisella's neck just below her ear. With a bloody finger, he followed it down the line of her soft cheek to her chin where it dripped and disappeared into the black grass. Through the blur of tears Wil could see Gisella's hand, still clutching the pink silk bag – she must have been about to give it to him when he asked her to look after Phinn.

While Wil didn't expect Gisella to react when he reached for the bag, he wasn't expecting her fingers to feel so cold. He delved into the pink silk – his own hands shaking almost uncontrollably – hoping that they would pull out a miracle. Almost immediately his fingers closed around something soft.

As always, a little label hung from the soft bundle of what felt like soft duck down. With tears still running unchecked down his face, Wil peered at the label; the words swam in front of him. He dropped his hands.

'Well, you're going to have to stop this blubbing, mate, or you're never going to be able to help them.'

So he wiped his eyes with the heel of his blood-streaked palms and took a deep breath. But reading the label, his heart started to pound – this time Lady Elanor's magical little bag couldn't help.

The label read:

> *Brindey Goose Down*
>
> *Snap the arrow and the bolt as close to the skin as you can*
> *without disturbing the wounds. Pack this down around both*
> *wounds and get experienced help as soon as possible.*
>
> *Best before: unknown, probably eternity*

Lost for what else to do, Wil re-read the label and set about Gisella's wounds. Snapping the head of the bolt, he did his best to pack the down around the ragged shaft sticking out from her back. The instant the down touched the wound he could feel it became wet, sucking up fresh blood like a wick. Convinced he'd done something wrong, Wil grabbed at the dressing – the down had set rock hard, there was no more blood.

Dressing the entry wound was more challenging. He rolled Gisella onto her side. Despite his shaking hands, he worked quickly and by the time he had finished the goose down was almost completely used up; although, to his relief, the bleeding from both wounds had finally stopped.

Next, Wil turned to Phinn. As he had guessed the arrow wasn't deep and slid out of the wound when Wil tried to snap it. Phinn gave an indignant yelp and licked Wil's hands as if to politely request that he didn't do it again and with soft words of reassurance Wil packed the hole with the remaining down.

With the wounds dressed, Wil turned again to the silk bag. This time it gave up a bottle that Wil had seen before. A picture of Mortimer with a bright green tongue flashed into his head – the bottle held the liquid used to treat blood loss. Wil curled back Phinn's top lip and tipped a few drops between the hound's teeth before giving the rest to Gisella – he had no idea how much blood she might have lost, but feeling the stickiness of the grass underneath her, he didn't think he could do any more harm.

With the tiny bottle empty and the dressings set, Wil rocked back on his haunches. He didn't know what to do next. It was only then he realised that the room above him had gone strangely quiet and a bad feeling crept over him.

The sound of galloping hooves coming up fast in the shadow of the castle wall made Wil reach for his knife – the distinct advantage of sitting under a gigantic dragon, flanked by two enormous dogs, seemed for some reason to have passed Wil by.

Mortimer pulled Shadow up short.

'Whoa, Wil, it's me.'

Behind Mortimer the moons were a hair's breadth from meeting; behind Wil, the Giant Redback spat a jet of orange flame that missed Mortimer by only a few feet.

'Erm, I know this might sound like a daft thing to say, Wil, but you do know there's a dragon behind you, don't you?'

'Yeah,' shrugged Wil. 'I had a sort of a plan but Gisella and Phinn got hurt and it doesn't seem like such a good idea now. Where's the girl with Pricilla?'

'Who?'

'Oh, er, I meant Lady Élanor's raven... her name's Pricilla. I thought you knew?'

Shadow took a step forward. The Redback growled ominously.

'I don't think your new friend likes me,' said Mortimer. He reined Shadow back two steps. 'Oh, yeah, the girl – she took the bird and went back to salvage what she could of her stall. The city's a mess! What hasn't been burned,' he raised his eyebrows towards the Giant Redback, 'has been picked clean by looters on their way to the mill. It's chaos. They're taking every bit of gold they can lay their hands on. Rexmoore's men are completely useless.' He shook his head and laughed. 'You should see Imelda – she's livid. I don't think they've had much practice with rebellion around here.'

'Any sign of The Jackal?' asked Wil almost hopefully. It was starting to dawn on him that his makeshift spear might have been a little too accurate.

'No,' said Mortimer with a frown. 'Come to think of it, I saw that woman – the one wearing the Wraithe Wolf head for a hat – she was taking a gold brick into the mill – very odd. Didn't seem to notice the riot at all!'

'So he must be still up there,' said Wil, almost to himself. He looked up at the balcony – The Jackal was skulking up there somewhere, he felt sure. 'Mort, can you look after Gisella and Phinn. I need to find that boy – he knows where my father is and I'm not leaving Armelia without him.'

'And what about your *little* friend here?' said Mortimer, pointing behind his hand. The Redback was now dozing, her scales bright in the light of the burning city – somehow her baby had managed to clamber onto her back and was nestled behind her folded wing.

'She'll be fine as long as you don't try to move him,' said Wil pointing to the fledgling dragon. 'Any ideas about how we're going to get out of here?'

Mortimer let go of Shadow's reins and slid to the ground. 'Absolutely none.'

CHAPTER TWENTY-SIX

The Many Faces of Death

It was hardly a surprise that the castle kitchen was deserted; although Wil was taken aback by the absolutely delicious smell that greeted him when he entered the silent room. Outside, a huge dragon had reduced the city to little more than glowing embers while its people ransacked and ran riot; and yet, in the warm serenity of Lord Rexmoore's kitchen, the cooking had continued.

In the middle of the vast kitchen table sat the biggest pie Wil had ever seen – although, on closer inspection he realised that it wasn't a pie. There was no pastry like on his mother's chicken pies and it seemed to rise out of the dish as if it had been inflated. Whatever it was though, Wil knew he just had to taste it – it smelled so good.

Suddenly starving, Wil grabbed the nearest spoon. He had never tasted anything so delicious – or so hot – in his life. He was just about to take another mouthful when the sound of heavy footsteps crunched across the courtyard. He thrust the spoon into the creamy mass and ran – behind him the steaming dish rapidly deflated.

The shouting started just as Wil put his foot on the first of the golden steps that spiralled their way up the centre of Imelda's precious tower.

'OH MY GAWD! MY SOUFFLE. FIRST MY EGGS AND NOW MY SOUFFLE. GALORIAN, IF THAT WAS YOU... GALORIAN, GET YER. FAERYDAE, WHERE'S YER BROTHER! OH MY GAWD!...'

Wil took the steps three at a time and as the shouting died away a twinge of guilt skipped into his mind; but then he remembered the terror of the bees in the burning skep and all thoughts of Galorian, Mhaddphat and the ruined soufflé vanished.

The stairs led directly up to the little room with the balcony; although, by the way their curve continued around the golden walls beyond the doorway, it looked like the tower was meant to go yet higher. Anger flared in the pit of Wil's stomach. He thought about the shabby city – the canal that doubled as a well and a toilet; he thought about his mother, and many others across Thesk who eked out a living to save enough to pay every time Rexmoore's thugs came knocking. Men had died – were still dying – just so that Rexmoore could indulge his wife.

The door that Phinn had so efficiently demolished earlier was still on the floor. Snuffy's tail jutted out from under one end. The converging moons outside provided the only light – a bright, silver beam cut the darkness in half like a knife. Grisly smears glinted in the moonlight. On either side of the beam the room's black corners were ominously quiet. Wil drew his knife from his boot.

'I know you're in here,' he said. 'If you take me to my father, I will spare your life.'

A scraping sound from the farthest corner gave away The Jackal's hiding place.

'And did... you give my... father a similar... choice, Wil... Calloway? Or... did you just... kill him in... cold blood?'

The voice was weak; uttered as if the speaker might be making a choice between a breath and a word. Wil couldn't help feeling pleased – at least The Jackal was suffering just as Gisella was.

'Your father gave *me* a choice,' spat Wil. 'And I took it.'

A shiver ran down his spine as he remembered; the freezing river, Sir Jerad Tinniswood on the rocks taunting him – Esk Falls dragging Tinniswood away. Wil shook his head to banish the memory – his only concern now was to make sure that the boy survived long enough to get him to his father before he got everyone home. There was a stomach-turning cough from the corner.

'And if… I take you… to your… father… will you … save me?' whispered the boy. There was an odd note in The Jackal's voice that caught Wil off guard.

'I…what do you mean, save you? You seem to have it pretty good here – Imelda's favourite nephew, Mommy's little *prince!*'

The Jackal attempted a scornful laugh but quickly gave in to another lung-raking cough before he spoke again. 'My aunt… loves gold; … my mother,' he spat the word, 'loves hats… in case you… hadn't noticed? And… the woman… who loved… my father… hates me for… being alive instead of… him.'

'And Lord Rexmoore?' A lame question Wil knew, but he was fighting a creeping guilt that had already made him lower his knife.

Another consumptive cough followed before The Jackal attempted an answer. Eventually he spat into the darkness and spoke in a bitter whisper.

'You know… I really do think… he loves… Imelda… Sad, isn't it?'

There was a gasp, a loud clatter and the sound of something sliding.

'Jackal? Colin?'

Nothing – not even the sound of the boy's laboured fight for breath.

Wil took three steps forward into the velvet blackness. With the third step his foot caught something hard, knocking it into the wall – there was a familiar click; something shot past Wil's knee and bounced off the door post behind him. It was a bolt – The Jackal had had a second bow!

In the gloom, Wil could see The Jackal slumped in the corner. The boy's chest was wet and warm to the touch – there was no need for light this time, Wil knew it was blood.

At his feet was the body of the only person who could have taken him to his father – and he now lay dead by Wil's own hand. The Jackal's last breath had already given way to the noise of the riot somewhere outside in the distance; inside the light from the rising moons crept relentlessly across the dark floorboards. It touched The Jackal's finger lying in the dust and then one by one illuminated the letters of the still sticky words 'THE MASON'. From the moment Wil had entered that room The Jackal had had every chance to kill, but instead he had left a message.

'Thanks,' Wil whispered and walked from the room without a backward glance.

In the dark corridor at the base of the tower Wil spotted the outline of a door tucked away under the stairs. He guessed that it would lead to the mill and that The Jackal's mother must have used it earlier, as the only other way to the mill would have taken her straight past Wil outside in the grounds.

Something told Wil he had to go that way. He ducked and tried the door – it opened.

The passageway reeked of mould and Wil's arms and face immediately felt damp in the claggy air. A dim light was provided by a very occasional, half-hearted glow-worm and twice Wil slipped on what he hoped was either moss or mould. What was strange, though, was that the route seemed to be taking him uphill – rather than dropping down towards the mill. In addition, there was absolutely no sound of the riot outside; what he could hear – and louder with every step – was the slow, rhythmic ping of a hammer hitting metal.

Wil gripped his knife in front of him and pressed on. Despite the cold, damp air, Wil was clammy and hot. His heart beat in time with the hammer. The climb grew steeper and the air got colder.

Finally, up in the distance Wil could see a pin prick of light that spread like a fan as he got nearer, turning the surrounding dimness into pitch blackness. Disorientated, Wil reached out. His searching fingers found the wall – thick with damp mould. He slipped again and landed heavily on one knee. He groaned.

The echo of his pain bounced all the way to the light at the end of the tunnel and out into... Wil wasn't sure he wanted to find out.

Then... the tunnel groaned back – a long, hollow moan, as if the sufferer had endured the pain for far too long.

Wil quickened his pace. Was this an Alcama ghost? His heart was now pounding. He daren't even try to imagine who had made that terrible noise – just in case he was right.

The end of the tunnel came too quickly now.

Suddenly, Wil was in a huge barn. All around him candles drowning in their own wax flickered and guttered. It was freezing. At the threshold of the open barn door, one solitary sheep's-head lantern burned – its light only a little brighter against the struggling candles. The regular ping of the hammer echoed out of one unlit corner; in another lay the source of the pain-wracked groan.

Wil ran towards the groan, hesitated, then lifted a filthy sack. The eyes that looked up at him were pools of the saddest, palest blue. But this was not his father. He dropped the cloth and took a step back in disbelief. He had seen those eyes before – in the painting above the fireplace in Lovage Hall – this was Lady Élanor's father.

'Hello Wil. Élanor was right, you are as reckless as you are brave. We wondered how long you would take to find me.'

The man's voice had a strange echo, as though it was in Wil's head, not in his ears.

'You're… are you…?' Wil started.

'Lord Lakeston, father of Lady Élanor and Talasina? Yes, of a sort,' said Lord Lakeston. He bowed his head with the merest hint of a smile. 'I am a revenant, Wil. Do you know what that is?'

In the dark, the hammer pinged.

The hairs on the back of Wil's neck prickled. He had no idea what a *revenant* was and was starting to wonder if his lack of food and sleep were playing tricks on his imagination. How could this man be Lord Lakeston? Tally had told him her father was dead.

The hammering stopped.

The man in front of Wil gave a solemn nod.

'Yes, Wil, you are right. I am dead.'

The hammering started again. This time the rhythm was less regular, higher too, as if a smaller tool were being used.

Lord Lakeston continued in the same solemn voice.

'I understand that you already know something of my family history, Wil – about how my beloved wife's sister took the rule of Thesk while I grieved.'

Wil nodded.

'And how Lady Élanor and Talasina came to live in Lovage Hall?'

Wil nodded again.

'And you also know that there is a secret that protects my daughters, although Talasina knows nothing of its content?'

'The legacy,' said Wil.

Suspicion gave way to realisation. Anger flared.

'Oh, I see.' Wil gripped his knife ready to fight. 'You're one of Rexmoore's men. So Imelda's still trying to get that blinking legacy – well, for the last time, *I don't know where – or what – it is!*'

The hammer continued to ping; the man's unblinking eyes cast sudden doubt in Wil's confused thinking – those eyes really did remind him of Lady Élanor and Tally. But no, this was definitely some sort of trick. The man stood up. The blade of Wil's knife caught the lamplight. Lord Lakeston stepped forward – straight into Wil's blade.

Wil felt the knife slide between the old man's ribs.

'No!'

Without altering his gaze, Lord Lakeston stood for a moment and then calmly took a step back. The knife was clean.

'Years ago a soul seller came to Armelia,' said Lord Lakeston, moving away towards the pinging hammer. 'My beautiful wife, Rosalind, was already dead. Even then, Imelda's control over Rexmoore was terrifying. It was only a matter of time before she took my girls, although thankfully she was unaware of their strange gifts – but I could never see

Imelda being a loving mother,' his eyes narrowed and he showed his teeth as he spoke. But his voice remained quiet and steady. 'So, wretched as I was, I struck a bargain – the legacy to which you refer and its protection.' Lord Lakeston shook his head, 'And before you ask, no, I will not tell you – I cannot. I was allowed to share the secret with two others. The price was my soul.'

Wil stood, wide-eyed in the dismal gloom.

'But what happens if…' Wil hesitated, 'If one of the secret keepers… dies?'

'Only then can their burden be passed on,' said Lord Lakeston.

'But what would happen if they *accidentally* told someone else – if it slipped out,' asked Wil, still struggling with what he had just seen, let alone what he was being told.

Lord Lakeston moved to the doorway and stared out into the dark.

'That cannot happen, Wil Calloway. That was part of my bargain. You see, the soul seller sealed their lips – they could not tell even if they wanted to – if their lives depended on it. Not until their dying breath.'

Wil stayed silent. His knife had just gone into this man's heart – and yet there was no blood. He was still standing and speaking. Lord Lakeston's words rolled through Wil's mind. Only the beat of the hammer filled the air.

'So Imelda would have to *kill* Lady Élanor to get her to give up the legacy?' he asked after a few moments.

Lord Lakeston closed his eyes and a single tear dripped down his cheek.

'Yes, Wil.'

'Or to give up the other secret keeper?'

Lord Lakeston nodded.

The hammering stopped. *Silence* filled the silence.

'That boy – Tinniswood's son – he told you about your father?' said Lord Lakeston after a moment. The sudden change of subject threw Wil.

'Er, yer,' he answered. 'Well, he said he knew where he was – he was going to take me to him. But then I…'

The words caught in Wil's throat. Lord Lakeston finished the sentence for him.

'You killed him.'

A shadow passed over his Lordship's face.

'Did he tell you anything else, Wil?'

'No, why?' asked Wil, wary again.

'I will take you, you need to know.'

A chill flurry whipped through the open door. The lantern went out. The man in the corner continued to chip away and, as they passed, Wil could see that he was carving something across a large, flat stone.

'The mason!' whispered Wil. He moved to double back but his Lordship grabbed his arm – for a dead man, his grip was extremely powerful.

'No, Wil. Come with me. Leave him, he can't tell you anything.'

'But... *he's* the mason. The Jackal left a message… he can tell me about my father.'

Lord Lakeston stopped, but for the first time he did not face Wil when he spoke.

'He can not tell you, Wil. He can not speak. *I* wrote the message.'

Then he strode away, leaving Wil to run to catch up.

By the time they eventually came to a halt, Wil had already realised what he would find. The headstones stretched out as far as the eye could see. Uniform lines, all with a name and the words 'Taxes paid' carved in beautiful precise lettering.

Some of the stones were covered with thick, green moss, some engulfed in ivy and some were so new they were not even coated in the evening dew; one, at the end of the second row back, had tiny green shoots around its base – crocus, thought Wil, his mother's favourite. The word 'Calloway' blurred in Wil's tears; as with all the others, below the single name, the words 'Taxes paid' had been skilfully hewn.

'He's been here all along,' said Wil in barely a whisper. 'The Jackal... he knew. He knew and he kept promising – using my father to make me tell them something I just don't know.' He choked out the last few words. He was glad The Jackal was dead – he was glad it had been him – Wil – who had killed him. He hoped The Jackal's mother would find him and that her heart would break...

'He was angry too, Wil,' said his Lordship, gently interrupting Wil's hate-filled thoughts. 'He was lonely and angry and he used the only thing he could to hurt you. And he picked you because he couldn't hurt anyone else – no-one cared. You are better than that, Wil. You are better than any of them. Go now and help your friends. Go and keep my daughters safe. You cannot do anything to help your father now, I am sorry. But you can help them.'

Wil felt a cold hand on his shoulder.

'You really are dead, aren't you,' he whispered.

'Yes, Wil – if you can call this a death. Being a revenant is an eternity of half-death.'

'But at least *you* get to see your daughters!' said Wil bitterly. He turned and walked away back towards the barn but stopped. 'It was you – at Black Rock – wasn't it? You gave me the staff.'

There was no answer.

Wil turned around – he was alone among the headstones. High above him the two moons were sliding into one.

CHAPTER TWENTY-SEVEN

The Redback's Wrath

'Blimey Wil, I thought I was going to have to come and rescue you again!' said Mortimer as Wil charged towards him across the grass – completely forgetting to stay in the shadow of the castle wall.

'Sorry, Mort, thought I'd stop for a bite to eat,' Wil lied. He was struggling with the surreal experience of meeting Lord Lakeston while, at the same time, trying to reconcile the reality that his father really was dead – the last thing he wanted to do right now was talk about any of it.

He handed Mortimer a wooden bowl full to the brim with what looked like green-flecked scrambled eggs.

'You want some?'

'What's this?' asked Mortimer, sniffing the dish. His tired face brightened. 'Ha! I was right. Quail egg soufflé… and… asparagus. Yum!'

'Oh, I brought you this, too' said Wil. He handed Mortimer a silver spoon that he retrieved from his bolt pouch.

'How're Gisella and Phinn?'

Mortimer scooped up a huge spoonful of the soufflé and held it to his mouth.

'Well, Phinn seems to be getting better all the time. He tried to get up a few minutes ago but I managed to stop him.' He popped the loaded spoon into his mouth and added thickly. 'Oh, this is delicious! Want some?'

'No thanks,' said Wil. True, he was tired and hungry but he felt too wretched to eat. 'So how's Gisella?'

Mortimer stopped mid-spoonful and frowned.

'Not too good. You did give her that blood stuff, didn't you?'

'Yer,' said Wil. He knelt down and put the flat of his hand on Gisella's cheek. It felt cold and clammy.

'So, you, er, didn't find your father then?' asked Mortimer.

'No,' said Wil abruptly. 'But The Jackal won't be bothering us again – Gisella'll be very pleased about that!'

Then he changed the subject.

'We really need to get her home,' he said, although putting Gisella on a horse right now was probably the worst thing they could do – but he couldn't see that they had any other choice.

Wil looked around; the Giant Redback and her baby were dozing peacefully, as were Mia and Farrow. Even the riot seemed to have calmed – other than flames reaching like tentacles out of the roof, the mill was quiet now; and, elsewhere, the city smouldered in a macabre peace. It was then that Wil spotted the little boat that he'd last seen down by the mill pond.

'Why's that up here?'

Mortimer scraped around the empty bowl, popped its contents into his mouth and then waved the pristine spoon at Wil.

'Because I've got an idea for how we're going to get everyone out of here,' said Mortimer and patted the silk rope that sat neatly coiled beside him. 'I've checked – this should be long enough – just. And as that boat survived being dragged from down there, I'm pretty sure it'll cope with what I've got in mind for it!'

When Mortimer had finished explaining his escape plan Wil went very quiet. He knew that they had to get out of Armelia and he knew that there was no way Gisella could ride; he also knew that, despite his apparently rapid recovery, Phinn was unlikely to be able to gallop too far for too long.

What Wil didn't know, though, was how to make a dragon take off; how to ride a dragon; or how to make sure that a boat carrying Phinn and Gisella under said dragon didn't fall – *if* they ever did get into the air.

In the west, leaving little room for the stars, the two moons were drifting together on their way to becoming one, before continuing their solitary journeys among the stars for another seven years. Mortimer's voice jolted Wil from his worries.

'Well, come on then. Grab the other end of this rope!'

Wil's mind raced; there just had to be an alternative to Mortimer's plan. In an attempt to buy some time, he said, 'Maybe we should get Gisella and Phinn into the boat first?'

'Good idea,' said Mortimer with a firm nod. 'Then, as soon as this rope's attached to the dragon's leg you can get up there and we'll get her to take off.' He bent to lift Gisella.

'No!' Wil said so abruptly that Mortimer jumped up, drew his sword and threw a wary glance over his shoulder. Wil stepped forward.

'It alright, Mort, I, er, I'll do that.'

Terrified he might hurt her, Wil carefully gathered Gisella into his arms before Mortimer could object.

'Suit yourself,' said Mortimer. 'But you're going to need a hand with Phinn.'

'Er, yer… of course, thanks.'

They laid Phinn next to Gisella in the bottom of the boat and wrapped Gisella's cloak around her as best they could. Mortimer had also brought up some sacking which they packed around the pair; although Wil wasn't sure how warm the rags would keep them once they were over the Fells. He was still trying to think of an alternative to Mortimer's mad plan.

'And you're sure you can get both horses, Mia *and* Farrow back to Saran on your own?' he asked. Mortimer looked offended.

'Gosh, yes! I'm a Fellman, Wil!' He wound the other end of the rope around his hand as he spoke. 'About three years ago, we had a Moon Chase that went really badly wrong. I was with Molly Edwards right up on the top of Thesker Pyke. We were chasing down a huge male Wraithe Wolf and got separated from the others. Shadow out-ran it and the hounds did their job. But Molly's horse stumbled – she went over its neck and straight into a ravine. Killed instantly, poor thing. I tried to get her body out but it was too close to dawn.' Mortimer absently flicked the end of the soft rope across his hand. 'There was no time so I took Molly's horse and Fellhound with me and got home. I don't think her parents would have forgiven me if I hadn't.' He stopped flicking the rope. 'And neither would mine.'

'So will you go straight over Tel Harion now?' asked Wil. It was, after all, the middle of the night – the favourite hunting time for Wraithe Wolves. It was also the Alcama – although Wil was sure that they'd had their fair share of awful happenings already.

'No,' said Mortimer, as if sharing Wil's thoughts. 'I'll head over to Grizzledale and then come back down along Mistle Forest – other than the odd wild boar or bear, it'll be far safer than travelling alone over the open Fells.'

He paused and then said, 'Was that carcass still up there?'

'Yeh, no head.'

Then Wil remembered.

247

'Oh! They'll come for the body, won't they! I forgot – dawn – Wraithe Wolves come for their dead. Mort – we really have got to get out of here!'

Mortimer moved quickly around the boat, hauling down on each of the rope fastenings as he went. The little boat creaked and groaned but the knots held.

The Redback's plate-size scales shimmered like some sort of iridescent armour and Wil wondered just how Mortimer was going to get her to take off. Then a shout from the mill made him turn. The glow of the city had suddenly got a lot closer – heading across from the mill and up from the canal, hundreds of torches were advancing on the tower. Wil made a decision.

'Mort, get on Shadow – you need to get going.'

'Yer, okay Wil, I just need to…' Clutching the other end of the rope, he disappeared under the sleeping Redback and shouted from the darkness, 'Just get on, Wil. And get her off the ground!'

Wil clambered up onto the dragon's back. From below, he heard Mortimer's voice.

'Good luck, Wil.'

And then the sound of Shadow's galloping hooves. Wil glanced down. Shadow, Mia and Farrow were nowhere to be seen.

'Right,' thought Wil as he wedged himself in between the dragon's scaly spine and its wing. Angry shouts echoed off the castle wall. An arrow shot past Wil's ear and wedged in the scales between the Redback's shoulder blades. She stirred. Then, without warning, she shook. Wil grabbed at the baby dragon to stop him sliding off. The arrow fell. A tiny trickle of green blood dripped down the dragon's neck. Then another arrow bounced off the Redback's snout and one more hit the wall.

The Redback sat up.

Wil wedged his fingers between the dragon's scales.

'Here goes!'

With every ounce of strength he had left, Wil concentrated. Arrows whistled over his head. A spear bounced off the bow of the boat.

'*Save your baby,*' thought Wil. '*They will take him. Take flight. Save your baby.*'

He pictured the man who had briefly been the proud possessor of the gold bar – the winner of the Unexpected Pets competition.

'*He is coming,*' thought Wil. '*Save your baby. Fly. They will kill you and take him.*'

The Redback arched her neck. She bent her head right around and sniffed her precious baby. Then, to Wil's alarm, he felt her hot breath as she sniffed him.

'*Save your baby,*' repeated Wil silently. '*They are coming. Fly. Save him.*'

The rabble was closing in. Wil could see spears, knives – someone was brandishing an axe while a woman waved a pitchfork.

'There it is,' called a ragged voice. 'I told you it's *hers* – look it's guarding her precious tower!'

'Take our gold; then use your pet to burns our homes!' yelled another. 'I want my gold back!'

'Hey, you up there – that's my dragon,' yelled a third man. 'My Ridge Creeper! I paid good money for that – it owes me a gold bar!'

Making a supreme effort to ignore the approaching mob, Wil tried again.

'*They are coming. Fly. Take him now!*'

At last he felt the dragon stir – just as a volley of arrows stopped the rioters in their tracks. Lord Rexmoore's reedy voice called out from the balcony of the golden tower.

'STOP! You will come no further!' And then, a little quieter, he added, 'And Master Calloway, you can stay where you are… with your new pet! Guards, watch him!'

Wil's concentration shattered.

Illuminated by the merging moons, Imelda and Lord Rexmoore surveyed the throng. Imelda spoke next.

'Every one of you will return the gold you have stolen from the mill – *every* brick and *every* coin.'

A mocking voice rose from the crowd.

'What! Give back what was ours in the first place?'

Shouts of approval drowned out whatever Imelda said next.

Below him, Wil felt the Redback shift her weight. He let his mind fill with the vision of huge wolves, vivid red eyes; two sets of needle-sharp teeth, designed to rip and tear.

'*The Wraithe Wolves are coming! Save him!*'

Wil sensed the dragon's unease.

Imelda snarled.

'That gold is mine! You live in *my* city – you pay *my* taxes!'

A spear flew out of the crowd. The Redback grabbed it in her jaws. It snapped like matchwood as she hauled herself to her feet.

'Look out,' shouted a frightened voice. Too late. The Redback spat a jet of fire right over the heads of the crowd. People screamed and scattered. On the balcony, Imelda's shrieking laughter echoed into the night.

'And this is what happens to people who steal! Ha, ha!'

Wil did his best to shut out Imelda's mad laughter.

'*They are coming. Fly. Save him!*'

Somewhere along the wall Rexmoore was yelling orders – guards lined the crumbling ramparts – all with their bows drawn; each one trained on the Redback.

'*Fly! Fly, NOW!*' Wil's mind screamed. He felt as though he would burst with frustration. If the Redback didn't take off in the next second they would all be dead, not just her baby!

Finally, the Redback flexed her huge wings. Wil braced himself. Next to him, the baby dragon slept on. But the Redback didn't take off. Wil felt a thud. The dragon's wing had hit the wall – she was too near.

'*Move, walk… jump! Move away from the wall…. if you want to take off – move away!*'

But the Redback stayed where she was. Wil knew she was listening to him but she didn't take off. He could feel her rage building.

Helpless, Wil clung on. Again, she beat her giant, leathery wings; again Wil felt them smack into the wall beside them. Then, to his absolute horror, the Redback stepped backwards, only just missing the boat that was right under her now.

'NO!' yelled Wil, unable to contain himself any longer.

Imelda's laugher stopped abruptly.

'The seer – *GET HIM*!'

The Redback's wing smacked against the tower again. A golden brick tumbled past Wil's ear – the large crack he had used as a foothold that afternoon sprang into his mind.

'Of course,' he whispered.

Whether the dragon had noticed the crack in the tower or whether she was actually trapped, Wil would never know; but once he pictured the building's weakness and suggested to the dragon that it might be a good idea to hit it a bit harder, she let loose with terrifying power.

With three more very quick and very devastating strikes, the crack opened so wide that Wil could have walked though it. Gold bricks and coins poured out onto the ground below – and with each strike Imelda's furious screams grew louder still.

The castle wall collapsed first. Guards scrambled in all directions as they fled the tumbling stones – their flat grey colour a shocking contrast to the golden bricks of the tower. Roaring, the dragon clambered up onto the ruined battlements and spread her wings for one last blow. With its only support gone, the golden tower gave way. Coins slid like sand in an hourglass. The Redback leapt skywards.

As they left the chaos beneath them, Wil peered past the dragon's scaly rib-cage. Imelda's screams could be heard even over the roar of the dragon; the green in front of the castle had given way to a carpet of gold and a dark wave of people was engulfing the rich pickings of the demolished tower.

The dragon soared into the night sky.

'Armelia – *taxes refunded!*' Wil yelled and whooped loudly.

The moons were almost one now. Freezing air blasted past Wil's ears as the dragon glided over the glistening ice-covered wastes of Tel Harion. He had absolutely no idea if the little boat was below them but quickly decided that trying to peer at the underbelly of a dragon in full flight was really not a good idea.

Instead Wil tried to call Phinn with his mind – after all, he'd managed it at the festival. But Phinn hadn't been injured then and right now Wil didn't even know if the Fellhound was conscious. But almost immediately Wil sensed that Phinn was close by – deeply unhappy about being in a boat that was a long way from the ground, being hauled along by a dragon, but nevertheless, he was close.

'*And Gisella?*' thought Wil.

His heart quickened slightly as Phinn's own concern merged with his – but Wil could sense that the Fellhound knew she was still alive.

Desperately worried, Wil drew his cloak tight around him. Despite her scales, the Redback felt warm beneath the cloth. The baby dragon was tucked down behind her wing on the other side of her bony spine. Wil did the same and was surprised how much of the bitter wind flowed over, rather than through him. He pictured Lord Lakeston's sad eyes and his own father's pathetic headstone; he thought of Mortimer galloping towards Grizzledale – to safety…and Tally…

The barn smelled of clean straw and sweet hay. Lady Élanor was standing in the stable doorway. She was deep in concentration. There was no sign of Tally but the sound of movement in the soft straw in Tanith's stable told Wil that Lady Élanor's pegalus had returned to Lovage Hall safe and sound.

The merging moons, now almost one perfect sphere, cast a silver-white beam that flowed into the unlit stable through a window set high up in the wall. The tranquillity was touchable. Tanith's gentle breath fogged the crisp night air and Wil could feel the pegalus's teeth as if they were his own, grinding down on the glorious meadow-fresh hay, untarnished by its winter storage.

Lady Élanor did not move – she was watching.

A bright beam crept across the straw. It brushed against one of Tanith's golden hooves. The pegalus stopped grazing.

'It is time,' whispered Lady Élanor. She glided into the stable, stroked Tanith's velvet muzzle and wound her arms around his neck.

'Good luck,' she whispered. Then she walked to the open window and looked out.

The Moon Crossing formed one perfect circle of pure gold. The stars dimmed. Tanith, suddenly sweating, pawed at the straw; a golden moonbeam hit his mane. He reared, opened his wings and… exploded into flames.

Lady Élanor opened her arms to the light. Tears were streaming down her face but she did not look around. The flames burned orange, then blue, then bright green, then pure gold. Wil tried to scream. He wanted to run, to raise the alarm. But he couldn't. He couldn't move. He opened his mouth to shout but the only sound that came was a feeble, rasping whimper. No one heard. No one came. Tanith's stable blazed. There was no sign of Lady Élanor. Blinded by the smoke and gasping for air, Wil made for the window. But just as his hands reached out for the timber the wall of the stable gave way and he crashed forward. He gasped a lungful of ice-cold air and opened his eyes.

The little dragon was eying him suspiciously. The night air was so cold that it was difficult to take in any more than tiny shallow breaths – so cold it *burned*. Wil shook his head. He had been dreaming again – or, more likely, having a nightmare!

Ahead of them Wil could see the telltale pink edge of dawn and wondered how Armelia would cope when the Wraithe Wolves came down from the Fells. He remembered the vision of the wolves streaming down from Tel Harion when he and Gisella had been waiting for Mortimer and Curtis, the night they lost Leon. He shook his head to get the terrifying image out of his mind.

Beside him the little dragon started to wriggle – he was hungry and very soon, Wil knew, he would start to make that dreadful sound again!

CHAPTER TWENTY-EIGHT
Not So Happy Landings

At almost the same moment that Wil realised it was feeding time *yet again* for the baby dragon, he realised that Mortimer's plan had a serious flaw – how on earth was he going to get the boat safely back onto the ground without it being smashed into pieces as the dragon landed? He'd never seen a dragon come in to land other than the Ridge Creepers up by Ewes Seat. But they all landed on craggy ledges – usually a very long way from the ground. Getting more concerned with every beat of the Redback's wings, Wil recalled the swans landing on East Lake; their wings smacking on the water as they slid to a halt – although, how that might work for Gisella and Phinn, Wil decided not to contemplate!

Somehow he had to persuade the Redback to fly low over a stretch of water *without* landing. If he could get down into the boat, he could cut the rope just before the Redback touched down and they would be home and dry – hopefully.

They were soaring now high over The Black Rock, inky in the dull, pink dawn – about half a day's ride by horse from Saran – but Wil had no idea how far by dragon.

Wil was pretty sure that the nearest stretch of water was the river leading onto Esk Falls. But he was forced to dismiss that thought. It was way too far from Saran to drag a boat with an injured Fellhound and Fellman *and* way too dangerous if he misjudged the drop!

No, somehow he had to get the dragon to fly slow and low over somewhere flat. That way he could cut the rope when they were close enough to the ground and hope that the boat came to a halt before it smashed to pieces – after all, Mortimer had said that it had survived being dragged up from the mill – hadn't he?

As Wil deliberated the various potentially fatal options open to him, the baby Redback resumed its whinging – and like before, the noise very quickly turned into a full-blown wail. Wil could feel the Giant Redback's anxiety building and she began to swoop and weave in search of food for her hungry baby. Wil's mind swam – suddenly he felt very sick.

The night was slowly giving way to the encroaching dawn. Below, Wil could see dark shapes dotted on the ground – rocks, he guessed. He wondered briefly about East Lake. There were likely to be some tasty sheep on Peachley Hills by now – if he could just get the message through to the Redback; but then again it was too far from Saran and Wil had no idea how much time Gisella had left. The words on the Brindy goose-down label had said 'get experienced help as soon as possible', and the only experienced help that Wil knew was at Lovage Hall – unless you counted Old Dulcie over in Little Howarth. But while her turnip linctus, renowned across the Hills, was great for curing anything from a sore throat to sheep scab, Wil wasn't sure it could help with a through-and-through bolt wound.

At the thought of Gisella's life ebbing away, Wil felt like someone was dragging their nails inch by painful inch across his heart.

Beside him the hungry dragon's pitiful cry was rapidly sending its mother into a frenzy. She swept across the open ground, hunting the frozen wasteland of the upper Fells. Wil knew it was only a matter of time before she spied the deer they had seen on their frantic gallop across to The Black Rock, and that would only mean one thing – she would go in for the kill. He had no choice. He had to get into that boat and get ready to cut the rope.

Keeping his head up and his eyes on the gathering clouds, Wil took a deep breath and slid down into the crook of the Redback's wing. Here, her vast ribcage was clad with leathery scales that proved fairly easy to cling to; they also acted like a natural ladder. Wil inched back until his legs dangled. Bone-chilling air ripped across the top of his boots; he was sure that at any second they would be swept into oblivion. Trying not to fall to his death, Wil made one valiant effort to persuade the Redback to slow down only to discover that the rushing air between his legs made thinking about anything other than survival impossible.

Gingerly, he scraped his toe against the dragon's flanks and found a ridge of scales that gave him a foothold; if he could just keep a grip he was pretty sure that he would be over the boat enough to let go and drop to join Gisella and Phinn. But what would happen if he missed the boat – or landed right on top of Phinn or Gisella and hurt them even more?... or–

An ear-splitting roar burst from the Redback's throat. The scales down her ribs vibrated violently. He knew without looking – she had spotted food and was going in for the kill.

Against every instinct that was making him cling on to the only thing that was stopping him from plummeting to the Fells below, Wil let go. The leathery scales whipped away from under his fingertips. He dropped.

As he slammed into the boat's gunwale Wil felt his arm shatter. But other than the snap of the bones, he felt nothing. He had fallen in, not past the boat. Phinn and Gisella were tucked down in the hull but Wil had no idea if they were conscious. The dragon's wings were hawked back. In the distance, standing proud on a broad sweep of moorland Wil could see a lone stag – antlers like fingers grabbing at the sky. The Redback had found her quarry.

Knife in hand, Wil forced himself to wait. He had no idea how high they were. Then the top of a tree whizzed by – he cut the rope.

The boat glanced off a lone hawthorn tree, smacked onto the ground and bounced high across a grassy ridge. Terrified rabbits scattered in all directions. Wil buried his face in his crumpled cloak and put his hands over his head, shouting for all he was worth.

'STOP! STOP! STOP!'

As if in answer, the little boat smacked into something very solid; the bow exploded into a thousand pieces and Wil's mind went black.

The first thing Wil became aware of when he woke up was that he was wet – very wet. With icy waves crashing over his face, he was pinned to the hull of the boat by his soaking cloak.

The second thing to attract his attention was a loud scraping sound, interspersed with the odd muffled knock and an occasional bang.

He also realised he was alone.

The boat must have crash-landed into water after all. Gisella and Phinn… they must have been thrown out! Wil tried to move, to get up to have a proper look. But a bolt of pure agony took his breath. Another wave of spray smacked into his face and filled his lungs. He choked.

'Wil! Was that you? Are you alive?'

Gisella appeared above the gunwale. The scraping sound had stopped.

'Look, Wil, I didn't have a choice!' said Gisella testily, but a nasty coughing fit prevented her from saying any more. Wil used his good arm to haul her cloak back over her shoulders; she was getting even wetter than she was already. The rain – not waves, Wil had discovered – was lashing across the Fells in great sheets. It was impossible to tell where they were.

'Yes, but pulling a wrecked boat halfway across Thesker Fell!' said Wil, over Gisella's coughing fit. 'What are you trying to do – finish the job The Jackal started?'

Gisella finally stopped coughing. The rain on the back of her hand briefly ran scarlet.

'Phinn was doing most of the pulling,' she said, wiping her eyes with her soaked cloak. 'Honestly Wil. I'm a Fellman – we're trained for this kind of thing!'

'Oh, right-oh! I suppose you crash a lot of flying boats on a moon chase do you – *after* someone's tried very hard to kill you!'

'I'm alright, Wil,' Gisella insisted. But Wil was even less convinced than Gisella sounded – her death mask face a stark contrast to her lips that had gone a very odd shade of blue. Cross as Wil was, he decided that now wasn't the time to pick a fight.

'Look Giz, you must be exhausted. Why don't you take a turn to rest? I'll help Phinn.' He peered into the sheeting rain. 'We really can't be too far now – how long has it been light?'

'I don't know,' admitted Gisella. 'It was already light when I came to. I don't know how long Phinn had been dragging us.'

Wil tried hard to banish the nagging thought that Phinn didn't really know the way to Saran. The poor hound was limping badly. The wound on his shoulder had opened up again and, by the blood down his leg, had been bleeding for quite a while.

'I don't suppose you managed to grab any food?' said Wil.

Gisella shook her head.

'It was all I could do… to get your bag and… the bolts.'

Wil didn't speak. The only sound in his ears was Gisella's fight for breath – the last time he'd heard that sound was just before The Jackal died.

Ignoring the biting agony of his own broken arm, Wil swept Gisella up into his arms and tried his best not to drop her back into the remains of the boat.

'What the…' gasped Gisella.

'Sorry, Giz, no time. We need to get back to Lovage Hall. You…you're freezing and if we're not careful we'll both end up with pneumonia!'

She moved to get out. Wil held up his palm.

'No, Giz. You are going to stay there if I have to tie you down. Phinn and I will get you home. Now, for the last time – stay where you are!'

Gisella opened her mouth to speak but another coughing fit robbed her of any words. She sat back, defeated, and by the look in her eyes Wil could see she was also frightened.

'I'll get you home, Giz,' he said. 'Trust me.'

She bit her lip and spoke again in a voice broken by her battle for air.

'Have you got any of that… potion we gave… Mortimer…You know… the stuff for… blood loss?'

Wil looked down at Gisella's blood-stained cloak and tried to fix his face into an expression that didn't betray his alarm.

'You're not... are you… is it–'

Gisella gave a weak smile.

'For Phinn,' she said.

'Oh, yes! I... of course. For a moment then–'

'Wil! Give Phinn some of that... potion! If he's going to get us home... he's going to... need it.'

Then she sank back against a wooden plank that ran as a seat across the centre of the boat – behind the seat the boat no longer existed.

'Oh, right. Yes. I'll do that now. I've got it here somewhere,' Wil lied. How could he tell Gisella he'd given her the remains of the potion back at the castle?

After a little searching, he found the little silk bag. It had been wedged up under the transom – during the landing, Wil guessed. He moved away before he sought out the bottle that he knew was empty; although he needn't have worried – when he looked back Gisella's eyes were closed.

'Don't die,' he whispered and turned away.

From behind him, almost lost in the wind, he just caught her weak reply.

'I'll try not to.'

CHAPTER TWENTY-NINE

Sights for Sore Eyes

Poised to start dragging the boat – or what was left of it at least – Phinn had one end of the silk rope clenched in his huge jaws. With one useless arm, Wil quickly realised that the only way he could help was by winding the other end around his waist. In the middle, the rope was still attached to a ring on the bow – one of the few things that hadn't come off during the landing.

Between them Phinn and Wil made fair progress. Downhill was relatively easy once they got up a bit of momentum over the waterlogged ground; although twice they had to dive out of the way as the battered hull overtook them down a particularly steep slope.

As if determined to make the journey as unpleasant as possible, the gusting wind smashed the rain into them again and again. Wil abandoned any attempt to wring out his cloak. Instead he took it off. Without the extra weight of the drenched wool the going was a little easier; although his leather jerkin was no match for the thin rope that quickly rubbed painful blisters across his chest and cut into the flesh under his arms.

Crimson rivers trickled down Phinn's shoulder again. Wil did his best with what was left of the Brindey goose down dressing but with no food and very little sleep for almost two days, he wasn't sure how much longer any of them could go on.

Every now and then Wil made Phinn stop to check on Gisella. Each time, her gasps were more desperate. A small voice in the back of Wil's mind nagged at him to send Phinn ahead; but another argued – if Phinn got lost too, Wil would have no hope at all of getting Gisella home.

The pain in his arm was bearable as long as he didn't move it, think about it, or touch it. As they ploughed on into the sweeping rain he did his best to ignore the numbness that had started in his fingers and was very slowly creeping up his wrist. The cold was also getting to his cracked cheekbone. It throbbed with every step. 'Well, Phinn,' he called into the wind, 'we left in the rain and we're going back in the rain – and it was miserable both times, too!'

At Wil's ironic laugh, Phinn moved closer to shield his master from the worst of the weather and, heads down into the wind, they trudged on together.

Wil had no idea when he fell, or indeed how he had fallen, but the next thing he knew someone was lifting him up. He screamed out in agony.

'Argh! My arm! Argh!'

His head was pounding.

A soothing voice floated across the wind and flowed through Wil's veins like warm honey.

'Let me see.'

Soft hands gently lifted his injured arm. He winced again but this time managed not to cry out.

'Get me two branches, Bryn. The straightest you can find,' said Lady Élanor.

Wil kept his eyes shut tight against the rain and braced himself. Lady Élanor pressed on the shattered bone – the pain in Wil's arm and cheek eased.

'Hmm, a bad break,' she murmured.

''Ere you are, my lady. A nice bit o' beech. 'll make a fine splint 'til we get 'im back,' said Bryn. Then the gamekeeper's voice came from a little further away. 'Good job Seth found Phinn – I still carn't believe 'e found 'is way back. *Miles* off the path! Blinkin' lucky 'ey din't fall into Hester Beck in this weather. Done Gisella no good at all – this rain!'

Wil opened his eyes.

'Where is she, where's Gisella?'

He sat up with a jolt and shoved Lady Élanor hard with his good arm. Caught completely off balance she toppled backwards.

'Leave *me*! It's Gisella – *she* needs your help, not me!'

Lady Élanor got to her feet and brushed her muddy hands down her cloak. Her calm face made Wil angry – *Why wasn't she tending Gisella? If Gisella was much worse than him, why was she wasting her time on his broken arm?*

Lady Élanor spoke again in a tone far kinder than Wil deserved.

'Seth has already taken her, Wil. Tally is with them. Now please, let me set this splint. You can see Gisella as soon as we get back to Lovage Hall.'

Phinn was surprisingly lively as they travelled back to Saran. Wil watched him trotting happily behind the horses. Occasionally, he would sprint off ahead at a full gallop, bounding into the driving wind as if challenging it to try to stop him.

''e was worried 'bout you, Wil,' said Bryn. Phinn came pelting towards them, darting to the right at the last minute, tail held high.

'What have you given him?' asked Wil. Phinn's antics made him feel a lot happier.

'Lady E's got a special mixture she keeps fur the 'ounds after an 'ard moon chase,' said Bryn. He tapped his nose and gave Wil an exaggerated wink. 'Jus' gave 'im a draft o tha'. Right as rain in no time.'

'So what's in it?' asked Wil, more to take his mind off his throbbing arm than anything else. Riding behind Bryn may not have been as fast as riding with Mortimer but Bryn was a lot broader and took up far more of the saddle.

'Oh, this an' tha,' said Bryn with a vague wave of his hand. Phinn bounded out of a solitary hedge ahead of them. A furry corpse dangled from his mouth. Bryn roared with delight. 'Ere, look, 'e's caught a rabbit, too! Well done, Phinn!'

The Fellhound trotted over and dropped his prize into Bryn's outstretched hand, then something behind them caught Phinn's eye and he was off again.

'Hmm, a nice one, too!' said Bryn weighing the rabbit in his hand. 'Martha'll cook up a lovely stew with this!'

'Or a game pie… with these!' said a familiar voice from the other side of the hedge. A moment later, Mortimer rode into view waving another rabbit in his hand. At the same time Mia charged straight past them and nipped Phinn on the back of the leg.

Lady Élanor laughed.

'I wondered how long you would be able to stay quiet Mortimer Merridown!'

Bryn tucked the rabbit into his belt and knocked Wil's arm with his elbow.

'Mortimer, how long have you been there?' said Wil, wincing and grinning at the same time.

'Oh, long enough to see that you're a big baby when you're hurt!' said Mortimer. He was breathing hard. 'I spotted you from right back there.' He pointed over his shoulder.

Wil wasn't too sure where he meant, but he was so relieved to see his friend that he didn't really care.

White with foaming sweat, Shadow and Rhoani were blowing hard.

'Gosh, you've made good time then,' said Wil, but looking up at the sun he realised that he must have lost a lot more of the day than he had thought.

'Not bad,' said Mortimer, smoothing his hand along the top of Shadow's mane. 'Been galloping all day. Having Rhoani *and* Shadow meant I could swap so we could keep going.' He handed Bryn a guinea fowl and the rabbit. 'So where's Gisella? Until I got closer, my Lady, I though you might be her.'

Mortimer bowed his head as Shadow danced. Wil could sense the horse's impatience at suddenly being brought to a walk so close to home.

'She will be back at Lovage Hall by now – in the infirmary,' said Lady Élanor.

'What?'

Mortimer looked at Wil.

'How?'

'Er, well, the boat probably wasn't the best idea you've had, Mort?' said Wil.

'Nonsense,' said Mortimer. 'It got you out of Armelia, didn't it? Phinn's fine and, well, what've you done? Broken your arm?'

Wil shifted awkwardly. A sharp pain shot right up his arm into his shoulder.

'Well, yes, the boat was fine. And the Redback was great,' he said trying not to show the agony on his face. 'It was just that the landing wasn't.'

'Wasn't what?'

'A landing,' said Wil. 'It was more of a crash.'

'Oh,' said Mortimer.

'And I got knocked out. Phinn and Gisella started to drag–'

'Yer, Wil, I think I'm getting the picture,' said Mortimer, for once looking almost as awkward as Wil felt. He changed the subject. 'So how did Lady Élanor find you?'

'Phinn!' said Bryn before Wil could get a word in. He was beaming with pride. 'Seth found 'im. On 'is way back to Saran 'e was! Comin' fer 'elp. Beat's me 'ow he knew the way, bur 'e did – 'e was nearly 'ome, too. Seth was worried about yer all an was up on the Fells lookin' fer any sign of yer. Poor Phinn were half dead. But 'e weren't givin' up. No. 'e saw Seth an' turned right back round an' led 'im right 'ere!'

Phinn was galloping across the Fells after his sister, while Farrow kept a more demure pace behind Mortimer. A thought struck Wil – even though he'd spent almost every moment of the dark winter days with a Fellhound he still had a lot to learn about them. Then another thought struck him.

'So how did you and Lady Élanor find us?'

'Well, turns ou' that Seth's go' a bit of a way with pegalus. 'e was out on Tanith when 'e saw Phinn. Took 'im no time at all to get back for 'elp.'

The gamekeeper chuckled.

'Poor Rhoani won't get a look in if Lady E don't watch out!'

The vision of Tanith in flames flashed across Wil's mind.

'Oh! So Tanith's alright then?'

'Yes, Wil, Tanith is fine. Tired of course, after such a long flight from Armelia, but otherwise perfectly fine,' said Lady Élanor.

Mortimer scraped a finger of foaming sweat from Rhoani's flank.

'Gisella'll be alright though, won't she, my lady?' He flicked the sweat into the grass. 'I know that the bolt went right through but we've come back from moon chases with far worse.'

'Yes, she will be fine,' said Lady Élanor. But there was something in her voice that worried Wil. Mortimer seemed to have missed it.

'That's good,' he said. 'Because I was thinking that she'd make a great chaser. What do you think, Wil? She's as brave as any and she's certainly got a way with the hounds.'

'Well you've changed your tune!' said Wil.

Mortimer shifted in his saddle.

'Yer, well, I was wrong. I'm not afraid to admit it. Olivia must have been upset and decided to try to make trouble. I'll speak to Leon... he'll be fine when he hears it from me.'

Wil frowned.

'You sure about that?'

From the moment they rode into the yard at the stables above Lovage Hall, Wil had refused all offers of treatment for his shattered arm and his battered cheek. His head was throbbing, too, but he needed to see Gisella. Unfortunately, his visit to the infirmary had been both brief and disappointing.

'Well, I'm sorry Wil, but I couldn't keep her awake just in case you decided to turn up!' said Tally. She had finally managed to get Wil to sit still long enough to dress his arm, but he was still resisting any attempts she made to look at his cheek or his head. 'She is very ill – you do understand that, don't you? We're giving her camomile and morphine in *very* large doses, so if you're *not* going to let me have a look at that bruise there's really no point in hanging around.'

Lady Élanor walked into the ward just as Tally took a breath.

'Don't worry, Wil. Gisella is fit and strong. If anyone can get through this, she will,' said Lady Élanor kindly. Her pale blue eyes flicked to the purple bruise on Wil's head and then to her sister. She continued in the same measured tone. 'But Tally is right, Wil. It is better if we keep her like this for the next few days – sleeping, she won't feel the pain. She needs her strength to fight, not to talk. In the meantime, perhaps you should let Tally take another look at that bump.'

She moved closer. Wil backed away.

'No, it's OK. I'm fine, honestly.'

He studied Gisella's smoke-white face.

'It's just that, well, she hasn't got anyone now…you know – to… to, well, er… look after her,' he struggled.

'No,' said Lady Élanor. 'With her mother still… away–'

'Away!' said Wil. A spark of anger flared inside him. 'She's in Armelia – Imelda's new best friend – that's where she is!'

'You saw her,' said Lady Élanor. Her irritatingly calm voice bore no hint of surprise.

'Yes! So did Gisella! And I don't think she's going to want to see her loving mother again – *ever*!'

It wasn't until after Wil left the infirmary with his arm encased in cumbersome splints that he started to wonder about Lady Élanor's reaction. She must have already known of Fermina Fairfax's whereabouts – *and*, Wil was prepared to bet, she knew about Fermina's romantic links with Sir Jerad Tinniswood.

'Lord Lakeston must have told her,' he muttered to himself as he stomped back up to the stables to check on Phinn. His head throbbed.

'Who told who what?'

Wil turned. Breathless, but beaming, Seth was just behind him.

'Oh, nothing,' said Wil casually. He was fairly sure that Seth knew almost nothing about Lady Élanor or the legacy;

if he told Seth that he'd met the ghost – or whatever he was – of Lord Lakeston, Seth would most likely march him straight back down to the infirmary again fearing that the bump on Wil's head was more severe than everyone had first thought. 'Where are you off?' he asked by way of a distraction.

A pink bloom the size of a walnut appeared on each of Seth's normally pale cheeks.

'Oh, nowhere,' he said, suddenly sounding as casual as Wil. 'Just thought I'd check on Farrow. Might pop over to see Tanith, too. Was, er, was Tally down in the infirmary?'

'Yes,' said Wil, feeling cross again. 'Exhibiting the bedside manner of a Bragg Hound as usual.'

Seth's shoulders dropped a fraction.

'Oh,' he said. Then, with a sideways glance at Wil he asked, 'Did she, er, did she, you know, say anything about me?'

'No,' said Wil. He kicked a pile of rotten leaves. 'She was in a really bad mood. I just can't understand why she dislikes Gisella so much!'

'Feather blindness?' said Morten Mortens as Seth and Wil walked into the yard. Mia was standing with Mortimer who was recounting the story about the eagard attack to the Grand Wizen. Phinn and Farrow were nowhere to be seen. Morten Mortens shook his head.

'Very nasty. Only seen it once myself. Poor chap lost his sight – but then he didn't have Lady Élanor watching over him.'

The Grand Wizen's face broke into a soft smile. Wil wondered just how much he, and the Order for that matter, really knew. Morten Mortens had said something before about a promise he had made to Lady Élanor's father; maybe it had something to do with Lord Lakeston becoming a revenant? Then Wil started to wonder just how you became a revenant – did it hurt? By the noise Lord Lakeston had been making in that barn, he'd certainly been suffering from something for a very long time–

'Didn't they, Wil?' said Mortimer.

'Sorry?'

Mortimer frowned.

'That bump on your head made you deaf?'

'No… yer… sorry, I was just thinking about something…sorry, what did you say?' Wil did feel a bit dizzy. He sat down heavily on the edge of the water trough.

Mortimer looked slightly more sympathetic. Morten Mortens peered over his glasses.

'Are you sure you are alright, Wil? Shall I ask Lady Élanor to have another look at you?'

'No, really,' said Wil, attempting to dispel the dizziness with a shake of his head, but it just made it worse. He tried to concentrate. 'What did you ask me, Mort?'

'I was just telling Morten about the eagard attack; about Leon getting injured. They were headed back here when they set off, weren't they?'

'Er, yes,' said Wil. Nausea was coming and going in waves now. He took a deep breath. 'They were coming straight back here. I don't think Leon was in a fit state to go anywhere else.'

The stable yard was spinning now and the waves of nausea were so bad he didn't want to risk opening his mouth. He barely noticed the Grand Wizen's lack of concern.

'Well, Oswald's sister lives somewhere up by Grizzledale – tiny place, Little Piketon, I think…only about three houses. Right on the edge of Mistle Forest – they've got a hobgoblin, you know – excellent wild boar sausages.' Morten Mortens grinned at the memory. 'I'll bet they stopped off there? It's nearer to The Black Rock than Saran, after all.'

Mortimer brightened.

'Oh, I know that place – yer, those sausages are delicious! I tried to get them to give me the recipe but no such luck. Lots of juniper, I think. Those hobgoblins know how to butcher a boar mind – use every bit – even the stomach contents are– Wil, are you okay? You've gone very green.'

Wil bent over the back of the water trough and vomited.

'I think we'd better get you back to Lady Élanor,' said Mortimer, and lifting Wil's good arm over his own shoulder, he added, 'And I think I'll ask Martha to keep sausages off the menu for a while!'

Despite Wil's continued resistance, Lady Élanor finally persuaded him to stay the night in the infirmary.

'Goodness me, Wil,' she said, her pale blue eyes looking almost the crossest he'd ever seen them. 'It's not as if I'm suggesting you spend the night in Saran Jail! We can keep a proper eye on you here. I'm only cross with myself that I didn't insist on it sooner. With that knock on the head I can assure you that the best place for you tonight is here. Now drink this!'

She presented him with a glass of bright orange liquid and did not take her eyes off him until he had drunk every drop. The medicine was as bitter as lemon rind but after one gulp Wil's nausea disappeared.

Lady Élanor gave a satisfied nod.

'Right, you can change into this for tonight and Martha will return your clothes – clean – in the morning,' she said, exchanging the empty glass for a long, linen night shirt.

'I can't wear… it'll be too–' started Wil, but a sudden steeliness in those blue eyes silenced him at once. Without another word he changed and clambered into bed, making sure that the shirt didn't ride up over his knees.

The sheets were crisp and the cool pillow soothed his burning head. Wil could feel his body giving in. Fighting sleep now, he looked over at the opposite bed. For the briefest second, just before exhaustion completely consumed him, he could see Gisella. She was smiling.

CHAPTER THIRTY

Gisella

Wil could not recall a time when he had slept more comfortably. It was almost lunchtime the next day before he stirred and when he opened his eyes Tally was just leaving Gisella's bedside.

'How is she?' he croaked, dry-mouthed and still groggy with sleep.

Tally spoke over her shoulder as she headed towards the door.

'As well as can be expected after having a bolt shot through her lung, being dropped from a dragon, and then being dragged halfway across Tel Hireth in the *wrong* direction in the worse storm we've had for ten winters!'

Tally stood aside for her sister to enter then she left the room.

'Why is she cross with me *now*?' said Wil. After all, he had just played a fairly big part in rescuing her from being burnt at the stake!

'Just ignore her, Wil.'

Lady Élanor was bearing down on him with another glass of the foul orange medicine.

'Here, drink this and as long as you aren't sick again this afternoon, you can get dressed and join us for supper. Martha is expecting you. I have not as yet had the chance to thank you all for getting Tally and Tanith home safely… and in time.' She took the glass from him but did not catch his eye. 'Mortimer and Seth have already accepted my invitation.'

Then, with an unreadable glance at Gisella, she added, 'You are welcome to stay. We've made up your usual room over at the Hall.'

'Thank you, my Lady,' he said, following her eyes. 'She is going to get better, isn't she?'

Lady Élanor turned away from Gisella's peaceful form. This time she looked Wil full in the face but her expression once again was unreadable.

'Gisella has only a slim chance of survival, Wil. Her injury was bad enough, and although you did all the right things, she was out on the Fells for far too long.' She turned back towards Gisella. 'She is also battling with the news of her mother… her father's murderer.'

'How did you–' Wil started.

Lady Élanor cut across him.

'Don't forget, Wil, I can *see* these things.' Her blue eyes held his gaze as she wound her hair absently between her slender fingers. 'She has a fair chance. She may have been injured during the Alcama – a time of bad luck, if ever there was one – but she had you to take care of her and,' her eyes fell back on Gisella, 'I am guessing you will be here for her when she wakes up?'

The room was suddenly much too quiet. Wil could feel his cheeks starting to burn.

'Well, er, yer. I thought I'd stay around for a while. After all, as you said, I did try to help her.' He paused and then added, 'Do you think she'll be cross with me for the boat crashing? I just couldn't stop it. And then I banged my head and passed out and left her to try to drag the boat.' He laid his head back on the pillow. Right above him, in the corner of the bright white ceiling, he could see a spider rolling a fly into a tight bundle of silk – all eight legs working frantically while the fly's muffled buzz drifted through the otherwise silent room.

'She's not going to forgive me, is she?'

'And why not?' croaked a weak voice from the bed opposite.

Lady Élanor was at Gisella's bedside before Wil could turn his head. It was difficult for him to see Gisella's face while Lady Élanor looked into her eyes; poked, prodded and tried her very best to discourage Gisella from trying to sit up.

'Please Gisella, just lie still. It is very good to see you awake so soon, but please… lie down.'

Despite the heavy cast around his arm, Wil managed to hoist himself up onto his good elbow. Gisella abandoned her feeble effort to sit up and, satisfied that she wasn't about to try to spring out of bed, Lady Élanor left the room, calling Tally's name crossly and muttering something about camomile not being on ration.

The door shut with a louder click than usual. Gisella looked over at Wil.

'Hi,' she whispered.

Her weak smile made his heart dance.

'Hi,' said Wil, suddenly terribly awkward.

'The others,' whispered Gisella. She gasped a few shallow breaths. 'They got back too?'

'Yes… er, well, not Leon and Oswald. Seth and Tally got back okay. Mortimer caught us up on the Fells. We were with Bryn and Lady Élanor by then. It was Seth who found you and me and…' Wil ran out of words. He wanted to tell Gisella how sorry he was about the boat and about collapsing; and about how she'd had to drag the smashed boat through the storm when she could hardly breath. But he didn't know how to start.

Gisella waved her fingers weakly.

'It's okay, Wil… You might have… half killed me… once we got out of… Armelia, but… at least… you got me out.' With a huge effort she raised her head from her pillow and looked over at him. 'I'd be there… dead… if it wasn't for you… Thank you.'

Wil grabbed the tumbler next to his bed and almost choked on the water –luckily he was saved from trying to speak by Tally, whose sudden appearance really did make him choke.

'Oh, Gisella, I'm so sorry! I was supposed to give you a double dose of camomile. You're supposed to sleep – to give your lung a chance to heal. I really am so sorry. Here, drink this.'

Obediently, Gisella drank the cloudy pink liquid. A trickle of the medicine escaped from the corner of her mouth as she settled back on the pillow. Tally took the glass and headed back through the door.

'I hope you're not overdoing it, Wil?' she called through the open door. 'Martha's making game pie and rhubarb crumble for tea.'

And then she was gone.

Gisella's laboured breathing was deafening now in the quiet room. Wil could see that her eyes were once more closed.

With his head feeling like it was full of custard, Wil lowered his legs over the edge of the bed and sat up. Once he was confident that he wasn't going to fall he slid the short distance to the floor and stood up, very conscious of the tails of the overlong nightshirt that were dangling way below his knees.

Sunbeams shone like wedges of light across the neat beds – each one deserted other than his and the bed in which Gisella lay fighting for every breath.

In half a dozen unsteady steps he was across the room at Gisella's feet. But he didn't know whether to go nearer. He could see the pale pink smear across Gisella's cheek – a stark contrast to her chalk-white face, normally brown and freckled by the sun. Either Tally hadn't noticed the dribbled medicine or, Wil suspected, she just hadn't bothered to wipe her patient's face even though Gisella couldn't do it herself.

He caught the corner of a clean towel that Tally had hung over the end of his own bed earlier and dipped it into his water jug. Then he returned, this time moving closer to Gisella's pillow. As gently as he could, he wiped away the spilt medicine; then he brushed the soft towel over Gisella's eye lids – first one, and then the other. Then he dabbed the cloth lightly across her brow.

'Just don't die,' he whispered.

Without opening her eyes, Gisella lifted her hand. Her icy fingers brushed against Wil's face as gently as a snowflake. When she spoke, her voice was as quiet as falling snow.

'I told you before… I'm… trying not to.'

By the time the sun had set and the twin moons were making their way towards the stars, Wil's dizziness had all but gone. Tally had returned to the infirmary to check on him twice during the afternoon and both times had given Gisella only a cursory glance. Gisella had not stirred at all and when Tally returned a third time, Wil's irritation got the better of him.

'So, is she alright Tally? Is her breathing okay?'

'Oh… er…yer,' said Tally. 'She's Eli's patient really. I don't know that much about lungs.'

'But you've been giving her that medicine. I just assumed,' said Wil, making an effort not to sound as cross as he felt. 'Did you, um,' he took a deep breath, 'Did you give her the wrong stuff earlier?'

Tally's face clouded. She flicked the corner of the extra blanket that Wil had put over Gisella when he had felt the chill in her hands.

'Well, that was Eli's fault! She should have told me it was supposed to be double camomile for the *whole* week – how was I supposed to know!'

'I thought you could read minds?'

Tally's eyes flashed but she didn't react immediately. She ran the flat of her hand across the blanket and pulled it a little further up under Gisella's chin. Then she gently brushed a curl of hair from Gisella's face.

'I'd never realised how curly Gisella's hair was,' she said and with a faint tut, she turned on her heels. 'Probably why it always looks such a mess.'

Supper at Lovage Hall was somewhat subdued. Lady Élanor had arrived late. She had been called down to the village to tend the blacksmith who had accidentally driven a nail into his hand while shoeing one of Godwyn Savidge's horses.

'But I thought he did that yesterday,' said Martha, spooning a second helping of rhubarb crumble onto Wil's plate even though he had barely touched the first. 'Cream, Wil?' she asked, plopping a huge dollop of clotted cream on the top before Wil could decline.

'He did,' said Lady Élanor. She helped herself to a tiny slice of pie that Wil was convinced must by then have been stone cold. 'But today it was a very odd colour.'

Wil pushed the crumble away. Lady Élanor took no notice.

'I've given him a bottle of iodine. If it's no better tomorrow he'll have to come up here. I can't keep going off down to the village while Gisella is still…' this time her eyes did dart to Wil, 'having such difficulty breathing.'

'She sounded more settled this evening didn't she, Wil?' said Tally, her voice filled with a concern Wil was convinced she did not feel. But not wanting a fight, he nodded. Lady Élanor brightened.

'Oh, good! Well now she's having the right dose of camomile.' Tally's fork crashed onto her plate. 'I'm sure the sleep will do her good.'

'So how's Tanith, Tally?' chirped Seth. He had eaten every crumb of the pie but the vegetables on his plate remained untouched. 'Do you want to come up to the stables to check on him later?'

'No,' said Tally.

Seth's face fell. Mortimer picked at the crumble with his spoon.

'I'll go, Seth,' he said, peering out of the window at the star-filled sky. 'Shadow was still a bit hot today. I want to check he's alright. Is Bryn still up at the stables, Martha?

'Oh, yes. What with two exhausted horses, three extra Fellhounds and Tanith to look after, he'll be up there for a while yet. Can you take him that last slice of pie and some of those potatoes when you go, Mortimer?' Her brow furrowed at the sight of Seth's uneaten vegetables. 'Seth, I didn't slave over a hot stove all afternoon for you to leave those on your plate–'

A sharp knock on the door saved Seth.

'We expecting anyone else?' said Martha, inspecting the nearly empty serving dishes and suddenly eyeing Seth's uneaten vegetables in a more positive light. Lady Élanor's dismayed expression suggested not.

'Oh, I do hope it's not Godwyn again. He was in such a foul mood earlier.'

'Hmph,' breathed Martha, hauling herself to her feet. 'The Alcama might be over for another seven years but some bad things hang around for a good while afterwards!'

There was a second impatient rap on the door.

'Goodness me, hold your horses!' called Martha.

But she had hardly put her fingers on the latch when the door burst open and Oswald Beck and Morten Mortens tumbled into the room.

CHAPTER THIRTY-ONE
The Bringers of Bad News

The first thing that Wil noticed was that Oswald was absolutely filthy; his face caked with mud, he was still in the same clothes he had been wearing when Wil and the others had said goodbye to him and Leon on Tel Hireth.

The second thing Wil noticed was that Morten Mortens was as white as a sheet. Lady Élanor knocked her chair over backwards with a clatter in her haste to get to her feet.

'Morten! What is it! What's happened! Is it Leon?'

Rejecting Mortimer's hand with a push, Oswald lumbered to his feet. He was shaking and it was obvious by the streaks down his face that he had been crying.

'No, my lady. Leon is fine, he's outside. I left his bandages on though. What with everything else....' His voice broke and his wild eyes sought out Morten Mortens for help.

The Grand Wizen went from white to scarlet.

'It's Olivia Drews, Eli. The Wraithe Wolves have taken her – she...'

'What?' chorused everyone in the room apart from Oswald. Morten Mortens let out a great gasping sob.

'She... I can't believe it... she went to them.'

Lady Élanor led the Grand Wizen to a chair.

'Martha, cherry brandy, I think. Glasses for everyone. And can someone bring Leon in?'

Mortimer carefully guided Leon into the room and helped him into a chair. The bandages over his eyes had held, but they were no longer crisp and white. Leon was as filthy as his father, and by the look of his cloak, he had come into very close contact with at least one gorse bush.

Bustling between the kitchen and the dining table, Martha kept stopping to listen while, between Oswald, Leon and Morten Mortens, the story of Olivia's fate unfolded.

'We left you, as you know, to come straight back to Saran. I set a course due south rather than heading over to Mistle Forest first,' said Oswald. The brandy had calmed him slightly. His voice now was flat – as if he were telling of an event in which he had played no part. 'It was early and the journey would be quicker. But the weather up on the Fell closed in and we soon lost our course.'

'I'm sure we were actually going around in circles for a while,' said Leon.

'I know that feeling,' said Wil with a grim shrug.

'We took shelter for the night and set off again the next morning,' said Oswald. 'We'd only just set off when out of nowhere, Olivia just walked up to us. She was drenched! She must have been in that storm – and there she was – all on her own.'

'But I thought she was going to visit her aunt,' said Tally. 'She told me the other day that she was going to stay there for a while to try to get over losing Giles.'

'And we all know who's fault that was, don't we!' spat Leon.

Morten Mortens' voice was barely more than a warning whisper from the other side of the table.

'Now, now, boy. We've been over this many, many times.'

Leon gave a sullen shrug. Oswald resumed their tale.

'She just walked right up to us. It was so strange. She had no horse, no bag, no bow – nothing. She was soaked to the skin, but she didn't seem to notice. She was…' Oswald stopped to think for a moment. 'That's it, she was lost… just lost.'

Leon nodded.

'We told her we were going home and told her to come with us but she kept saying that she couldn't find him.'

'Find who?' asked Lady Élanor.

She indicated to Martha to pour some more brandy into Oswald's glass, but gave an almost imperceptible shake of her head when Martha gestured towards the goblet in Leon's hand. Oswald stared at the brandy.

'Well, we couldn't work it out for ages,' he said. 'At first I thought she was talking about her father. Before we left for Armelia he told me he was going to ride over to Lower Minton with her. But when I asked her she swore she'd come out alone. She just kept saying that she just wanted to find *him*. She was behaving so strangely.'

'So who was she looking for?' asked Seth, his eyes wide as he listened. 'And why was she just south of The Black Rock – if she was on her way to Lower Minton she'd gone really badly wrong!'

'Well, I think the answer to your first question is fairly obvious, Seth,' said Mortimer.

Seth looked confused.

Mortimer turned back to Oswald. 'So why didn't you just bring her back with you when the rain stopped?'

Oswald clutched his glass with both hands and studied the floor.

'It really wasn't as simple as that, boy. Things took a turn for the worse after we'd persuaded Olivia to join us.'

'Oh, yes,' said Leon, turning his head to follow the voices. 'You see, without my sight I can pick up things

I wouldn't usually notice – sounds seemed louder… and smells… I knew we had gone wrong when I couldn't smell the forest any more.'

'But I thought you said you hadn't headed for the forest?' interrupted Seth.

'That's right,' said Oswald. 'But we were following one of the ridges that looks down over it – for a time.'

He took a large sip of his brandy and let Leon continue.

'It had stopped raining. There was a really weird smell – so familiar. But father told me it was still daylight so for a while I just thought it was my mind playing tricks… and it was the day of the Alcama–'

'What smell?' interrupted Mortimer. It was obvious from his expression that he had a fair idea what Leon's answer was going to be – so did Wil.

'Wraithe Wolves,' said Leon. Mortimer nodded.

'Cae Wheeler, this morning, said he'd seen footprints out on Thesker Fell – over by the river. I told him he must have made a mistake – Wraithe Wolves don't come this far south.'

'Well, I'm afraid he wasn't wrong,' said the Grand Wizen. 'Tell them Oswald.'

Oswald threw the contents of his glass into his mouth and swallowed.

'They were both right – Leon and Cae.' He looked straight into Mortimer's face. 'They just wouldn't let us get back. Every time we tried to turn towards Saran two or three would be there – on the nearest hilltop – forcing us to change course. They were herding us. As long as we kept going east they left us alone.'

'Father decided that it would be better to head for the river. Olivia was getting really excited – hysterical almost. I thought she was just scared, I... I was,' said Leon, his bandaged eyes sightless to the rapt faces in the room.

'It was starting to get dark and the Alcama was rising,' said Oswald. 'We decided to light the biggest fire we could and stay right by the river. The plan was to go downstream the next morning with the hope of getting back to Saran from Goatmed Scarp. We even managed to get Olivia to calm down a bit. It was fine... until the moons crossed.'

Oswald's voice, flat and drained of emotion, filled the quiet room.

'The fire was going well but it was eating logs. I'd only just come back from collecting more wood – I didn't dare move too far from the river. You could feel them watching us,' he said with a shiver. Martha ignored Lady Élanor's disapproving frown and topped up his empty glass. He nodded gratefully and continued. 'Olivia wouldn't sit down. She just kept pacing and looking out at the hills. It was getting dark and there wasn't much you could see, even in the moonlight.' He took a sip of the brandy. 'When I got back I dropped one of the logs on my foot. It wasn't bad to begin with, but I was hobbling around. So when I mentioned having to go to get more wood a bit later, Olivia insisted she do it. She seemed a bit brighter – calmer – and my foot was sore, so I agreed...' He raised his hand and pressed his eyes. Teardrops leaked down his cheeks. 'She laughed as she went. She was so happy just then. I should have known – realised.'

He wept openly. Nobody stirred. Martha lowered herself onto one of the little milking stools by the fire, the brandy bottle momentarily forgotten in her hand. After a few moments, Oswald took a deep, quivering breath, his eyes on the same patch of floor somewhere in front of him.

'Leon heard it first. The howl. Then another, and another until I thought I was going to go mad. They were all around us. But then the storm hit. I could hear Olivia calling but in that wind I couldn't make it out at first. Then I realised. She was calling Giles's name. She kept saying, "Giles, it's me. I've come. Take me with you. Giles it's me."

'I ran out into the dark, away from the fire, but I couldn't see anything. I called,' Oswald was whispering now. 'But she just kept calling for Giles and the wolves kept howling. And then they stopped and...'

'I heard Giles,' said Leon.

'But you couldn't have!' interrupted Seth so loudly that Martha jumped. 'He's dead – well, you know.'

'Are you sure it was Giles, Leon,' said Mortimer. 'Did you hear him, sir?'

'You calling my son a liar, boy?' snarled Oswald.

Wil glanced at Lady Élanor but her expression was impossible to read. Her fingers were knotted so tightly that her knuckles gleamed white.

'I heard Giles,' Leon repeated. 'He called Olivia. He called her and she went to him.'

'Did he attack her, Leon?' asked Lady Élanor, her fingers still knotted in her lap.

Leon shook his head.

'He wasn't near enough. He called Olivia out onto the Fell. There were wolves close – I could smell them. *They* got her. And you know what...' he turned his head as if looking around the room. 'She never made a sound. They dragged her away and she *never* made a sound.'

'So what happened after they took her?' asked Seth, all eyes. 'Did they come back for you two?'

Oswald put his glass down and, gripping the table with one hand, pulled himself to his feet.

'You know, that was the strangest thing. Once they had Olivia, they went.'

Leon nodded.

'Yer, as they took Olivia their scent just went away.'

Seth raised his index finger.

'But that was two nights ago,' he said innocently. 'How come you've only just got back now?'

Oswald hobbled across to lean on the huge oak lintel above the fireplace and the answer became immediately apparent. He was only wearing one boot; his other foot was bare and at least twice its normal size.

'As you can see, that log did me a bit more damage than I first thought. The horses must have taken off when the howling started. There was no sign of them after Olivia…' Oswald seemed to grind to a halt, as if it was all simply too much. He'd got his son home, he'd told his sad story and that was it – he didn't seem to have anything left. Leon came to the rescue.

'As soon as it got light we worked out where we were. If they'd driven us any further we'd have gone off Nell's Drop! It's taken us ages to get back.'

'Well, what with you blind and your father hardly able to hobble, I'm not surprised,' said Morten Mortens. The puffy bags under his eyes were wet and glistening. 'Eli, do you think you can find two beds in the infirmary for tonight?'

'No, Morten,' said Oswald. He leant heavily on the back of a chair and winced. 'One will be fine. Leon needs your help, my lady, but I… I need to see my wife.'

To Wil's surprise, Lady Élanor did not object.

'That is perfectly understandable, Oswald. But perhaps you might let Tally bind that foot to make it a little more comfortable?' She turned to Tally without waiting for Oswald to respond. 'Tally, go and get some bandages and the poplar buds – I left a new batch soaking in the pharmacy. Pack them around Oswald's toes as best you can, they'll help with that swelling.' She turned back to address Oswald and the Grand Wizen. Oswald was already hobbling to the door.

'I'll send Tally down to the house Oswald,' she called after him and then said under her breath to nobody in particular. 'But I'm willing to bet the pain will drive him back up here before tomorrow.'

CHAPTER THIRTY-TWO

A Friend Returns

Sure enough, before breakfast when Wil pushed his head around the infirmary door the next morning, he saw three occupied beds. Both Leon and Oswald were sound asleep; Gisella didn't look as though she'd moved since Wil had left her the night before.

'He came up around midnight. His wife brought him,' whispered Tally, who had crept up behind him. 'Eli's pretty sure he's broken his foot in at least three places. She's amazed he managed to walk from Goatmed Scarp in anything less than a week! Did you know he sleeps with his eyes open?'

'Yes, I noticed when we were at The Black Rock – scared me half to death!' said Wil.

'Me, too!' said Tally, with a mischievous grin. 'It was really giving me the creeps. I shoved some lemon balm and ashwagandha under his nose in the end – seems to have done the trick!'

'Good idea. And, er, what about Leon?'

Tally's eyes narrowed.

'*Gisella* is getting on just fine, Wil – as that's *obviously* who you really came to see at this time in the morning! As for Leon, he will mend. Thank goodness Eli put that feather blindness potion in your bag.'

'So, will he be scarred?' asked Wil, remembering the terrible weals across Leon's eyes just after the eagard attack.

'No. Eli's confident that his sight isn't damaged either. He'll be as good as new in a couple of weeks, once the new skin comes through.'

Tally tucked the blankets into the end of Leon's bed, checked the knot on his new bandage and fussed with Gisella's pillows for far too long. Torn between annoying Tally and desperately wanting to see Gisella, Wil hung around for as long as he dared.

In the end it was Martha who broke the stalemate by calling them in for breakfast with the bell that hung outside the kitchen door for just such a purpose.

As usual the courtyard was bursting with vibrant colours and smells that made Wil feel quite light headed as he made his way back across to Lovage Hall.

'Look, Wil,' said Tally, skipping up to join him. Wil braced himself for another fight. But instead of berating him or being mean about Gisella, Tally looked slightly embarrassed. Wil stopped just short of the kitchen door.

'I, er,' Tally started, steepling her fingers. 'Well, the thing is, I should have said thank you. You know, for getting me out of Armelia. I know I would be burnt to a crisp by now if you and … and the others hadn't come to get me.'

She pressed her fingers together so hard that the tips went pink. Wil shrugged. Why did she always have to make everything so difficult?

'It's OK, Tally. I'm sure you would have done the same.'

Tally opened her eyes wide.

'Oh, yes… for you, definitely! You know that.'

'And for Gisella?' said Wil.

Tally dropped her hands to her hips.

'Oh, typical! You always have to spoil it, don't you?'

With a sweep of silver hair, she turned and marched back into the infirmary.

'Tally, oh, come on. I thought you were coming for breakfast?' Wil called after her.

A tearful, disembodied voice replied.

'Tell Martha I don't want any!'

And with that the infirmary door slammed; one of the panes of glass shattered and thousands of tiny shards of glass exploded across the cobbles.

As the days went on Gisella's breathing got easier and easier and by the fifth morning, to Wil's relief, Lady Élanor instructed Tally to halve the camomile and start reducing the morphine.

When he called in to the infirmary that evening, Gisella was awake and Tally was nowhere to be seen. Oswald had gone home the previous day just after Tally had removed Leon's bandage.

Wil nodded to Leon, lying in the bed opposite.

'Hi, Leon, can you see anything yet?'

Leon's eyes were almost their normal colour again.

'Yer, much better,' he said with a vague wave. 'Tally said it's mostly down to you that I'm not going to be blind?'

'Oh, I don't know about that,' said Wil, feeling very awkward. He knew what it must have taken for Leon to thank him – after all, it was fairly obvious that Leon still blamed Wil for what happened to Giles on the moon chase. 'Gisella had a good hand in it, too.'

'It was mostly you though!' said Gisella. 'It seems we've all got something to be grateful to you for, doesn't it!'

Her sunny smile made Wil's heart dance a little jig.

'You've woken up at last then,' he said grinning back.

'Well, a girl can only have so much beauty sleep,' said Gisella, hauling herself up on her pillow. Wil jumped forward to help.

'Here, lean forward.'

She was still bound in a thick bandage. Wil tucked the pillow carefully behind Gisella's back and his blood froze. In the middle of the binding, right over Gisella's lung, was a circle of blood the size of Wil's fist.

'Giz, are you… are you feeling okay?' he stammered as he backed towards the door. Gisella was still bleeding – or maybe the effort of sitting up had made her start bleeding again – and it was his fault.

His boot had found Lady Élanor's foot.

'Ouch! I was just coming to check on my patient, Mister Calloway. I hope that you are not trying to stop me – or do you think that there aren't quite enough occupied beds in here?'

Wil removed his foot from Lady Élanor's slipper, leaving a muddy scrape across the delicate silver embroidery.

'No! Oh, I'm so sorry, my Lady!'

Fortunately, Lady Élanor had other things on her mind.

'So Gisella, how are you feeling tonight?' She gently pulled Gisella forwards and examined the same bandages. 'Hmm, still some blood. But I do not think it is anything to be concerned about – it was a big hole, after all.'

'Does that mean she's going to be alright?' asked Wil.

Lady Élanor helped Gisella to settle back against the pillows.

'Yes, Wil, it does,' she said. 'Although it might be a while before she is riding out on any moon chase – or riding any dragons, for that matter!'

A patter of light feet in the hall outside suggested that Tally might be on her way. Wil's heart sank. He'd managed to avoid her for the past few days. But when she did poke her head around the door her smile could not have been friendlier.

'Hi, Wil. Hi, Gisella. Good to see you're awake.'

Wil waited for the barbed comment about him, or about Gisella's snoring – which Wil had put down to her lying on her back for five days. But instead Tally simply said, 'Anyone seen Seth?'

Wil, Gisella and Lady Élanor all shook their heads.

'Oh, he must be up there already,' she said and ducked back behind the door only to reappear a moment later. 'Oh, Eli, is it OK if we take Tanith out for a ride.'

'We?'

'Oh, just Seth and me,' said Tally, and before her sister could answer, she said 'Thanks,' and closed the door.

Eyebrows raised, Lady Élanor looked from Wil to Gisella.

'They were out on Tanith only this morning … and yesterday, too.'

Oswald Beck, still hobbling and pale with pain, came up to the Hall to collect Leon the following morning. Leon had said very little during his stay in the infirmary and his silence continued as he blinked his way into the overcast morning.

Oswald stopped at Gisella's bed and held out his hand to Wil.

'I know that you and Leon have your differences,' he said gripping Wil's hand in both of his own. 'But he owes you his sight. I won't forget that and I'll make sure that he doesn't either.'

Lost for words, Wil shook the hands offered and stood at the doorway until father and son were safely at the kitchen door on the other side of the courtyard. Then he turned to return to Gisella's bedside. There, in the hallway of Lady Élanor's pristine infirmary stood Phinn. The great hound wagged his tail lazily by way of a greeting and pushed his head into Wil's chest.

'Phinn, how did you get down here?' said Wil. He glanced around to make sure neither Tally nor Lady Élanor were about to appear. 'I know I've been neglecting you, but I think Gisella needed me just a bit more than you did.'

Phinn moved closer and leant his entire weight against Wil. Wil scratched the hound's ear and Phinn groaned appreciatively.

'No, you can't see Gisella. Lady Élanor would dose me up with something highly poisonous if I let you in there. Come on, let's go back up and see Bryn.'

Phinn padded through the main door and Wil followed him out into the mottled light of the beech wood.

'Crronk!'

Phinn stood and let out a single booming bark.

'Oh,' said Wil, with a laugh. 'You came to get me!'

Gliding down from a branch high up in the nearest beech tree, Pricilla landed a good horse's length to Wil's left.

'Oh, come on, Pricilla! You can't possibly be cross with me, too? It's been bad enough having to battle with Tally! I had to leave you with that girl – what other choice was there? Honestly, you'd *never* have survived what we went though – believe me!'

Utterly disappointed, Wil retreated back towards the infirmary. Pricilla hopped after him. It was then that Wil noticed that she was dragging something behind her.

He bent down and, without being invited, the raven hopped onto his arm. There, attached to her leg was tiny roll of parchment. Wil untied the knot and unfurled the paper.

'Please find attached – your raven. No bones broken and in time she'll be flying straight again. Got nearly all my stuff

back, but the Redback dagger was lost – that's looters for you. Am safe back home. From – oh, never mind, we're unlikely to meet again. Regards, The Girl with the Dragon Tooth Earring.'

Guilt and gratitude flowed over Wil in equal measure. Pricilla was back and – almost – alright. He hoped that Lady Élanor wouldn't notice her slight drift to the right and decided it might be best if Bryn checked her over. So with Phinn happily leading the way, Wil set off towards the stables.

Wil walked into the stable block expecting to find Bryn, but it was Lady Élanor he found instead. She took one look at Pricilla perched on Wil's arm and smiled.

'Thank you for looking after her, Wil.'

His job done, Phinn wandered back over to his own stable and plonked himself down, nose out of the door so that he could keep an eye on what was going on. There was no sign of Bryn.

Wil felt very awkward.

'So, Tanith's alright, my Lady?' he asked, for want of anything else to say.

'Yes. Tally and Seth seem to be giving him plenty of exercise now he's had a good rest.'

'Oh, that's good. It was just I… well, I had a dream and–'

Lady Élanor moved to stroke the raven's healing wing.

'Tanith is fine, Wil. That is the second time you have asked,' she said extending Pricilla's wing. To Wil's relief there was no sign of the bolt wound. 'You must work to control that gift of yours. It is the only way you will learn what is a genuine dream and a real vision. It will come.'

'Er, can I ask you something else, my lady?'

'Of course.'

'Did you, um, did you believe Leon… you know, about hearing Giles?'

Lady Élanor's expression did not change.

'Leon had suffered a terrible injury, Wil. And with the storm and… well, the Alcama can play some odd tricks on an injured mind.'

Pricilla hopped onto her outstretched arm.

'Now, you are neglecting Gisella. I will take Pricilla to Bryn. You must go check on *my* patient.'

The infirmary was strangely quiet when Wil went back in. Gisella was lying with her back to the door. Wil smiled – she had not been able to tolerate lying on her side since The Jackal had shot her.

But as he got closer he realised that Gisella was crying.

'Giz, what's the matter? Do you feel ill again? Shall I go and get Lady Élanor?'

Gisella did not move.

'No, it's okay Wil. I'll be fine. I need to start doing things on my own now anyway.'

'What do you mean by that?'

Gisella sniffed.

'Well, now I'm getting better, you'll be going back home. Your mother must be wondering what's happened to you by now.'

It was only her shaking shoulders that gave away her silent sobbing.

Wil wasn't sure what to do. True, he did have to go home soon; to tell his mother that her husband really was never coming back – but he wasn't ready to do that just yet. Tentatively, he reached out to put his hand on her shoulder. She spoke again – this time in barely a whisper.

'But who's going to wonder about me?'

Wil stayed his hand.

'What do you mean, Giz?'

'Well, my mother's hardly going to come visiting, is she?' She sniffed. 'And as she killed my father, well, that sort of leaves me on my own, wouldn't you say?'

As Gisella seemed determined not to face Wil he moved around the bed and crossed his arms.

'Gisella Fairfax, if you think for one moment that I'm going to abandon you to fend for yourself, you really don't know me very well at all!'

CHAPTER THIRTY-THREE

home to mother

Lady Élanor stood with Mortimer. Behind them, the Grand Wizen, Oswald Beck and Agatha Peasgood stood alongside Seth, Tally, Mia and Farrow. Tally's own hound, Pickles, was there too.

Wil sat behind Gisella on Rhoani. For once, he'd managed to get on without too much trouble – which had amazed everyone as his arm was still in splints. Mortimer held Rhoani steady while they got ready to set off. He pointed a finger at Wil.

'Now, understand this, Wil Calloway. I'm only *lending* you my new chaser. I fully expect you to return her at regular intervals for hunting practice once she's fighting fit. And, of course, if you feel like joining in...' Mortimer winked.

Wil risked letting go of Gisella for a brief moment. He held up his hand.

'I've told you before, Mort. I've seen enough Wraithe Wolves to last me a lifetime! But if that's what Gisella wants to do,' she looked around at him with a warning glare. 'Well, that's up to her.'

'An' don' ferget, when you come home, Gisella, there'll be a new Fell'ound to train. You think of a name while yer way!' said Bryn.

'I will,' said Gisella.

Lady Élanor stepped forward. A burgundy silk bag swung from her wrist.

'Well, you had better go, Wil, or you will be staying another night and your poor mother will be frantic.' She offered up the bag to Wil.

'Oh, I don't think I'm going to need that, my lady,' said Wil. 'Gisella's got all her medicines in her own bag.'

Lady Élanor's face was suddenly serious.

'No, Wil, this is not first aid,' she pressed the bag into Wil's hand. He could feel it was full of coins.

'Lady Élanor, I can't– '

'No, Wil, you must. It is the least I can do. My father would have wanted you to have it – he would have insisted. It is because of you the legacy is safe,'

'But I didn't–'

'Take it, Wil. Give it to your mother. I have no news of Lord Rexmoore as yet, but his thugs will be back to collect his taxes before too long.'

'Well, I'm not sure about that, my Lady' said Wil, recalling the screams as the golden castle collapsed into the dirt.

'Only time will tell, Wil Calloway,' said Lady Élanor with a steady gaze.

As if knowing that they needed to go, Phinn stood at the end of the stable block and barked loudly – his amber eyes staring at his master. Wil grinned and wrapped his arms around Gisella's waist.

'I think we're being nagged.'

'Are you sure about this, Wil?' said Gisella. 'I mean your mother–'

'Look Giz,' said Wil. 'The last time I came home from Saran, I arrived with the biggest dog my mother had ever seen and she still loves me – you, by comparison, will hardly even raise an eyebrow.'

'*Thanks!*' said Gisella. The little group on the ground laughed.

'Well, obviously I didn't mean it like that!' said Wil. He recalled the last time he had left Saran – when he had managed to upset Gisella and she had galloped off the other way. At least this time they were both on the same horse!

Gisella kicked Rhoani into a walk.

'Now you look after him, Gisella,' called Seth. 'He's on loan, too, remember!'

Tally planted her hands on her hips.

'Oh, right! So you might get bored of Tanith, is that what you're saying, Seth Tanner?' said Tally. Wil gave Seth a sympathetic grin and then looked up into the grey skies – it was going to rain again.

'Right Gisella Fairfax, let's go and see my mother!'

As they neared the edge of the woods a figure was standing in the shadows of a giant beech tree. The figure stepped out into their path.

'Lady Élanor,' said Wil, suddenly concerned. 'Did we forget something? I checked Gisella's medicines twice.'

'No, Wil. Gisella has all the medicine she will need for you and your mother to take care of her.' She paused and then said, 'Wil, do you remember asking me if I believed Leon's tale?'

'Yes,' said Wil. 'I told Gisella, too, and she agreed with you.'

'Yes,' said Gisella. 'I thought I'd heard Giles's voice when I was lying in the boat. But I didn't even know who I was then, I felt so ill, and in that storm – well, *everything* sounded pretty frightening!'

Lady Élanor folded her hands into her cloak and dropped her gaze.

'What you and Leon heard I cannot say, but I advise you to get back to Mistlegard before dark – stay in the forest. Do not go out on the Fell.'

The hairs on the back of Wil's neck suddenly felt very uncomfortable.

'Why my lady, what's happened?'

Lady Élanor's pale blue eyes moved from Gisella to Wil.

'Armelia was not invaded at dawn on the day you left.'

'What?' breathed Wil.

'The wolves – they did not go into the city to collect their dead.'

Special thanks to: Tim, my ever patient and utterly supportive husband; Marion who overcame her fear of dogs to come and sell books; Lynn Hunter, for readings to which I can only ever hope to aspire; BJ, for sorting out my commas and hyphens. Thanks too to those who have given advice and support including my family, the dog walkers of Dinas Powys, Max (gone but not forgotten), Toby Faber, Windsor Bookshop in Penarth, Waterstones, Alun Owen, Trish Dunford, Kath Little and Tracy Johnson and all those who took the trouble to write to tell me how much you enjoyed Book One, *Moon Chase* – I hope I don't disappoint!

And for those of you who haven't read it yet…

Moon Chase

Cathy Farr

Accused of a crime that he didn't commit, teenager Wil Calloway is sentenced to join the Moon Chase to try to prove his innocence. On the face of it, this sounds easy enough, especially with the help of the huge Fellhounds of Thesk, but as Wil learns more from the mysterious Lady Élanor and her telepathic sister, Tally, he soon realises that proving his innocence is the least of his challenges – staying alive is another!

www.fellhounds.co.uk

Lightning Source UK Ltd.
Milton Keynes UK
UKOW05f0620291213

223687UK00001B/15/P